DEFENDING DANI

ALASKA BLIZZARD BOOK 1

KAT MIZERA

ALSO BY KAT MIZERA

The Las Vegas Sidewinders Series:

Dominic

Cody's Christmas Surprise

Drake

Karl

Anatoli

Zakk

Toli & Tessa

Brock

Vladimir

The Inferno Series:

Salvation's Inferno

Temptation's Inferno

Redemption's Inferno

Romancing Europe Series:

Adonis in Athens

Smitten in Santorini (2018)

The Alaska Blizzard Series:

Defending Dani

Holding Hailey (2018)

Stand Alone:

Barefoot Bay: Tropical Ice (Roxanne St. Claire, Kindle World)

Special Forces: Operation Alpha: Protecting Bobbi (Susan Stoker Kindle World)

Brotherhood Protectors: Catching Lana (Elle James Kindle World)

For Kelsey Koelzer, and all the strong, talented women of hockey. You're an inspiration.

1

————————

Sergei Petrov got out of the taxi and hurriedly paid the driver as he grabbed his bag. He hadn't seen his son in more than two months and couldn't wait to look into his sweet little face. They'd spoken on the phone and via video chat, of course, but it wasn't the same as holding him, touching him, feeling his warmth. He'd had no choice but to leave Nikolai here with his brother Toli's family when he'd been unexpectedly traded to a team in Anchorage, Alaska, but it was one of the hardest things he'd ever had to do.

He didn't bother to knock, merely threw open the door and called out to his family, "Hey—anybody home?"

"Dadddeeee!" Nikolai bounded down the hall and vaulted into his arms.

"Hey, big guy." Sergei held him tightly, nuzzling his shoulder and inhaling his familiar scent.

Toli came down the hall more slowly, smiling at them. "Good to see you," he said when Sergei finally put Niko down.

"Good to be here." Sergei hugged his older brother as well, unsure where a sudden influx of emotion had come from. "I've said it before, but I'll say it again—you and Tessa saved me with this."

Toli shook his head. "You're my brother—what choice did we have? Although, to be fair, it was more Tessa than me. She's the one who really stepped up to the plate, along with some of our other friends."

Sergei nodded. "I know. I don't know how I'll ever repay everyone."

"That's what family does," Toli said, walking back towards the living room.

"Hey, Sergei!" Tessa called out, her hands buried in a meat concoction she was putting in a pan.

"Hi, hon." He leaned over to kiss her cheek. "That looks good. Your famous meatloaf?"

"I know it's your favorite." She smiled.

"You're the best sister-in-law ever."

"I try."

"Daddy, I can skate." Niko was tugging his arm.

Sergei frowned. "What?"

"Dani and her friend Sara took all the kids," Toli said, handing him a beer. "Raina, Niko, Derek, and Duncan. They had a blast."

"I'm gonna be a 'fenseman like you!" Niko yelled, gliding across the kitchen floor in his socks.

"Easy, tiger, this isn't a rink," Tessa called after him, laughing. "And defensemen are supposed to protect the goalie, not run around like lunatics."

"I was going to teach him this summer," Sergei muttered, taking a pull from his beer.

"He's three." Toli chuckled. "I'm sure he'll need more than one lesson. Besides, serves you right for not teaching him last summer. Alex will be on skates this summer and he's only a year."

Sergei made a face. "Not like I have a lot of time, you know? Have you forgotten about that whole single dad thing?"

Toli arched his brows. "Cranky much?"

"Whatever." Sergei sank into a chair in the family room.

Toli sat across from him, leaning forward and cocking his head. "How's it going? You haven't said much since you moved to Alaska."

Sergei shrugged. "What's to say? They're a struggling expansion team. They came into the NHL the same year as the Sidewinders but there's a different vibe than what you have here." Sergei and his brothers all played professional hockey. While Sergei had been playing in Russia and then in Boston the last few years, Toli and their half-brother, Vlad, played for the Las Vegas Sidewinders. A little over two months ago, in late February, Sergei had been traded to the Alaska Blizzard, and it hadn't been anything like what he'd been expecting. In fact, it hadn't been like any team he'd ever played for—in college, in Russia, or in the NHL. Though he didn't want to say the words out loud, it sucked.

"You want to talk about it?" Toli pressed, watching him carefully.

"Nah. I want to hang out with my family for a week, and then head back to…Anchorage." He tried to hide his distaste but his brother knew him too well and his eyebrows instantly shot up.

"I've heard rumors it's a rough room," was all Toli said.

"Not as bad as some, a lot worse than others," Sergei muttered.

"That bad?" Toli looked surprised.

"It's honestly like nothing I've ever experienced as a professional."

"Will you stay?"

"I've had feelers out but I think I'm stuck in Anchorage for at least one full season."

"You want me to talk to Mr. Finch? Find a way to get you on the Sidewinders?"

Sergei shook his head. "Nah. That would scream nepotism and I can handle almost anything for a year. Assuming I can find a nanny for Niko."

"Speaking of which, I think I have a solution for that."

"You do?"

"Yes. Our friend—"

He was cut off as the front door opened and a cheerful female voice called out, "Lucy—I'm ho-ome!"

"Who's Lucy?" Sergei frowned as Niko bolted for the front door.

"Mama D!"

"Hey, kiddo!" A tall blonde came around the corner, her face nuzzled in Niko's tummy as she carried him.

"What did he call you?" Sergei stood up, a scowl creasing his face.

"Excuse me?" The blonde slowly put Niko down and scowled right back.

"Did he call you *Mama*?" Sergei demanded.

She arched her brows and fixed big green eyes on him. "Yes. Mama D—for Danielle."

"You're not his mother."

"Sergei—" Toli began.

"We're both well aware of that." Her eyes flashed with annoyance. "It's a *nickname*."

"Daddy?" Niko looked distressed as he watched them.

"It's okay, sweetie." Tessa swooped in and grabbed Niko's hand. "Let's get a snack."

Sergei whirled on Toli once his son was out of earshot. "You let him call her *Mama*? What the fuck?"

"It's not—" Toli tried again.

"We didn't *let* him," Dani interjected with a dark frown, folding her arms across her chest. "We tried to guide him to *Auntie* D and he refused. For some reason, he hung on to *Mama* D and we decided to let him get past it on his own instead of calling attention to it like you're doing now."

The look she was giving him would have made his dick hard under any other circumstances as he took in big green eyes currently sparking with anger, pink lips pursed in annoyance and a taut, gorgeous body poised for a fight... But not today. Today he was pissed. Today he wanted somebody to take out his frustrations on and hearing his son call this stranger *Mama* poked him in just the wrong way.

"He's *my* son," he growled, giving her an equally distasteful look as his lusty thoughts turned dark.

"No shit, sherlock." She narrowed her eyes. "What does that have to do with anything?"

"In case you weren't aware, he has a mother and—"

"Unfortunately, he doesn't anymore," she snipped, tossing her long blond hair. "And based on the fact you dumped him here on your brother's wife, he doesn't have much of a father, either."

"Who the hell do you think you are?" Sergei took a step toward her but Toli quickly planted himself between them, shaking his head, even though Danielle never flinched. Before anyone could say anything, Tessa came back into the room glaring at them.

"Sergei, what on earth is wrong with you?" she asked in disbelief. "We tried to get him to call her something else and he refused. We thought it would only make it worse if we kept correcting him, so we stopped. I'm sorry if that bothers you, but it's not Dani's fault, so please stop yelling at her."

No one said anything for a moment as Tessa fixed the brothers with a look of disapproval.

"I have things to do," Dani muttered, picking up her purse. "Tessa, call me tomorrow. Bye, Toli." She walked out the front door and slammed it behind her.

"If I lose the best helper I've ever had because you two are stupid, I'm going to be pissed!" Tessa snapped.

"I tried to tell him," Toli protested.

"Well, you weren't quick enough and he hurt her feelings." Tessa shook her head. "Neither of you should get any meatloaf tonight."

"Hey, what did I do?" Toli called after her, a smile of affection on his lips as he watched her go.

Tessa chuckled as she disappeared around the corner.

"He can't call a woman I don't even know *Mama*," Sergei grumbled, following Toli out to the back patio.

"You could have handled that four hundred and seventy-two different ways," Toli said, twisting the top off a beer and taking a long pull before switching to their native Russian. "What was that about? And don't give me any bullshit about how he can't call anyone *Mama* but Tatiana. She's been gone nearly two years. He doesn't even remember her—" He held up a hand when Sergei started to say something. "I loved her, too. I miss her. Not like you do, but I knew her most of my life, and I watched her die just like you did. There's nothing fair about it and I'm not trying to tell you how to grieve, but you can't expect Niko to mourn like you do. He's *three*. All he knows are her pictures. He tried calling Tessa *Mama T*, but we changed that to *Auntie T* and it stuck. For whatever reason, we couldn't dissuade him with Dani. Yelling at her like that was uncalled for."

Sergei let out a long, frustrated breath. He wanted to yell some more, tell all of them to fuck off and kiss his ass, but that wouldn't be the right thing to do. Not only were they family, they'd gotten him through the darkest days of his life after his wife had been murdered, and Tessa had dropped everything more than once to help him with Niko. No, it wouldn't be right to take his anger out on them no matter how much he wanted to. And now that he'd calmed down a little, he realized he shouldn't have gone after Dani, either. Tessa had mentioned Zakk's sister helping out on more than one occasion and now he was a little embarrassed by how he'd behaved.

"Are you going to talk to me?" Toli asked quietly, meeting his eyes.

Sergei gave an impatient little shrug. "I'll apologize to her. It caught me off guard."

"I don't care about that." Toli grunted. "I mean, I do, but not right this minute. I want to know what's wrong. You miss Tatiana, you're not thrilled playing in Alaska, and being a single dad is rough. You have every right to be on edge, but not here, in my house—this should be where you can relax. What happened to set you off?"

"Nothing specific," Sergei admitted, "but I hold it in all the time. The anger, the frustration, the pain... There's nowhere else to let loose. I have to focus on hockey. When I'm not playing, I've got to be a dad to Niko, which is all-encompassing. Then Boston traded me to fucking *Alaska*. I had to sell the house, make sure everything was packed up, dump my kid with family, and move to fucking Anchorage. I'm constantly on guard because the new team is a mess. On top of all that, they had a shit season and we didn't make the playoffs. I've been living in a shithole corporate apartment and couldn't find a house I liked. I haven't had time to melt down or let off steam or get my shit together. I took a little time off when she died, but sitting at home grieving wasn't good for me and it definitely wasn't good for Niko. Fast forward about eighteen months and I'm still struggling."

"And because we're men we don't think we can admit weakness," his brother responded wryly.

Sergei managed a faint smile, taking a pull from his beer and staring off into space. "Maybe I'm a little jealous, you know? You have it all—the beautiful wife, the kids, the skyrocketing career... I don't have anything except that little boy in there. Maybe that's why I lost my shit when I heard him call someone I didn't know *Mama*."

"What can I do?" Toli asked quietly.

"I don't know. Probably nothing."

They were quiet for a while, sipping their beers and watching the sun get a little lower in the sky. Finally, Toli glanced over at him. "Stay a while," he suggested softly.

"What?"

"What is there for you in Anchorage? Right now, you need your family, and I hate to say this, but Niko needs his aunts and uncles, his cousins, and the people he's met here. If the team out there isn't like a family to you, then borrow mine. Until you're strong again." He rested a hand on Sergei's shoulder, though he didn't look at him. "I know it's hard for you to ask for help, so I'm going to give it to you. The Sidewinders have become family to me, and you already have a relationship with many of them. Stay here with us; take some time to heal. Let Tessa and the other wives mother Niko—he knows they're not *Mommy*. He doesn't understand it, but he knows. Tatiana will always be his mother, but since she can't be here, let him get that kind of love elsewhere."

Sergei swallowed hard, swiping at something that was making his eyes scratchy.

"Fuck, Toli." Sergei couldn't articulate anything else.

"I know." Toli squeezed his shoulder as he got to his feet. "Now I'm going to go inside and sweet-talk my wife until she lets us have meatloaf for dinner."

"Thank you."

Toli just smiled.

For a while, Sergei didn't move. Long after his beer was empty and Toli stuck his head out to tell him dinner was ready, he sat in the lounge chair staring at the crystalline waters of the pool and the slowly setting sun. It was as close as he'd come to relaxed in nearly two years. It had been nineteen months since his wife had died, and sometimes it seemed like yesterday. He still saw her smile in his dreams, but when he was awake, it was harder. He had to focus to picture her face, and those were the times guilt overwhelmed him.

She'd died to protect him, and it still haunted him. He should have stopped her—he'd known her father hated him—but living in the U.S., far away from his father-in-law's involvement with the Russian mafia, he'd dropped his guard. She'd paid for it with her life, and though he didn't think she would be happy knowing how difficult it had been for him to move on, he didn't know how. She and Niko had been his life outside of hockey, and there had never been a scenario where he was going to raise his son on his own. Her death had thrown him for a loop emotionally, mentally, and in a lot of ways, profession-ally. At this point, he had no choice but to accept Toli's offer of help. Whatever stage of grief this was, it sucked balls. Maybe the comfort of his family was what had been missing all along. God knew he needed something, because he wasn't handling it on his own.

2

Dani was in a sour mood when she left the Las Vegas Sidewinders' offices a little after four. She normally left at two, but today she'd stayed late, answering phones and hanging out with the rest of the staff. It was busy right now with the team in the playoffs, and since there was a game tonight it seemed silly to go home just to change clothes and come back.

Her older brother, Zakk, was a forward on the team, and she'd come to Las Vegas to live with him and his wife back in December. She'd only had a few classes left to get her master's degree, and all three had been available online, so she'd been able to leave North Dakota. There were only three weeks left in the semester and though she was excited about graduating, she was floundering. She didn't know what she was going to do with her degree, where she was going to work, or where she was going to live. Throwing the Olympics into the mix left her at the biggest crossroads of her life.

Changing into jeans and her Sidewinders jersey in the ladies' room, she smiled despite her dark thoughts. She loved wearing Zakk's jersey. It was as close to the big leagues as she'd ever get and since they shared both a last name and a number, she sometimes liked to pretend it was the real thing. She'd played hockey, too, and people often said she was as good as her brother. The problem, of course, was that there was no viable professional option for women, at least not in her opinion, because she refused to play for the pittance women in the National Women's Hockey League were paid. It was embarrassing and wrong, but while her decision kept her pride intact, it didn't keep her from missing hockey.

She headed down towards the locker rooms. Though she only worked part-time in the sales department, she was an employee as well as the sister of one of the players on the team. She stayed away most of the time, but the guys never seemed to mind if she stopped by to say hello before a game, and she made sure she left relatively quickly so she didn't overstay her welcome. Zakk had said it was okay, so she occasionally wandered down around the time the guys started arriving at the arena.

"Hey, sis." Zakk was already in the hallway.

"Hey." She smiled at him.

"How was your day?"

"Pretty good. You ready for tonight?"

"Hell yeah." He caught the soccer ball that came flying through the air as he grinned at her. "Wanna play?"

She shook her head. "No thanks, I'm going to—"

"Dani! Just the young lady I was looking for!" Sidewinders' team owner Lonnie Finch approached her with a broad grin. Looking up at her, since she was a good six inches taller than he was, he held out his arm and she had no choice but to take it.

"Have a good game!" she called over her shoulder to her brother.

"See you tonight!" he called back.

Though part of her was a little concerned that the team owner wanted to see her, she couldn't think of anything she'd done wrong. She only worked part-time and her job was basically answering phones. As long as she wasn't rude to anyone—and she was fairly certain she hadn't been—there wasn't much to screw up.

"How have things been going, my dear?" he asked as they took the elevator up to the executive offices.

"Okay," she responded. "I've only got a few more weeks left until I finish my master's degree, so I've been working on my resumé."

"That's what I wanted to talk to you about," he said, letting her walk into his office ahead of him.

"Okay." She sat in one of the chairs by his desk and he sat beside her.

"You hate working in the sales department." He met her gaze directly, though there was no censure in his eyes.

"It's not what I've studied for," she said quietly. "Sales isn't my thing, but I'm grateful for the opportunity to work for the team."

"Have you given up on hockey?"

She sighed. "Sir, I can't work for that kind of money. All those women either have day jobs or wait tables to survive and it's unfair."

"I agree," he nodded. "What about the Olympics?"

"I don't know." She looked away. This was a touchy subject for her.

"You made the team."

"Yes." Tryouts had been last week.

"Are you going?"

"I'm not sure."

"What's the hesitation?"

"I'll have to go to Colorado in September and stay there, with the team, until the Olympics in February. I'm about to get my master's in kinesiology and exercise science. I have student loans, bills to pay... I don't know how much longer I can afford to keep this up."

"Keep what up?"

"Mr. Finch, I'm sorry, I don't mean to be rude, but are you telling me I don't have a job here anymore? I've pretty much decided I'm done with hockey, even though I'm planning to go to the Olympics..."

"I thought you didn't want to go?" he pressed gently.

"Zakk wants me to. Everyone wants me to."

"But do you want to?"

She blew out a breath. "Yeah. My heart wants me to even though my brain says I'm an idiot."

"How old were you when you started playing hockey?"

"I don't even know," she admitted. "However old Zakk was. I'm three years younger, so essentially that's when I started."

"I've seen you play. You're every bit as talented as your brother. I'm sorry there isn't a career choice for women that equals the ones afforded to men, but the Olympics is something special, something very few people can say they've done."

She narrowed her eyes slightly. "Zakk asked you to talk to me," she said after a moment, shaking her head.

"He may have mentioned that you're unwilling to accept financial assistance from him for that time period and therefore considering not going. I'd like to change your mind about that. Perhaps offer you some incentive."

Dani couldn't help but chuckle. "My brother is nothing if not persistent."

"He loves you."

"And I love him. But I'm going to be twenty-three this summer and it's time for me to take care of myself. Zakk sent me money all through college to cover things my scholarship didn't, and then he paid my living expenses so I could stay and start my master's. Now I live with him and he helped get me my job here on the team. At some point, I have to do something on my own. Do you understand?" She met his gaze imploringly.

This time he was the one to sigh, reaching out to pat her hand. "Believe it or not, I do. I just don't think this is the time to spread your wings. Not yet. Eight or nine more months of hockey, Dani. What will it hurt?"

"I don't know."

"Tell me this, then. What are your plans if you decide not to join the Olympic team after all?"

"I'll start looking for a job as an assistant trainer."

"For a hockey team?"

She chuckled. "Well, yes, that's my specialty so that would be my first choice. Since the trainers here in Vegas are solid, I'll be putting out feelers to all the other teams in the league."

He leaned back. "There may be something opening up."

She froze, turning in surprise. "Here?"

"If you join the Olympic team, I can hold the position until you get done."

Her mouth opened but nothing came out at first. "Mr. Finch, that's not how this works!"

He burst out laughing. "Of course it is, little one. You'll have a graduate degree in exercise science shortly, which is exactly what you need for the job, and what you've been studying for. You also played the sport and come with excellent recommendations. If working here in that capacity is what you want, I can arrange it." He gave her a quick, almost paternal, wink. "Come see me after the Olympics, Dani, and we'll make this happen."

There didn't seem to be anything else to say, so Dani nodded. "Thank you, Mr. Finch. I appreciate it."

3

Sergei was checking email on his phone as he waited for the elevator doors to open, so he didn't notice her right away. He was immersed in a note from his mother in Russia as he stepped inside, and it wasn't until he heard his name that he looked up. He froze when he found big green eyes intently focused on him. Jesus, had Danielle been this pretty yesterday? How had he missed those eyes? It was like staring into a pool of the shiniest, most sparkling emeralds he'd ever seen, and for a moment he couldn't remember why he didn't particularly like her.

"Are you going up to the owner's box?" she asked, cocking her head when he didn't respond right away.

"Er, yes. Mr. Finch invited me to watch the game from there."

"I get off on the floor before," she said, pushing a button on the panel.

"Do you have seats?" he asked.

"I sit with the WAGs," she responded, referring to the wives and girlfriends of the players.

Damn, he needed to stop staring, so he cleared his throat. "I wanted to apologize," he said hesitantly. "I shouldn't have reacted the way I did yesterday. It caught me off guard since I don't even know you, but I'm genuinely sorry for raising my voice."

"Is it Toli or Zakk who's forcing you to apologize?" she asked, those green eyes still burning into his.

"What?" He made a face. "No one forced me to do anything. But Toli explained how much time you've spent with Niko and how helpful you've been to Tessa, so I thought—"

"You thought you'd make peace since I'm the sister and you're the brother." She made an impatient gesture. "No worries, it's all good." The elevator came to a stop and she took a step towards the doors as they slid open.

"No. Wait." Sergei wasn't sure why everything was so difficult with this woman. He was trying to be polite and she wasn't making it easy. "Will you please come up to the box with me so we can talk?"

"I'm meeting friends." She stepped out and turned to look at him. "But if you'd like to talk tomorrow, meet me at the practice rink on Hellman Street. Ten o'clock. You have equipment you can borrow?"

He blinked. "Hockey equipment?"

"No, rugby equipment." She rolled her eyes. "Yes, of course hockey equipment. A group of us play several times a week. You want to talk, be there. If not, I understand." The elevator doors closed and left Sergei staring blankly at where she'd been. What the hell had just happened? And where was he going to get hockey equipment that fit by tomorrow morning?

HE'D HAD TO SCRAMBLE, but with Toli and Zakk's help, Sergei managed to put enough equipment together for an informal hockey game. From what Toli had told him, Danielle played with a group of mostly male players from the local university team and a few retired NHL players who lived in the area now. She was one of only two women who played, and there was no checking allowed, but they played hard and fast. It kept her in shape since she'd made the Olympic team—which he hadn't known—and Sergei had looked her up online last night to get a feel for how good she was.

To his chagrin, he'd discovered she was fantastic. Watching video of her during last year's Frozen Four championship game had been mind-boggling to him. He'd had no idea Zakk's sister was so skilled and couldn't help but wonder why she wasn't playing professional hockey. There was a woman's league now, though he admittedly didn't know much about it. Zakk had said they didn't offer much in the way of salaries, and when he'd looked it up, he'd been surprised at the pay scale. Ranging from ten to twenty-six thousand dollars a year, none of those women could make a living wage playing full-time, especially in cities like New York and Boston. The more he read, the less sense it made, especially if they played anywhere near as well as Danielle did. These women were athletes just like him and anyone he'd ever played with, yet the salaries were unbelievably low. How could anyone work as hard as they did in hockey and still have to work another job to have money for rent? He had no idea what that was like and made a mental note to be a little more grateful for the career he had.

He got to the arena early, wanting to get a feel for the place and see who his teammates were. His gut told him Danielle wanted him to apologize somewhere she felt comfortable and he was okay with that; he honestly hadn't meant to hurt her feelings. Maybe if they played on the same team he could make it up to her by helping them win. She was good, but he didn't know what the others were like, so he wasn't expecting much in the way of competition.

"Good morning." She came out of the locker room in form-fitting bike shorts, a sports bra and sandals, her blond hair pulled up in a ponytail.

"Good morning." Sergei had to catch himself so he didn't do an obvious double take, but he'd never seen a woman with a body like hers. She had six-pack abs, with a torso so sculpted he wanted to reach out and run his hands over it. Then there were her legs, long and lean, but with muscular thighs and perfect calves. She didn't have much in the way of breasts, but that was okay since the rest of her was essentially perfect. Holy shit, who was this woman?

"The guys change in there." She motioned to a door down the hall. "We'll start warming up in about twenty minutes."

"Okay."

"I'm sure Toli told you, but there's no checking. We play three twenty-minute periods but we only take five-minute breaks in between. There's a ref, but it's hit or miss on whether or not whoever we get will actually call much."

Sergei snickered. "Sounds about right."

"You'll play for the Wolves, so light jerseys."

"Who do you play for?"

"The Glaciers." She flashed a smile as she turned to go back into the locker room. "See you on the ice."

"I'll be there." He watched her go and had to snap his mouth shut to keep from gaping at her ass. It was about as perfect as a woman's ass could be, and if it was anything like the rest of her, he'd be willing to bet it was rock solid, too. Round, toned and probably muscular—he didn't know when he'd last wanted to take a bite out of a woman's backside.

"Hey, you must be Sergei." A tall, skinny man with glasses and a friendly smile held out his hand. "Kincaid Lawrence."

"Nice to meet you." Sergei shook his hand and fell into step beside him as they headed towards the other locker room.

"It's an honor to play with you today," Kincaid said, letting Sergei walk into the room in front of him. "We play a pretty high-level game, but I'm sure you'll up the intensity."

"I'm always happy to play, but mostly I'm here as a favor to Danielle," Sergei hedged, suddenly unsure what he was actually doing here. It had almost been as if she'd dared him to come and now he was questioning whether or not he'd made the right decision. He did owe her an apology, though, and this seemed to be the way she wanted it even though it didn't make much sense.

"Well, you'd better tap into your NHL skills because Dani and Sara don't mess around, and now that Dani's going to be on the Olympic team, she needs us to push her limits."

Okay, maybe it did make sense. What better way to push her limits as a hockey player than by practicing with an elite player from the NHL? It was a little odd to think of himself from what might be her perspective, but it's not like he said that kind of thing out loud, even though it was technically true.

"Who's Sara?" he asked as they started changing.

"She and Dani are good friends. They played in college together."

"So she's pretty good?"

"Sara? Yeah. Not like Dani, but she can hold her own, for sure."

"Sounds like a good time. You play anywhere?"

"In college," he nodded, "but never professionally. I'm an attorney—went straight to law school, and I wasn't that good. I still enjoy it, though."

A few other men arrived and once Sergei was introduced, conversation drifted to his team in Alaska and other random hockey topics. By the time they got onto the ice to warm up, Sergei felt comfortable with his teammates, confident it would be a fun morning doing the one thing he still enjoyed. If it somehow bought him some brownie points with his brother and sister-in-law, that would be a nice bonus since Tessa was still annoyed with him about the whole thing.

Stepping out on the ice, Sergei didn't think about skates that were half a size too small, equipment that was unfamiliar, and a stick someone else had taped. These were minor annoyances, nothing he couldn't play through, and he focused on watching the other team as he circled the ice.

Danielle was slender but strong and fast, moving smoothly as she shot puck after puck into the net as she warmed up. She was accurate as hell and he was briefly distracted by how great her shot was. He was momentarily annoyed they were on opposing teams; it would be a lot of fun to play on a line with her, watch her move the puck and see what kinds of plays she made. Some people were more fun to play with than others, and from what he'd seen so far, Danielle would be one of them.

"She's hard to ignore, eh?" Kincaid skated up beside Sergei and followed his gaze.

"Our brothers are friends and I'd heard of her, of course," Sergei admitted. "But I had no idea she was so good."

"Yeah, we've gone from playing once a week to three times to help her get ready for the Olympics. She's having a hard time making a decision on whether or not she's going to go in September."

"Why?" Sergei cocked his head.

Kincaid hesitated. "That's her story. I shouldn't have said anything." He skated off and Sergei followed thoughtfully. Why would she have doubts about playing in the Olympics? Who wouldn't want to win a gold medal? He had one and so did Toli. There was probably more to the story, but he didn't know her well enough to be able to come up with a reason to ask.

It had been a long time since Dani had been nervous on the ice, but Sergei had her so self-conscious she barely remembered warming up. Now that she was sitting on the bench, waiting for the game to start, her heart was still racing a little and it wasn't because she was out of breath. Why did someone as good-looking as Sergei have to be such a jerk? He hadn't done anything since their initial awkward encounter yesterday but she still had a bad taste in her mouth from the way he'd shouted at her. She probably shouldn't have responded the way she had, but she'd been caught off guard as well, since they'd all tried to get Niko to call her something other than *Mama D*. It didn't seem fair for Sergei to assume she was trying to replace Niko's mother.

"He's soooo hot," her best friend, Sara Chandler, nudged her. "I can't believe you got Sergei Petrov to come play with us!"

"He owed me after being such a jerk the other day," Dani muttered.

"That right there is the guy you need to punch your V-card!" Sara giggled.

"Shh!" Dani's cheeks reddened and she looked around quickly to make sure no one had heard. The last thing she needed was to advertise the fact that she was an almost-twenty-three-year-old virgin.

"Don't worry, no one can hear me." Sara shook her head, her brown eyes sparkling. "Look, you said you just want it gone, so he's perfect. Really hot, so it'll be fun to make out and stuff. A lot older, so experienced enough to make it bearable even though the first time is probably gonna suck no matter what. And, for the icing on the cake, he's still a wreck over his dead wife, so he's not going to get hung up on you or get clingy. Exactly what you need."

Dani gave her friend a look. "At this point, I might as well go to the doctor and have my cherry surgically removed."

"Oh, stop!" Sara laughed. "That's not nearly as fun."

"You just said the first time is gonna suck no matter what—how is that fun?"

"It might not be awful, but I don't know anyone who said it didn't hurt. Besides, that's not the point... *Sergei Petrov* is the point. I mean, holy shit, look at him move."

Dani had to concede the point; he was beautiful both on and off the ice. Unlike his quirky older brother who had a crooked smile and a bump on his nose, Sergei was magazine cover material. Deep-set, wide blue eyes, a strong chin with a cleft in it, light blond hair that was usually swept back off his forehead, and cheekbones for miles. Not to mention the body of a god. He was an inch or so shorter than Toli, but more muscular, with broad shoulders and thick thighs from spending his life skating. She couldn't see it now, but when she'd seen him in jeans yesterday, his backside looked good enough to want to take a bite of and—

"Snap out of it!" Sara nudged her again. "Let's go."

Together, they swung their legs over the boards and onto the ice. Dani skated to the face-off circle while Sara moved off to the right. Out of the corner of her eye, Dani saw Sergei move to a defensive position to her left, close to the blue line. Sara was set up to cover Sergei, which made Dani snicker since her friend appeared somewhat starstruck. His record was impressive on paper but even more so in person. He was good-looking, talented and strong—what more could you want from a guy who played hockey?

Dani won the opening face-off easily, passing the puck to the defenseman behind her. She followed the play, taking the pass back to her and scoring the first goal of the day. A small smile played on her lips as she watched the surprise register on Sergei's face; he obviously hadn't been expecting her to come out ready to play, but that was one of the things she was known for. As soon as she had the chance, she'd show him what else she'd come to be known for on the ice.

4

Sergei had watched video of Dani, but she was even better now that he was watching her in person. The way she handled a quick release—the motion of shooting immediately after stickhandling—was as good as anyone he'd ever played with, at any level. Even some NHL players took a little longer to get set up to take a shot, but Dani's reflex was like lightning, sending it off as though the stick was part of her. It had been so incredible to watch up close; she'd scored three goals before he caught the satisfied little smirk she sent in his direction.

"What's the matter, big guy?" she taunted as she skated past him. "Afraid to show me what you've got?"

He arched a brow. "Ask and you shall receive, sweetheart."

She won the next face-off, as she'd done since the beginning of the game, but this time he was on top of her, stealing the puck and taking it back in the other direction. He passed it to Kincaid, who shot wide, sending the puck almost directly onto Dani's stick.

Rookie, Sergei thought with annoyance. He followed the play, keeping an eye on Dani, still intrigued with how fluid her movements were. She was getting close to another scoring opportunity, and this time he would show her how they handled things in the big leagues. She was attempting to fake around him, on her side of the ice, stickhandling forehand to backhand, leaning and looking towards the middle. He'd seen her do it the last time she'd scored and it was a pretty crafty maneuver, but this time he was ready.

When she suddenly ducked back towards the boards to go in the opposite direction she'd been looking, he was expecting it. He slid one skate out to block the puck from going around him, kicked it to his stick and took possession. In a move he made almost daily in the NHL, he accelerated, breezing past

Dani's much slower teammates, placing the puck almost delicately in the net. As his teammates surrounded him with a group hug and high fives, he caught her look of surprise, but opted to keep his head down. The time wasn't right to let her know he was on to her; he'd let her sweat it a little first.

Dani didn't seem to take it to heart, winning the face-off on her next shift and keeping the puck in play. Both goalies were getting a workout, blocking more shots than they let in, but it quickly became apparent this was the Dani-and-Sergei show. They were the stars, the most powerful players on the ice, and she was going to give him a run for his money. He thought it was hot as hell, but he'd let her get comfortable before showing her up again. She was far too confident for someone who was going to be going up against the best in the world in a few months.

She scored again, flashing him another smile that made him shake his head. Okay, it was time.

When she tried to fake him out again, leaning and looking in the opposite direction of where she planned to go, he didn't wait and simply reversed direction. She had to come to almost a complete stop to keep from colliding with him, and he stole the puck, taking it down the ice before passing it back to Kincaid without a backward glance.

Sergei nearly laughed at the look on Dani's face as she realized he'd purposely foiled her signature move not once, but twice. And this time she was *pissed*. She'd asked for this, though. He'd planned to keep things mellow, let the amateurs have some fun with him, but she'd brought her A game and the moment she'd asked him to test her skills, he'd been ready and willing. She hadn't expected him to be able to read her, and he didn't know whether to be cocky or humble about it. Taking into consideration the relationship of their brothers, he figured maybe a happy medium was the best move, but he couldn't resist a little wink as he skated past her on his way back to the bench.

DANI WASN'T sure if she wanted to laugh or punch him. What the hell had just happened? How had Sergei known what she was going to do like that? Her brother had taught her that move—faking out her opponents—and it had earned her a full athletic scholarship and helped her team win two Frozen Four championships. Sergei had gotten around her twice, which was as impressive as it was infuriating, and now she was lost as to what to do next. Losing to him was not an option.

"Damn, he's really good," Sara panted, sinking down next to her.

"Fucker," Dani mumbled.

"Oh, don't be like that. I rarely get to see anyone play better than you."

Dani gave her a dirty look.

"Hey, you make me look bad every time we get on the ice together, so now you know how it feels."

Dani frowned. "You feel bad when we play together?"

"Not anymore, but I did in college. Dani, you're so good—if you weren't my best friend I'd hate you."

"Is that a compliment?" Dani wrinkled her nose.

"Of course it is!" Sara got up to get on the ice again, and Dani followed, skating to the face-off circle.

"Next time," a deep voice spoke softly in her ear, "go in the direction you're looking. No one will expect it. Change it up every play. It'll keep them guessing."

She turned to respond, but Sergei was heading back to the bench, his back turned as if he hadn't just spoken to her.

He had a point, though. Changing her approach would be the smart thing to do, and while she hated that it had come from him, he was right. This was why he was one of the top players in the world. She didn't have to like him, but she would be foolish not to respect or listen to him. Especially if it helped her team win in the Olympics.

An hour later, Dani tried to shake off the frustration of losing 7-6. Sergei had scored five of the other team's seven goals, and she'd scored five of the six on her team, but his last goal had been just before the final buzzer. It stung a little, and she huffed back to the locker room before anyone had a chance to talk to her. It was silly to be mad; the whole reason she was here was to stay in shape until September. Sergei making her do better wasn't a bad thing. If only it were someone else. Anyone else. Something about him made her frustrated, angry...excited. Why did he have to be so good-looking?

"Great game!" Sara gushed, sliding onto the bench next to her.

Dani cut her eyes to her. "We lost."

"Yeah, but it was tied right down to the wire. I mean, I was on the ice with Sergei Petrov! That's the closest I'll ever get to professional hockey."

"You and me both," Dani groused.

"Are you mad?"

"Frustrated," Dani said. "He makes me want to hit something."

"'Cause he's hot and you want him."

Dani gave a half-hearted chuckle. "I do *not* want him. He's an arrogant ass."

"Who gave you a run for your money."

"He plays seven days a week with the cream of the crop in hockey—of course he did! I'm playing three days a week with minor league, college, and retired players. There's a big difference."

Sara met her friend's eyes. "And he knows that. I'm sure he didn't make that last goal just to piss you off."

"After the way he behaved yesterday, I wouldn't put it past him." Dani got up and started changing her clothes.

SHE TOOK her time cooling down, changing into shorts and a T-shirt and packing up her equipment. She'd hoped Sergei would be gone by the time she was ready to go, but she wasn't that lucky. He was leaning up against the wall, talking with Kincaid and a few of the other guys.

"Great game today, Dani!" Kincaid called out. "It was awesome testing my skills against Petrov."

She nodded. "It was a good workout. Thanks for coming, Sergei." She high-fived a few of her friends and kept walking.

"Danielle! Wait up." Sergei was coming after her and she managed to keep herself from sighing.

"You need a ride?" she asked politely, pausing to let him catch up.

He shook his head. "No, I took Tessa's SUV."

"Okay." She started walking again.

"Danielle—"

"It's Dani," she called over her shoulder. "Only my parents call me Danielle."

"Would you stop walking?" he demanded gruffly.

She stopped and turned, narrowing her eyes. "I have to get home. I have homework to finish."

"Homework?" He looked confused.

"I'm getting my master's degree," she said. "I have one final paper due in two weeks and I have a job, plus helping Tessa and Tiff with the kids."

"Wow, congratulations on the master's," he said. "You only graduated last year, right?"

"Yes, but I started my freshman year with a semester's worth of classes through AP credits and still took a full course load. I was able to start my master's in the spring of my senior year, as well as classes last summer, and since I chose the non-thesis option, all I have left is this paper and an oral exam my professor offered to do via Skype."

"You're busy," he said quietly, his deep blue eyes meeting hers.

"I am." She tried not to stare back because there was something intoxicating about him. "Thanks for playing with us today and for the tips, but I have to get going."

"Yeah, sure. I, uh, Kincaid asked if I wanted to play Tuesday... Is that okay with you?"

She hesitated a moment but nodded. "Absolutely. It's good having someone who can challenge me out there."

"We're good then?"

"We're good."

"See you Tuesday."

Something unfamiliar fluttered in her stomach but she pushed away what could only be described as excitement and tried to think about finishing her paper. His blue eyes and broad shoulders were absolutely not what she needed to think about.

SITTING in bed late that night, Sergei was thinking about Danielle instead of watching the show on TV. *She likes to be called Dani,* he reminded himself. She was everything he usually avoided in women, but she was all he'd thought about today. With Toli and the Sidewinders out of town for a road trip, he'd kept busy helping Tessa with the kids and playing with Niko, but now that everyone was in bed and the house was quiet, his thoughts drifted to the tall, athletic blonde with the piercing green eyes. He'd seen her at games a few times in the past, but he'd been married then and he'd never looked at other women. Not even beautiful ones who played hockey as well as any man he'd ever known. She needed a little coaching, but her natural skills were excellent.

Mindlessly switching the channels, he stared at the TV without really seeing anything. He'd watched so much TV in the year and a half since Tatiana had died he'd practically memorized some of the more common shows. At times, the loneliness had been almost more than he could bear. Those were the nights he dug into a bottle of bourbon until the pain eased and was able to rest. Luckily, his devotion to his son and the game of hockey kept him from doing that too often, but there had been days off that had nearly driven him out of his mind. Loneliness and grief were a terrible combination, and he'd wallowed in it for a while. Too long, probably, but he still couldn't completely wrap his head around the fact that Tatiana was gone. Dead. Shot right in front of him. The worst day of his life. The end of everything as he'd known it.

He'd been trying to get past this stage, the one where he wasn't an emotional wreck anymore, but he hadn't really started living again, either. There had been a handful of one-night stands—he was only human—but he made sure to keep away from women who might get attached. The thought of dating scared the shit out of him so he'd done everything in his power to avoid it. Especially in Alaska, where all the attractive women looked like they were still in high school. At thirty-three, he had one ex-wife and one late wife, so if he was looking, it would be someone his own age, who might have an ex or at least some life experience. A twenty-year-old puck bunny didn't sound like any fun at all outside the bedroom.

There was a certain green-eyed hockey player who made parts of him that had been mostly dormant come alive every time he thought about her, though, and that needed to stop. Something about her fiery spirit made him want to know more. She was beautiful, athletic, and from what he'd heard, extremely intelligent. She would be the perfect woman for him to dip his toe back into the dating waters with. Except dating wasn't the same as having a one-night stand and he didn't want to date. Besides, she didn't seem to like him very much, which would be problematic if he wanted to date her. Which he didn't. In fact, everything about hooking up with Dani was terrible in theory.

First, she was too young. He was more than a decade older than her. He'd already turned thirty-three and she wouldn't be twenty-three until late summer. A girl her age was almost definitely looking for a husband, and he wasn't husband material. Not again. Twice was enough for him. Maybe he'd be willing to stay faithful to one woman at some point, have a long-term girl-friend, but he'd given up on forever. Especially with Niko in the mix. He wasn't comfortable bringing into the boy's life a woman whom he could potentially lose again. It was a little dramatic to think that way, but he wasn't willing to expose his son to that kind of pain. Niko wouldn't remember losing his biological mother, but he'd remember losing anyone who moved into that role now. Which brought him to the second reason getting involved with Dani would be a bad idea.

She wasn't just young in age, she was inexperienced in life. She wasn't even completely out of college and didn't know what she wanted to do. Though there was nothing wrong with that—not everyone needed to know their life plan at twenty-three—he'd been through too much in the last couple of years to get close to someone who could change her mind at a moment's notice. He and Niko needed stability. There were times it pained him to think that way because it made him feel like an old man, but his emotions were real. He didn't want another woman who was focused on change, finding herself, possibly even experimenting with different careers. She wasn't sure about the Olympics, and Toli had mentioned she was also considering staying in school to get her Ph.D. It sounded exhausting to him. He'd already been through it with both Maria and Tatiana; when the time came to get involved again, it would be with someone who'd be willing to focus on him and Niko. There was no room in his life for a smart, sassy young woman who'd ultimately leave him and a boring little family in Anchorage behind.

That didn't mean they couldn't be friends, did it? The thought came and went quickly and he shook his head. He had a major hard-on for this girl and the only way to get her out of his system would be to sleep with her. Except that would be a huge mistake for him and wholly unfair to her. Maybe it was time for another one-nighter with a stranger, someone to scratch his proverbial itch and make it easier to ignore the stirring in his groin every time he was in the same room as Danielle Cloutier.

5

Sitting up late at night to work on her paper wasn't Dani's idea of fun, but this was the only time she had any peace and quiet. It was Friday, so she wasn't working tomorrow and could stay up as late as she needed to. She'd immersed herself in schoolwork the last few days in order to avoid thinking about whether or not she would go to Colorado Springs in September, but it had backfired. She hadn't gotten much done on her final paper and she hadn't made a decision about hockey, either. At this point, she was second-guessing herself, her talent, her decision-making abilities, and almost everything about her life. She loved hockey, and playing on the Olympic team would be her last hurrah in the sport. By the same token, it worried her because not getting a medal would mean ending her career on a sour note.

She jumped when there was movement behind her and turned to her brother in surprise, frowning. "What are you doing up?" she asked softly.

Zakk sank into the chair beside her. "You haven't been sleeping," he said quietly. "Tiff said you've been quiet, keeping to yourself, and I've been too busy with the playoffs to really pay attention, but that ends now. Talk to me, Dani."

"What do you want to talk about?" She was purposely being obtuse but she still didn't have any answers for what she knew what he wanted to talk about.

"You know damn well what I want to talk about."

She clenched her teeth before blurting out, "Tell me what to do, Zakk."

He seemed momentarily confused. "I can't make your decision, kiddo. I don't know what you *want*."

"That's the problem. I don't know what I want either."

"Then name one thing you definitely do *not* want."

She met his gaze. "To end my hockey career as a loser."

"Like not medaling at the Olympics?"

"Exactly."

"There are no guarantees in sports. You know that."

"I can guarantee I end my career as a college champion if I stop now."

"If that was enough for you, we wouldn't be having this conversation." He folded his arms across his chest. "What is it that's got you so confused about this?"

Dani sighed, impatiently tapping her finger on her laptop. "There's no future for me in hockey. At least, not as a player, and I don't know how much more I can sacrifice, how much more debt I can run up, how much more I can borrow from Mom and Dad, how much more you can give me... It'll be almost six months of living in Colorado, running up more debt, living on the bare minimum. Maybe this makes me a bad person, but I'm tired of not being able to buy a new pair of jeans, not having money for a few drinks with friends, saying no to movies and concerts and everything fun. I've been a struggling college student for *five years* and I'm over it, Zakk."

"But I've offered..." His voice trailed off as she fixed him with a glare.

"Don't you see how demeaning that is for me? My rich, successful older brother paying for my pathetic little hockey dream?"

"Jesus, Dani, that's not how I feel," he protested.

"But it's my reality. I'm not angry with you—this is how it goes for women in hockey—but I can't let you keep taking care of me. It's time for me to grow up and take care of myself."

"If that's what you really want," he said softly, "I understand and I'll do whatever you ask of me. Just think about this: only a handful of people ever get the chance to represent their country in the Olympics. It's special. It's a dream I'll never fulfill because I'm not willing to sacrifice my professional career for a gold medal. So you'd be doing it for both of us. Kind of the way I hope I represent you every time I get out on the ice."

She flushed, a wave of emotion barreling through her. "Zakk..."

"Let me do this for you," he said quietly. "I'm your big brother and I love you. I can afford it. I *want* to do it. I don't care about the money if it makes you happy. It would make me happy to see you play at that level, but it only works if you let me help. If you're going to do it, I want you to be comfortable. I want you to eat, sleep, and breathe hockey because all your bills are paid, and you can escape once in a while to go shopping or out to dinner or whatever girls like to do when they have free time... One last time, Dani. You and me, doing it together."

Tears spilled over and she swiped at them angrily. "Dammit, Zakk."

"Aw, don't cry." He hugged her tightly and she wrapped her arms around his neck.

"Okay," she whispered. "One last time. You and me bringing home a medal for the U.S."

"Gold," he whispered back.

She sniffed. "Nothing like putting on the pressure."

PLAYING HOCKEY THE NEXT MORNING, Dani felt lighter than she had in a long time. Between the talk with Zakk and finally making headway on her paper, she felt calmer about her decision. Though a tiny part of her still struggled with accepting more money from Zakk, it would be churlish to deny herself this opportunity out of misplaced pride. Zakk had the money and gave it freely, so why not do something she'd never forget? Win or lose, it would be the experience of a lifetime, and now that she'd allowed herself to go forward, she was excited about it. Even if their team didn't win, her brother wouldn't let her make a fool of herself, and they'd been working to prepare her for months.

"Tessa needed the car and dropped me off, so would you mind giving me a ride home?" Sergei's deep but well-modulated voice snapped Dani back to the present.

She nodded. "Oh, sure. You ready?"

They packed their things into her SUV and she turned it towards home.

"You look good," he said quietly. "You're going to kick ass and take names come September."

She glanced over at him in surprise. "Thanks. It's pretty scary, but I'm getting excited."

"You'll move to Colorado Springs in September?"

"Yes. There's centralized living and practice starting in early September and going all the way until we leave for the Olympics. It's pretty intense."

"Sounds like an amazing opportunity."

"I guess so."

"You don't sound convinced," he said in surprise.

"It's complicated," she murmured.

"I can't think of any reason I'd turn down the opportunity to play in the Olympics, other than an injury or family emergency."

"You can afford it." She shrugged. "It's totally different for me."

"Zakk's helping you, isn't he?"

She was glad she'd had to stop at a red light so she could turn and glare at him. "Is that how you do the things you want to do? By asking your brother to pay for them?"

Sergei opened his mouth but nothing came out and he narrowed his eyes slightly. "I've obviously put my foot in my mouth again, but I'm not sure what I said."

She sighed. "I'm sorry. I'm a little defensive about it because what if Zakk couldn't afford it? How would I do it then?"

"How do other athletes do it?" he countered.

"I don't know," she grumbled, "but I'm tired of being in debt. Tired of my brother paying for things for me. He bought me this SUV, he paid for me to stay in North Dakota to work on my master's… Now he's paying for this. I hate it. I'll probably never be able to repay him."

"Why would you repay him? You're family."

She snorted. "I'm sure you'd be perfectly okay letting Toli pay for everything while you follow a dream."

"You're not sitting on the couch smoking weed all day," Sergei protested. "You're doing something exciting, something very few people are skilled enough to do, much less find the time and money. I wouldn't hesitate for something like this."

"Well, I've made the decision and I'm doing it. I just feel a little guilty. It feels like I've been taking money from my family for too long."

"From what I can tell, your family loves you and wants to do it."

She was quiet for a bit before opting to change the subject. "So, what do you think of Anchorage?"

He didn't say anything at first. "It's okay."

"The city, the team, or everything?"

"Everything," he chuckled. "The team seems to be going through some growing pains. They haven't found their footing as a new team the way the Sidewinders have."

"That's to be expected. The Sidewinders have been a bit of an anomaly."

"For sure."

"What about everything else? The weather? Location? Nightlife?"

"It's beautiful, but I have no idea about nightlife. I pretty much played hockey and worked out. Period. I'm in an apartment with a month-to-month lease, with most of my personal belongings in storage. I haven't got a clue where Niko will go to preschool, where we're going to live, if I'm going to buy or rent or even where to start looking… I guess there's a part of me that can't believe I got traded to Alaska."

He let out a short laugh that made Dani snicker.

"It does sound a little surreal."

"It's a rough organization," he said hesitantly. "I don't want to bad-mouth the team that's paying me the kind of money I'm making, but if you were my sister, I wouldn't want you there on your own."

"I can take care of myself." She smiled. "Trust me."

"I'm sure you can. It's just… Well, you're not my sister."

She snorted. "No, and I already have an overprotective big brother, so I don't need another one."

"I'm sure you don't."

6

The next two weeks were busy. The Sidewinders had lost in the second round of the playoffs so Toli and their half-brother, Vlad, were both around. Spending time with his brothers and their wives and children was nice, but Sergei was starting to feel the itch to find his own space. He'd been in limbo since leaving Boston in late February and now that it was June he needed to start organizing his life. It would be hockey season again before he knew it and his first priority had to be a home and a schedule for Niko. He needed to find an agency that would give him options for a nanny because he had no doubt it would be difficult to find a good one. He'd been lucky in Boston since he and Tatiana had already employed a part-time nanny who'd been willing to go full-time. She couldn't leave Boston, though, so he would be starting over.

He wanted to stay with Toli, Tessa, and the kids, but it would only postpone the inevitable. Much as it pained him, he needed to head home in a few days. Anchorage might not be where he wanted to be, but it was where he had to be, and he'd make it work one way or another.

His phone rang, startling him out of his dark thoughts, and he was surprised to see Aaron Ferrar's name on the caller ID. Aaron was the starting goalie in Anchorage and they hadn't really had a chance to get to know each other because Aaron had been out with a broken hand since Sergei had been traded there.

"Hey, Aaron." He wasn't even sure how Aaron had gotten his number, though he assumed it was on the player information lists they all got.

"Hey, Sergei. How's it goin'?"

"Pretty good. I've been in Vegas with my brother and family, soaking up the sunshine before I head back up north."

"Yeah, that's what I was calling about." Aaron paused. "I don't know if you heard, but I'm in the middle of a divorce and trying to unload my house. Jake said you might be interested. It's not too big, but not small, and doesn't need any work. I'm not interested in making much profit; I just want out so I can give her half the money and move on."

"Oh, uh..." Sergei hadn't been prepared for something like this.

"No pressure, man. I thought I'd text you some pictures and stuff. It's four bedrooms, three baths, with a basement I converted into a workout room and a hot tub in the screened-in porch."

He gave a few more details and when he told Sergei the price, Sergei was surprised again; he'd done some research and prices were a lot higher for the kind of space Aaron was talking about. "That's all you want for it?"

Aaron chuckled. "Like I said—the less I sell it for, the less she gets, and that's all I care about."

"Doesn't she have a say in the selling price and such?"

Aaron took a breath. "She's in prison awaiting trial and needs every penny she can get her hands on for legal fees."

"Oh." Sergei was taken aback, but it occurred to him the details didn't matter. If the house was relatively clean and passed inspection, what did he care what it looked like? He needed a place fast and this was a steal, even without looking at it.

"If you're not interested, it's no problem. I just—"

"No, I'm interested." Sergei gave Toli a nod as he came into the room. "I'd just like to see some pictures, set up some kind of inspection."

"I can email you all the pictures I took and specs of the house. If you're interested, you can hire someone to handle the details. I really don't care as long as I can pay off the mortgage and walk away with what I put down on it. We've had it a little over two years."

"Send me the stuff and let's talk again later," Sergei said.

After exchanging email addresses, they hung up and Sergei poured himself another cup of coffee as he filled Toli in on the conversation.

"You're just going to buy it sight unseen?" Toli asked.

Sergei shrugged. "I'm going to see pictures and I'll hire an inspector to head over there, but yeah, why not? Niko and I need a place right away and the price is definitely right."

"I guess as long as you have it inspected..."

"I have to go, Toli." Sergei gave his older brother a smile. "I love being here but I need to get Niko settled. I have to find a nanny, a preschool or a daycare... I have a lot to do. I sold almost all our furniture when I left Boston, so I don't even own a bed anymore. I kept Niko's stuff, and all our personal stuff, but I didn't move furniture all the way to Alaska. It was just too overwhelming."

"I know, but I have an idea that might help not just you, but someone else we know as well."

"Oh?" Sergei looked up.

"Why don't you hire Dani to be Niko's nanny for the rest of the summer, until she leaves for Colorado?"

Sergei's gut reaction was to say yes, but his brain kicked in a second later, making him shake his head. "Even if this was a good idea—and I don't think it is—what's in it for her?"

"Change of scenery and she adores Niko. Why not let her take care of him while you get settled? She can probably help you set up a new house, she'd be tough on potential nannies since she's attached to Niko, and, frankly, I think it would be good for both of you."

Sergei scowled. "Bro, if you're trying to play matchmaker—"

"What's wrong with her?" Toli demanded. "Smart, beautiful, a nice girl—"

"*That's* the problem," Sergei muttered. "I'm not looking for a girlfriend, and if she's a nice girl, she's looking for more than an occasional roll in the sack. Not to mention, she's practically still a kid."

"She's graduated from college." Toli shook his head. "Don't make excuses."

"She's not my type."

Toli laughed. "Why? Because she's tall, blond and probably smarter than you?"

Sergei scowled; Toli had just described Tatiana as well as Dani.

"Fine, maybe she's not potential wife material, but she's perfect nanny and friend material. She'll help you, you'll help her financially, and it'll be good for both of you to step out of your comfort zones. Zakk says she doesn't do much other than hockey."

Sergei tried to think of a protest but nothing reasonable came to mind. She *was* smart, capable, and in a perfect position to help him. She also knew Niko and the boy adored her, which was a plus. And damn if he didn't want to be alone up there. If he didn't have Niko, it would've been different. Sex and female companionship had never been a problem for him and there were plenty of guys on the team who went out drinking regularly. Though he tended to avoid that during hockey season, he allowed himself to let loose now and again. Having Niko meant one-night stands had to be minimal and drinking with the guys nonexistent. Which left him with nothing to do and no one to do it with. Not in Anchorage, anyway.

"I can see the wheels turning a hundred miles per hour." Toli chuckled. "What's the hesitation?"

"The truth?" Sergei eyed him.

"Of course."

"She's beautiful, young, and single. How would that look to people?"

"You going to harm her in some way?"

Sergei made a face. "Of course not."

"Then who cares? Zakk would take your word for it, and I know you better than that, so who else matters?"

"Her reputation matters. If she's going to be working for an NHL team in the future, living with me without being in a relationship might look bad if word got out."

"You're both adults and she's a strong, professional woman who's perfectly capable of defending herself against any of that. Besides, if she's really not your type, since you'll have live-in help with Niko, you're most likely going to be hittin' the puck bunnies hard and that'll stop any rumors about the two of you."

"Already did that in Boston. I'm over it."

"Really?" Toli's eyebrows lifted, his eyes glinting mischievously. "Then you're ready to find a nice woman to spend time with?"

"That's not what I said."

"You're already over one-night stands… What else is there? If you say abstaining, I'm going to punch you in the dick."

Sergei snorted out a laugh. "Thanks."

"So, what's the problem? Obviously you're not going to replace Tatiana, but she's gone and you're still alive. You're only thirty-three. You can't make me believe you want to be alone."

"No." Sergei fidgeted. "It's just, you know, guilt."

"You didn't kill her. She put herself in front of that bullet to protect you and Nikolai. I refuse to believe she did that so you would spend the rest of your life alone, mourning her and feeling guilty for wanting to start living again."

"No. That's not who she was." Sergei sighed. "I know it's time, I've just forgotten how."

"No, you haven't." Toli grinned. "It's just like a one-night stand, except with a woman you like and maybe no sex the first night."

They laughed together.

"You think there are single women in Anchorage?"

"There have to be, no?"

"I hope so."

7

The whole way to Anchorage, Dani kept wondering if she was dreaming. Everything had happened so fast, she still wasn't sure what she was doing. Toli and Sergei had approached her with the idea of taking care of Niko and helping Sergei set up a new house over the summer. He needed help and it would be the perfect opportunity for her to make some money without having to work in the Sidewinders' sales office. He'd promised she would have ample time and opportunity to work out so she wouldn't have to worry about staying in shape, and though the salary he offered wasn't huge, he'd added incentives like paying her car insurance, gas, and either moving or storage expenses when she left for Colorado.

Which brought her here. They were currently driving through a small town in Alaska she'd never heard of. They'd made it a mini-vacation, stopping in a lot of great places like Salt Lake City, Idaho Falls, Helena, Calgary, and then all sorts of little towns. She'd taken hundreds of pictures, coaxing Sergei into relaxing and both of them having a better time than either of them had anticipated. Though Niko was a little tired of being in the car, they'd spread it out over ten days instead of six, so they could sightsee a little and give him time to run around. Sergei had been quiet at first, almost cold. Dani had quickly realized he was nervous for some reason, and she went out of her way to make him feel more relaxed.

She didn't know much about dating since she hadn't done it a lot, but she had more male friends than female, so she was comfortable hanging out, and their mutual love of hockey made it easy to find things in common. By the third day they were talking and joking like old friends, and while she still found him a little bit full of himself, she liked him more and more. His arrogance was more an act he put on, part of his hockey persona, and she saw glimpses of a kinder, gentler man when he was with Niko or when he talked about his family.

"You sure you're okay driving another ninety miles?" he asked as the sun got lower in the sky.

"I'm fine." She smiled over at him. "Although I'll be glad to sleep somewhere that's not a hotel."

"Being in my apartment the first couple nights won't be much better," he admitted. "Even if I give you my room, the bed isn't great, and I think the couch is worse."

"We'll need to look at the house right away," she said, "so you can decide if you want it. Then we go shopping for essentials."

"I already ordered a bed for myself." He chuckled. "It's on hold until I can give them an address for delivery. Aaron said he's fine with me having them deliver it to the house before we close, but I want to see the place first."

"How exciting," she mused, staring off at the endless expanse of highway. "Getting to decorate a new house, buy all new furniture…"

"You know that's a guy's nightmare, right? Especially a single one."

"I'm happy to be your pretend wife in that regard. I love that kind of thing. Especially since I've never bought new furniture or anything."

"Never?"

"In college I lived in the dorms, which already had furniture, and then I moved into Zakk's already-furnished guest room. The most I got to buy for my dorm was a cool rug and new sheets."

He made a face. "Well, you can shop to your heart's content for me. As long as we agree on a color scheme, I don't really care."

"What was your old color scheme?" she asked.

"Oh, uh…" He paused. "Honestly, we didn't have a lot of color outside of Niko's room. Tanya—that's what I called Tatiana—liked everything really sleek and modern, so it was all shades of black, white, and gray, with lots of glass and metal."

"Glass and metal? With a toddler?"

"We had to get rid of the coffee table but she wouldn't part with the dining room set. After she died, I sold everything except personal items and Niko's bedroom set."

Dani wasn't sure what to say at first but smoothly transitioned into her next question, since the last thing she wanted to do was criticize his late wife. "Well, what colors do *you* like?"

"You know, I've been thinking about it. I think I'd like something in the red family for my bedroom. Masculine, and not too bright of course, but a deep, rich maroon with hints of copper and maybe mahogany."

"Red's my favorite color," she said. "This is gonna be fun!"

"If you say so."

The smile he gave her made her heart skip a beat; he was so damn hot, she hated looking at him sometimes. It was only times like these she wished she wasn't so strong and muscular. She was proud of her body and how hard she worked to be the athlete she was, but once in a while she yearned to be long and willowy, with slender legs and bigger breasts. Less of an athlete and more of a woman.

"Whatcha thinkin' about?" he asked a moment later.

"Oh, um, just decorating stuff."

"I don't think that's true," he teased. "Your cheeks are kind of pink, like you're thinking about something naughty."

She hurriedly shook her head. "Oh... No. I don't do naughty."

"Why not?" he asked curiously.

Dani was momentarily thoughtful and decided honesty was best. Sergei certainly wasn't interested in her romantically or even sexually, so if she told him about her issues it might make conversations like this less awkward.

"Look at me!" She forced a laugh. "I'm kind of like a guy."

"Like a...guy? What the hell are you talking about? You look like a woman to me."

"I do?" She managed a quick glance at him. "I mean, sure, my face is pretty enough, but have you seen my muscles? I was the unofficial arm wrestling champion of my graduating class—not including the football team. Guys see how much I can lift in a heavy squat and think I'm kind of a freak."

Sergei raised his eyebrows. "How much?"

She hesitated. "A little over three hundred."

"Seriously?" He briefly met her eyes since she quickly looked back at the road. "That's hardcore amazing, Dani, but...is that supposed to be some kind of turn-off to guys?"

"It was when it came to me. Guys would get a look at my thighs and kind of back away slowly."

"You obviously dated the wrong ones."

"Obviously, but my point was just that I don't do the naughty-flirting-with-cute-guys thing. For one thing, it doesn't do me any good, and for another, you're basically my boss for the summer, so that wouldn't be cool."

"You think I'm cute?" He chuckled, nudging her with his elbow.

"I'd be willing to bet you've heard that more than once in your life."

"Maybe twice."

"Whatever you say."

"Dani, I'm not in a position to date you and I hope you don't take this the wrong way, but I want you to know I think you're beautiful. Your strength and athleticism are turn-*ons*, not turn-offs. Like you said, I'm your boss for all intents and purposes, so I'm not trying to make you uncomfortable, but any guy who thinks you're too strong or muscular or something is a fool. Take it from a guy who loves women's bodies—yours is very, very sexy."

For some strange reason, his compliment warmed her from head to toe. "Thank you," she murmured softly. "That's sweet of you to say."

"It's true. You'll see when you get to the Olympics. Those guys will be all over you."

"One can only hope," she quipped.

"The guys on the men's hockey team didn't find you attractive?" he asked after a moment.

"I'm not sure, to be honest… Well, when I was a freshman, Zakk was a senior so he pretty much beat them off me and let them know he was only a flight away if anyone messed with me after he graduated. And I'm sure you've heard the story about how Zakk witnessed one of his professors commit a hit-and-run but didn't tell anyone because Zakk was drunk and afraid he'd get into trouble? Well, that professor's in jail now and his son played on the team so there was a lot of animosity starting in my junior year."

"That sucks."

"Yeah, so anyway, it's not a big deal. I'm just not one of those girls who's always flirting and acting all cutesy. I don't even think I know how."

"Stick with me, kid—I'll give you some pointers."

Oh shit, oh shit, oh shit. Was he flirting with her or genuinely trying to act in a big-brother capacity to help her game with men? This sucked, because she didn't know, and that made it difficult to respond. Luckily, Niko's whine from the back seat interrupted them.

"I'm hungry!"

"We ate two hours ago," Sergei protested mildly.

"Hungry." Niko stuck out his lower lip.

"Bored," Dani said softly.

Sergei nodded. "A little while longer, buddy, and we'll stop for the night, okay? You want to go for a swim? There's a pool at the hotel."

"Yay!" Niko instantly cheered up and began talking about swimming in Uncle Toli's pool and his new water pistol.

THEY ROLLED into Anchorage just after five o'clock the next day, starving and road-weary. Sergei was behind the wheel and Dani had been dozing but jerked awake when he pulled up in front of the Sheraton in downtown Anchorage.

"Go on and pull together what you'll need for a couple of nights," he said gently. "You're staying here with Niko tonight while I get his stuff out of storage, and tomorrow you're spending the day at the spa."

"What? No." She shook her head. "I'm here to work. I don't need a day at a spa or—"

"Says the girl who doesn't flirt." He gave her a look. "*Girls* like spa days."

"Not all girls," she protested.

"Already paid for it. It'll go to waste. Now get your stuff while I wrangle all of Niko's things."

She hesitated. "You didn't have to do this, Sergei."

"It was a long trip and it's going to be a busy few weeks getting settled. I wanted to."

"Thank you."

"You're welcome." He watched the smile she was trying to hide and hid one of his own. She was adorable. Not in a sexy kind of way, but in—oh, who was he kidding? She was sexier than sin and had absolutely no idea, which was hotter than anything he'd seen in a long time. He was going to be beating off the men with a stick to keep them away from her, especially since the ratio of men to women in Alaska was off the charts in her favor. It occurred to him he had no business keeping her away from interested men, especially after what she'd told him, but the strange need to protect her was impossible to ignore. Probably because of how close she was to Toli. What else could it be? She definitely wasn't his type. She was far too innocent for him; he liked his women with a taste for the wicked and a hunger for everything carnal. His sexual appetite was voracious when he was in a relationship, and Dani definitely wasn't that kind of girl.

Was she?

Shaking off thoughts that were too personal, he focused on getting Niko and a small bag of essentials out of the SUV. They had so much laundry, so many suitcases, and so much stuff—he couldn't wait to unload it all. He was almost ready to buy Aaron's house sight unseen, just to have a place to put everything. Dani's hockey equipment had taken up a good portion of the trunk, but that stuff hadn't been optional, and they'd had to squeeze in everything else. Toli was shipping two boxes of toys and things Niko had collected while living in Las Vegas because they simply had no room left in the SUV.

"You coming up?" Dani was asking him.

"Yeah, I'll help you guys get settled but then we're going to eat."

"I'm so tired of eating out," she groaned. "I can't wait to go grocery shopping."

"That's a phrase you will never hear come out of my mouth."

"Normally, I would agree with you, but I need protein powder, eggs, some fruit...and fish. We've had nothing but steak and chicken lately."

"First thing tomorrow, I'm going to look at the house," Sergei promised.

"Oh, I'm going, too," she said firmly. "I want to see it so we can start thinking about everything you'll need to furnish it."

"Thanks. That means a lot." Sergei was strangely pleased she was that excited to decorate the house. Tatiana had hated house-hunting and liked furniture shopping even less. She'd hired a decorator for everything except their bed and the furnishings for the nursery. Tatiana had been a physician and after so many years of school, she didn't have the patience for tasks like choosing a couch or accompanying accessories. They'd had fun with the nursery, though, and for a moment he was lost in the memory. Their relationship had been complicated, but he'd loved her more than life itself at one time. It was a little disconcerting to realize that while he still missed her, he didn't feel that mind-numbing pain he'd felt when she'd first died. Now it was more of a hollowness, as though something that had once been full had turned into a bottomless chasm. The emptiness had become more and more prominent, and it wasn't until this minute that he realized why: he was lonely.

Toli, the older brother who'd always looked out for him, had known this instinctively even though he hadn't said the words. That was why he'd all but insisted Dani come to Alaska with him and Niko. He'd known Sergei needed company, a friend, someone to help him transition to this new life in a new city on a new team. The time he'd spent here at the end of the season had been like an extended business trip, living in a temporary home, without Niko or their belongings. Now it was real and that same hollowness that had been slowly working its way out of his subconscious might have become overwhelming without something, someone, to keep him busy. Someone beautiful, smart, athletic, and wonderful with Niko.

Jesus fucking Christ. The whole lot of them had been playing matchmaker. Toli and Tessa, Vlad and his wife, Rachel, and Zakk and Tiff. Even Zakk, who should've known better than to offer up his younger sister to a broken, grieving man like Sergei. Yet here they were, and after ten days on the road— something else that had been Toli's idea—he liked her more than he'd thought he would. She was gorgeous and had impressed him with her on-ice abilities, but more than anything she was sweet and kind. She had so much patience with Niko, laughing and distracting him no matter how cranky he got. They played together like the best of friends, but then she morphed into a maternal role, making sure he ate right, went to bed on time, napped when he was supposed to, and didn't do anything too dangerous. She was the perfect nanny.

"Sergei?" Dani was staring at him and he snapped back to the present.

"Let's go," he said gruffly, hoping she didn't see his mushy thoughts mirrored in his eyes.

8

The house was perfect. Sergei, Niko and Dani had stepped inside, taken one look around, looked at each other and the two adults simultaneously nodded. It was spacious, with high ceilings and an open floor plan. The glass and chrome gas fireplace in the center of the living room was breathtaking and the stone pedestal upon which it sat was a work of art. The bedrooms were large and the master bathroom had the kind of tub Sergei could stretch out in when he was sore. Niko's room had lots of closet space and the perfect bay window for a reading nook, and the kitchen was sleek and modern. The screened-in portion of the patio held the hot tub while the rest had plenty of room for a grill and a table and chairs. Best of all, Aaron was leaving the appliances, window treatments, and a lot of the furniture, including the bed in the guest room.

"It's been used twice, when my mom came to visit," Aaron had said. "No need for you to buy something new."

There was also a huge leather couch, a dining room table with eight chairs and a matching china cabinet, bar stools for the island in the kitchen and a few random pieces of furniture that Sergei didn't bother to ask about. He wrote him a separate check for the furniture and immediately headed home to pack. Aaron had said they could move in before they actually closed, so he'd wanted to get started packing while Dani enjoyed her afternoon at the spa. With Niko playing in front of the television, he threw his clothes into suitcases and packed up the few things he'd accumulated since he'd been here, he called to reserve a U-Haul truck. He didn't have to do it himself, but if he waited to find reputable movers, Niko might be without his bedroom furniture and other things for weeks. There was nothing in storage he couldn't move or carry, and if there was anything that was too heavy or bulky, he would call Aaron.

When his phone rang he didn't recognize the number, but it was local, so he answered in case it was Dani calling from the hotel. "Hello?"

"Sergei, it's Gage Caldwell."

"Oh, hello, Mr. Caldwell." Sergei had only met the man once before.

"I heard you'd arrived in town and wanted to take a moment to officially welcome you to Anchorage. I know you were here in February, but now you're here for good and I hope you feel at home."

"Not yet," Sergei admitted, "but I'm sure that will change once the season starts."

"I'm having a get-together on July Fourth and thought it would be a good way for you to spend some time with the other guys in a casual environment. A good portion of the team will be in attendance, so I think you'll enjoy it."

"Yes, of course, I look forward to it." Not that he had any choice. A personal invitation from the owner of the team wasn't optional barring a family emergency.

"You're welcome to bring a date."

"Thank you," Sergei responded automatically. "I'm looking forward to it."

"My secretary will email you the details. Feel free to contact her if you have any questions, whether it's schools for your son, the best place for seafood, or an interior decorator."

"I appreciate that. I'll keep it in mind."

"Very good. See you on the Fourth." Gage disconnected and Sergei put his phone back on the counter thoughtfully. He'd just taken over the team in January. His uncle, Malcolm Caldwell, had died unexpectedly of a heart attack and had apparently left everything to his only and favorite nephew. There had been a bit of scuttlebutt about it because Gage was barely in his mid-thirties and had never been involved in professional sports before. He'd told the team and management he wouldn't be making any changes until the following season, after he'd had a chance to assess everyone and the roles in the organization, but it seemed that a lot of people didn't like him, including their head coach.

Sergei hadn't had much to say and kept his head down, focusing on playing and getting to know his teammates. He'd heard a few rumors about the young billionaire owner, but he'd ignored them because he'd hoped to get traded again. Unfortunately, that hadn't happened so now he would have to pay more attention.

"Daddy?"

"Yeah, buddy?" Sergei looked down into his son's big blue eyes.

"When's Mama D coming home?"

"In a few hours." Sergei ruffled his hair.

"What's she doing?"

"She's at a spa, doing...girlie things."

"Like dolls and tea parties?"

Sergei laughed. "Not exactly, but kind of like that."

"I want her to come home."

"Soon. How about we get some lunch and then go see our new house?"

"Is Mama D coming, too?"

"After the spa." Sergei sighed. Niko had gotten a lot more vocal after spending time at Toli's, probably because Tessa's daughter from her first marriage, Raina, never stopped talking. When he'd dropped him off back in February, he hadn't been the toddler who consistently asked why. Now, it had become a way of life. Why is the sky blue, Daddy? Why is it bedtime? Why do I need shoes? Why isn't Mama D home? Mama D was a huge part of Niko's vocabulary and his life. He adored her, and though Sergei tried to be annoyed about it, he couldn't. She was great with him, and more importantly, good for him. She loved him. There was no doubt about that. Though she had two nephews from Zakk's relationship with Tiff and a biological niece that Tiff had given birth to last year, Dani was probably closer to Niko than all three of them. They were like two peas in a pod and it fascinated him. It had annoyed him at first, but with each passing day, watching his son blossom under the young woman's affection, he had a hard time resenting her for it. Tatiana would be grateful someone loved her child that much.

"Daddy?"

Sergei glanced down at his son almost guiltily, as if thinking about Dani in front of him was somehow inappropriate. "Yeah, buddy?"

"Are we eating now?"

Sergei scooped him up, nodding. "Absolutely."

THE NEXT FEW days flew past. Dani and Sergei worked tirelessly to set up the new house. He'd retrieved everything from storage and their first priority had been Niko's room. He had a daybed, dresser, toy box and rocking chair. Sergei said he would paint the room after they were settled, so they focused on washing the bedding, putting away his clothes and toys, and hanging up some pictures. Sergei had gone out to get them lunch and was coming down the hall to tell them he was back when Niko's voice wafted down the hall.

"This is Mommy. Daddy says she's the prettiest angel in heaven."

"She's beautiful," Dani responded softly.

Sergei froze outside the door, unsure whether to interfere or not. Part of him wanted to hear what Niko thought about Mommy in heaven, but a bigger part of him wanted to know how Dani handled it.

"Daddy says she watches me from heaven."

"I'm sure she does. All mommies watch over their little boys and girls."

"But you'll watch me from down here, right?"

Sergei winced.

"Of course."

"You're not going to heaven, are you?"

"Gosh, no. I'll be right here making sure you're safe and happy until I go to Colorado to play hockey. Remember?"

"I don't want you to go," Niko whispered.

"I know, buddy, but you know how Daddy plays hockey for work? That's what I do too."

"Did Mommy play hockey?"

"Um, I don't think so…"

Sergei cleared his throat. "Hey, guys, lunch is here."

"Yay!" Niko took off towards the kitchen and Sergei glanced at Dani apologetically.

"I'm sorry. I heard the last part of that—Tatiana didn't play hockey."

"I didn't think so, but I wasn't sure." She smiled, placing a picture frame on Niko's dresser. It was of Tatiana holding Niko just minutes after he was born; Sergei had taken it and it was one of their favorites.

"I don't know how much to tell him," Sergei admitted. "He's three and a half. He wasn't even two when she died. He doesn't remember anything about her, and while I don't want him to forget her, it's not really fair to implant my memories in him."

"I don't think it's unfair," she said mildly, putting a few stray pairs of socks away. "You have to tell him the things about her that are most important but then let him conjure up her memory in whatever way works for him. You have pictures and stories, which will be enough when he's older. Eventually you'll probably remarry and—"

"No." He spoke more sharply than he intended, shaking his head. "I'm not interested in doing it again. Tatiana was my second wife and I think two strikes is plenty."

"Two strikes?" She cocked her head. "Did your first wife die, too?"

"What? Oh, no. We divorced."

"Well, that might be a strike, if you want to label it that way, but having your second wife pass away isn't a *strike*… It's more of a walk."

He smiled at the odd but endearing baseball reference. "Maybe," he agreed. "It just feels like I wouldn't be a good bet for a woman after one divorce and one death. What's next? Me dying?"

She shook her head. "Such a pessimist! How about next time is your soul mate? Your happily ever after? The woman who makes all your dreams come true?"

He arched a brow. "Seriously? That's for romance novels, honey. I got as close as I was going to get to that with Tatiana and there were no happy endings there. At this point in my life, I'm looking for a friend-with-benefits situation, someone who might be willing to put up with a single dad who has a black heart in exchange for good sex and maybe some nice vacations."

"Yikes." She wiped her hands on her jeans. "You're cynical as fuck."

"Aren't you the one who said you have no luck with men?" He followed her towards the kitchen.

"Well, yeah, but I still have hope that there's a guy out there who doesn't mind that I'm more muscular than he is and will fall in love with me anyway."

Watching her walk ahead of him, Sergei wanted to point out she wasn't more muscular than he was, and if he wasn't the cynical bastard she'd just told him he was, he'd be more than happy to show her how much he didn't mind her beautifully strong body. He could have a lot of fun with a beauty like her, if only she wasn't so young. And Zakk's sister. And his *nanny*. Not to mention the ramifications for Niko if things went south. Jesus, he needed to get laid or he'd be panting outside her bedroom door every night. Maybe one of the guys on the team knew some local girls who enjoyed no-strings sex. He'd have to give Aaron a call. The pickings were supposedly slim, at least based on statistics, which was why the puck bunnies were all barely legal. He wasn't interested in girls that young, though.

9

Within a week, Dani had the house whipped into shape. Sergei had dropped a small fortune on kitchen supplies, linens, and all kinds of things he hadn't even thought about, but he didn't mind. He was closing on the house in a few days, he'd contacted a service that was going to start sending nannies for them to interview, and he'd signed him and Dani up at a local gym so they could both stay in shape. He toned it down in the summer to give his body a chance to rest after the abuse it took the other eight or nine months of the year, but Dani was ramping up and he wanted to make sure she had every opportunity.

They'd worked out this morning and now she was reorganizing the kitchen cabinets for what seemed like the tenth time as they waited for the first nanny to arrive. Sergei was a little nervous, unsure what to expect. He'd specified that he wouldn't need anyone for a month or so but waiting until the last minute wasn't a good idea. The agency said it was no problem and they would let all the candidates know they wouldn't be starting immediately, but Sergei still wasn't sure how he would handle it if he found someone he liked.

"You don't cook, right?"

"I use the grill, and if I have to I can make eggs and stuff, but nothing to write home about."

"Well, the kitchen is organized if you ask the nanny to cook so—"

"She'll have to cook, won't she? For Niko?" He ran a hand over his short blond hair. "Shit, Tanya dealt with all this with our old nanny... I don't even know what I'm supposed to ask."

"You mostly have to see how she is with Niko," Dani said gently, meeting his eyes and surprised to see a flicker of uncertainty. He was always so confident about everything; she hadn't expected him to show weakness when it came to hiring a nanny.

The ringing of the doorbell ended all discussion and Sergei moved to go answer it. Dani followed, since Sergei had told her he wanted her opinion on each candidate, but she hung back, wanting to make her assessment from a distance.

The woman was probably in her late twenties, with long, jet-black hair and a pair of Coke-bottle glasses. She wore skintight jeans, a halter top and...four-inch red stilettos. Dani dipped her head to hide her astonishment as the woman sashayed into the room, looking around with interest.

"Well, this place is swanky! They didn't tell me the guy was wealthy—but I shoulda guessed based on the assignment. You this Sergio guy I'm looking for?" She looked Sergei up and down, slowly and purposefully removing the massive lenses covering most of her garishly made-up face.

"That's me," he said dryly, not even batting an eyelash at her misuse of his name. "*Sergio.*"

Niko had moved towards Dani and now buried his face against her leg.

"This is Niko," Dani said, lifting the little boy and trying to understand why Sergei didn't just throw this bimbo out. "He's a little shy sometimes."

"Oh, he'll be all right," the woman said absently. "He don't have to watch."

"Watch?" Dani blinked.

The woman turned and eyed her. "But no one said anything about a threesome."

"A threesome?" Dani's mouth fell open.

"I'm sorry," Sergei shook his head slightly. "Did you say *threesome*? Are you from the Xavier Agency?"

She gave him a wide grin. "Sure, honey. Now you sit on down over there and I'll make sure you have a good time. What do you want to do about your girlfriend and the kid?" She started unbuttoning her jeans.

"I'm not—" Dani began, her eyes widening.

"She's..." Sergei's lips had begun to twitch. "I'm afraid there's been a misunderstanding," he finally said, biting back a laugh. "I'm sorry to waste your time, but I don't think we'll be needing your services today. I'll be sure to add a nice tip when I get the bill." He was ushering her towards the door.

"But they said—"

"I know." He was chuckling as he opened the front door again. "Initiation, right? Sorry, but we have company coming and I can't play along today, but you'll be paid for your time. Have a nice day." He shut the door and snickered.

Dani just stared, Niko still snuggled against her shoulder. "Was she a...stripper?"

He nodded, still holding back laughter.

"So who... I'm so confused."

"Any time you're new to a team the guys tend to do some hazing. I'm older and have been around so they're not going to do something stupid like try to shave my nuts, so—"

"They shave guys' nuts as a hazing ritual?" She grimaced.

"Usually just in the minor leagues, but it still happens on occasion at our level." He was still shaking his head. "Since I'm single, I guess they figured sending me this stripper when they knew I had a nanny coming to interview would be funny. I wondered why Aaron was asking so many questions about the nanny—" He cut off as the doorbell sounded.

"I'll get it," she said firmly, handing him Niko and walking to the front door.

This time the woman standing in the foyer was most likely a nanny. She was middle-aged, probably in her fifties, with her hair pulled back in a severe bun and her face devoid of makeup. She had on loose-fitting slacks, a button-down shirt, and black mules, a no-nonsense look on her face as she introduced herself.

"I am Dannica Compton." She shook Sergei's hand and slowly turned to Dani. "I was told there was no woman in the picture. Has this situation changed?"

"Dani's a friend of the family," Sergei said mildly. "She's helping me with Niko until I hire someone. Please, come sit down."

The woman nodded and followed him to the couch. "Leather. Very nice. Surprised to see it in such good shape with a child in the house. You'll have to consider finding something easier to clean. I can't be responsible for furniture this expensive."

Sergei cocked his head. "Niko isn't destructive and as long as he doesn't eat in the living room, which isn't allowed anyway, it shouldn't be an issue."

"This is the boy?" She peered at Niko as if he were a pet, looking him up and down and then summarily dismissing him. "He's three?"

"Yes," Sergei spoke quietly. "Say hello to Ms. Compton, Niko."

"Hi." Niko gave the woman an equally assessing gaze, his blue eyes full of distrust.

"I was told the hours are negotiable."

Sergei frowned. "I think you misunderstood. The hours will vary depending on my travel schedule. I can show you the team's game schedule to give you an idea of how much I'll be away, but the job is full-time, 24/7. Days off have to be arranged well in advance because once hockey season starts, I won't be—"

She cut him off. "Hockey season? You're with that new team of heathens they brought to Anchorage? I'll have no part of it." She quickly got to her feet. "There was no need to bring the circus to town like this, with you men running about with all the single ladies." She snapped her gaze to Dani. "You'd be well advised to steer clear, young woman, and find yourself a *nice* man to marry. And remember—there's no need for him to buy the cow when he's getting the milk for free." She marched to the door, opened it and walked out without a backward glance.

"What just happened?" Sergei demanded.

"Getting the milk for free..." Dani dissolved into giggles. "Unless something changes quickly, you better think about buying that cow!"

Sergei burst out laughing and they laughed until tears ran down their faces.

"Aaron is definitely getting payback for the stripper," he muttered when they finally settled down, "but the agency is going to get a serious earful about judgmental asshole nannies."

"Yeah, that was totally uncool." She shook her head. "But it was still pretty funny."

He grinned as he picked up his phone. "For sure."

THERE WERE a few more interviews over the next few days, with mediocre results since Niko didn't seem interested in either of them and Dani didn't like them either. Today, however, Sergei was looking forward to the interview because the nanny was Russian. Though she was an American citizen now, she'd been born and raised in Moscow, coming to the U.S. for college and marrying an American. She was divorced and didn't have children, so he was anxious to meet her. Having a native Russian speaker taking care of Niko would be a great way to keep him immersed in the language since Sergei often forgot to speak to him in anything but English.

"What time is she coming?" Dani asked as she cleaned up their lunch dishes.

"One thirty, so about ten minutes from now."

"Maybe I should make myself scarce," she said. "You'll probably be talking Russian and—"

"Don't be silly," he interrupted. "You're an integral part of this process and I value your input. We might speak Russian for a few minutes so I can get a feel for how Niko responds to it, but the interview will be mostly in English."

"Okay." She nodded just as the doorbell rang.

"I got it. Will you make sure Niko doesn't have grilled cheese in his hair?"

"Sure." She went upstairs to check that Niko was presentable and found him playing in his room. "Hey, buddy. You ready to meet another possible nanny?"

Niko wrinkled his nose. "I want you to be my nanny." He looked up at her, his blue eyes darkening.

"I'm here until I leave for hockey."

"I hate hockey." He stuck out his lower lip.

"Don't let Daddy hear you say that," she whispered, kneeling down so she was eye level with him. "We love hockey, but we love you more. That's why we're going to find somebody to help take care of you until we get back."

"You're coming back after hockey?"

"Yup. After the Olympics I'll be back!" *I hope.* She hated lying to him but it would be impossible to explain something as complicated as her professional future to a three-year-old.

They went down the stairs hand in hand and Dani heard Sergei's laughter alongside a distinctly feminine giggle. Good grief, the nanny was giggling during a job interview? Dani already didn't like her, and as she got to the bottom of the stairs, she froze. Sergei and the woman were on the couch, sitting closer than Dani would have liked. She was wearing a tight skirt with a pretty top that revealed her ample cleavage. She had on high-heeled sandals and her long fingernails were painted a bright, blood red. Her auburn hair was long and silky, curled and obviously mussed just enough to give it that super-model runway look. Her makeup was flawless and every time she giggled she put her hand on Sergei's arm in a far too familiar fashion.

Who was this woman and how did she expect to get a job taking care of a three-year-old when she was behaving like a bimbo?

"*Dobry den,*" the woman said, smiling at her.

The woman had just said *good afternoon* in Russian. *Bitch,* Dani thought, though she smiled politely.

"*Dobry den,*" Dani replied, grateful she'd learned a few common Russian phrases to use with Niko. "*Kahk dehlah?*" *How are you?* She almost smirked at the look of surprise on both the woman's and Sergei's faces, but she looked down at Niko instead. "Can you say hello in Russian?"

"*Nyet,*" he responded, scowling. *No.*

Dani bit her lip to keep from laughing.

"When did you pick up Russian?" Sergei asked her, smiling.

"Spent way too much time at your brother's house listening to him coo at the baby for hours on end."

He chuckled. "Sounds about right. Though I doubt he said *good afternoon* and *how are you* to Alex in Russian."

"Hello, Nikolai," the prospective nanny spoke to Niko in a sugary tone.

"My name is Niko," he replied blandly, pressing back against Dani and turning his face away.

"Don't be rude, Niko," Sergei said softly. "Say hello to Miss Veronika."

"Why are your lips black?" Niko asked instead.

Dani was having a hard time keeping a straight face, but she gently squeezed his arm. "That's special makeup," she told him. Veronika was wearing lipstick in such a dark shade of purple it appeared almost black; Dani thought it was extremely unattractive.

"Why don't you tell us something about your background with children," Sergei suggested. "It will give Niko a little time to warm up to you."

"All right." Veronika turned, her dark eyes trained on Sergei. "I majored in early childhood education and taught preschool for three years after college.

Then I got married and had to quit when we moved here. My husband cheated on me and I divorced him, but I like it here and don't want to go back to New York. I wasn't planning to work full-time so I've been taking temp jobs, but when I heard there was a Russian looking for a nanny, it seemed like the perfect opportunity to work with children again."

"You understand I won't be home much?" Sergei asked her.

"The agency didn't give any details about your job, only that you travel a great deal for business, but now that I'm here, of course I know who you are. No self-respecting Russian doesn't know Sergei Petrov. I've watched you play hockey since the beginning of your career."

"When did you come to the U.S.?" Sergei asked her, glossing over her praise.

Dani tuned them out, focusing instead on keeping Niko from scurrying away. He didn't seem to like Veronika, refusing to look at her and turning his back whenever possible. Dani didn't like her either. She was behaving as if she was interviewing to go on a date with him instead of going to work for him, and everything about her screamed gold digger. Her clothes were expensive and far too sexy for a nanny position. Her makeup was overdone, her gestures too intimate and she didn't seem to have much interest in Niko at all.

"I'm sorry?" She turned, realizing they were talking to her.

"Can you keep an eye on Niko while I show Veronika around the house?" Sergei asked. "Then I thought the two of them could play a little while, get to know each other."

Dani nodded. "Of course." She watched them walk up the stairs, switching to Russian and talking like old friends. A shot of white-hot jealousy ripped through her and she had to take a moment to steady herself. Where had that come from? She and Sergei weren't dating or romantically involved. They were friends. If he wanted to date a Russian bimbo, it was none of her business.

"Mama D?" Niko tugged on her hand.

"Yeah, baby?"

"I don't like Veronika."

"Why not?"

"She has a funny face."

"That's not a nice thing to say. There's nothing wrong with her face."

"All the making up is funny. It's not pretty like yours."

"You're such a sweet boy." She kissed the top of his head. "But you shouldn't comment on how a lady looks, especially her makeup. It's not polite."

"But I can tell you, can't I?"

"Of course. You can tell me anything."

"I love you, Mama D."

Her heart constricted and she felt a little light-headed as she hugged him tightly. Nope. No way was she going to let Sergei hire La Femme Russkie to be

Niko's nanny. If he wanted to date her, she had no way to stop him, but she didn't want that woman spending that much time with Niko. Of course, if she dated Sergei, she'd be with Niko by default, but he said he didn't do serious so maybe he'd just sleep with her and move on. *Hopefully*. Whether she wanted to admit it or not, she was jealous, and that didn't bode well for the rest of the summer.

10

Dani was quiet through dinner, focusing on something on her phone and then shooing Sergei and Niko upstairs for bath time while she cleaned up the kitchen. She'd disappeared after Veronika left, saying she had some phone calls to make, but Sergei had a feeling something was on her mind. She definitely hadn't liked Veronika and at first he'd continued the interview because it seemed fun to tease her, but now he regretted it. There wasn't a chance in hell he was hiring a qualified but wholly inappropriate woman to take care of his son, but his first thought had been she might be just what he needed to scratch the itch he'd felt since the first time he'd laid eyes on Dani. She'd practically thrown herself at him when they'd been upstairs and instead of being turned on, he'd apparently pissed off Dani and frustrated himself.

The chemistry between them was fairly obvious even though they were both ignoring it. It sizzled in the room when they were together, like the tiny sparks from a cord that was shorting out, but as soon as it became too overt, she shut it down by either leaving the room or changing the subject. Casual sex might work out okay if she was more experienced, but her own admission that she didn't date a lot made him uncomfortable. Not because he wanted her to be sexually experienced—he had no problem showing a woman what he liked in the bedroom—but because treating her like a casual lay when she'd already become his friend was disrespectful. It had only been two months or so but it felt like much longer. They'd spent a fair amount of time together for over a month in Las Vegas and now they were together all day, every day.

She'd put his home together for him in short order, took care of Niko and still found the time to work out, cook, and clean on days the cleaning service didn't come. They were only friends but in her capacity as his nanny she'd already become virtually indispensable to him. The thought of her leaving in two months was disturbing and using her for one night of pleasure before letting her go was unconscionable. He truly didn't know what to do about it.

Unable to sleep well with the strangeness between them, he tossed and turned until six before finally getting up. He got dressed and freshened up before checking on Niko and heading downstairs. She was already up and he found her in the kitchen on the phone.

"Hey, Sara, I have to go," she said into the phone. "I'll call you later, okay? Yeah, sure... Bye." She disconnected and stood up. "I was going to go for a run."

"Before you go, will you tell me what's wrong?"

"Nothing. Why?" She met his gaze unflinchingly.

"You barely spoke to me after Veronika left yesterday and then you went up to your room and never came back down."

"I had to call my mom and we wound up on the phone for over an hour, and then I started texting Tiff and lost track of time. I guess I fell asleep. Did you need me for something?"

Yeah, to bend you over that counter and fuck you senseless. "I wanted your thoughts on Veronika. I take it you didn't like her."

"She's not exactly interested in *Niko*." She gave a little shrug.

"What does that mean?"

"Come on, don't be obtuse." She scowled at him. "The way she kept touching you, flirting... And that ridiculous top she wore, showing off her tits. Who wears that kind of thing to an interview? I mean, it was so obvious she wants to go out with you and if that's your thing, that's fine, but to hire her to care for your son would be—"

"You really think I'm going to hire her? You don't think much of me, do you?"

"I honestly don't know you that well. You seemed into her."

"I was playing along, to see if she was just a little flirty by nature—there are women like that, by the way—or if she was truly making a play for me." He watched something he couldn't quite decipher flicker across her face before she schooled her features again.

"And what did you decide?" she asked, cocking her head slightly.

"That she's a bimbo looking for a rich guy to pick up where her husband left off. She somehow thought the Russian connection would make her a prime candidate."

"You told her you'd call her," she said, her voice almost accusing.

"But I'm not going to." He met her eyes. "If I didn't know better, I'd say you were jealous."

"That's ridiculous." She narrowed her eyes. "You're not my boyfriend. You can date whomever you like, but I didn't want you to hire her because Niko really didn't like her and she was just...icky." She wrinkled her nose.

"Icky?" he repeated. "You have a master's degree and *icky* is the best word you could come up with to describe her?"

"Fine. She was a cheap, slutty-looking gold digger who practically threw herself at you during a job interview."

He laughed. "You're right. Which is why I'm not going to hire her and definitely not going to get involved with her."

"You could sleep with her without having a relationship," she pointed out.

"I could." He glanced at her and that ever-present spark between them nearly singed his corneas as their gazes locked. "But she's not really what I want."

"What, um, what do you want?" Dani worried her lower lip nervously, her eyes never leaving his.

"I don't know exactly," he hedged, unsure how far he could go without coming on too strong. "But definitely someone with more class."

"Yeah, um, that's probably a good idea," she said slowly. Then it was as if someone flipped a switch. She quickly turned away and bent to tie the laces of her sneakers. "Anyway, I need to get going so I can be back in time to make Niko's breakfast."

"You don't have to feed us three meals a day," Sergei said, somehow both frustrated and relieved she either hadn't picked up on or chose to ignore his signals.

"I know, but if I'm going to feed him, it's not a problem to feed you, too." She grabbed her earbuds. "Do you need anything before I go?"

"No, you go ahead. Have a good run." He watched her jog out the back door and disappear around the corner.

Well, that had been a bust. He normally didn't have a problem approaching a woman he wanted, but Dani was in a category of her own and he didn't want to mess up their friendship. He couldn't talk to his brothers or closest friends about it—since they were all friends with her brother—and he realized just how much he'd secluded himself since Tatiana's death. He'd stopped hanging out with anyone but his brothers and friends from the Sidewinders, whom he only saw intermittently, and though the group here in Alaska wasn't that friendly, there were a few guys he could've gotten to know better if he'd put any effort into it. He just hadn't wanted to until now. For the first time in nearly two years he couldn't ignore the pull to start living again.

Shit. It was all because of the sexy blonde who'd just scampered out of here like a pack of grizzlies was after her. Maybe it was for the best. She was too young for him, right? And leaving soon to go be an Olympic champion. Yeah, he needed to let this go and find someone to get horizontal with. Someone who wouldn't get under his skin like a certain hockey-playing nanny he knew. Determined to stop thinking about getting naked with Dani, he went to check on Niko.

He was halfway up the stairs when his phone rang. It was barely seven in the morning and he looked down, surprised to see Dani's name on the screen. Panic rushed through him and he snatched it to his ear.

"Dani?"

"I've had a little accident," she said quickly. "I'm okay, I just—"

"I'll be right there—where are you?"

"You can't leave Niko alone," she said firmly. "I can walk, I just might need a little help getting up the stairs."

"Where. Are. You." He ground the words out succinctly through gritted teeth.

"I'm at the end of the block. Really, I'm fine, I—"

He disconnected without letting her finish and ran down the stairs. He stuffed his bare feet into his sneakers and raced out the front door. She usually took the same route when she ran so he had a good idea where she was and they'd be back in two or three minutes flat. If he didn't spot her where he thought she was, he'd double back and grab Niko.

His stomach clenched in fear as he ran down the lengthy driveway onto the street, looking both ways. Sure enough, she was coming around the corner, one leg covered in blood. A *lot* of blood. He got to her in a few seconds, pausing to grip her face between his hands.

"Are you okay?"

"I'm fine, but you need to go back—what if Niko wakes up?" she protested.

"Come on." He scooped her up in his arms and speed walked back to his yard and up the driveway. "Jesus, you scared the shit out of me—what the hell happened?"

"A car came around the corner too fast and didn't see me there. I jumped out of the way and landed on some rocks. It looks worse than it is, really."

"We need to clean it and see." He climbed the steps to the back door and set her down inside. "Sit," he said firmly.

She looked like she was going to protest, but didn't, merely sinking into the nearest chair. Sergei wadded up a bunch of paper towels and knelt in front of her, assessing the damage to her thigh. It was already starting to turn an ugly purple color, but the bleeding had almost stopped and he didn't think it would need stitches. It needed to be cleaned, though, since there was a lot of dirt in the wound.

"Let's get upstairs to the master bath," he said, standing up straight again. "You need to get the blood washed off and I can clean out the dirt."

"I can do it," she said, also standing up. She winced, and he quickly shook his head.

"You can barely stand up. Stop being stubborn." He lifted her in his arms again, trying to ignore how good her skin felt against his. He climbed the stairs and carried her through his room and into the bathroom, where he set her on the closed toilet seat. He leaned into the large open shower that had two full walls, one half wall with the garden-style bathtub on the other side of it, and nothing at all on the side where you entered and exited. It was roomy, easily spacious enough for two people, so he picked her up and set her on the half wall before taking down the showerhead.

"Shit, that stings," she muttered, wrinkling her nose.

"Almost done," he said quietly, using his finger to wipe away the dirt.

DANI'S MOUTH was a little dry as Sergei tended to her. His hands were big, with long, tapered fingers. Though well-groomed, there was no doubt he used his hands a lot. The skin was lightly calloused, but his touch was ridiculously gentle so the contrast actually felt wonderful. Her eyes fluttered closed as he cleaned her injury, goose bumps breaking out on her skin as he trailed his fingers down the inside of her thigh. It wasn't a sexual motion, he was simply wiping away some of the dried blood, but it felt deliciously intimate. *Sensual.* She could only imagine those same fingers touching her for pleasure.

Her fantasy came to a halt as he turned off the water and hung the shower-head back up. He patted her upper thigh dry with more paper towels before handing her a bath towel. "Go ahead and dry off while I dig around for some bandages. I don't know if I have anything big enough. Did we buy any Neosporin?"

"I don't think so."

"I'll run to the drug store after Niko wakes up."

"I can watch him if you want to go."

"You've been taking care of us for almost three weeks. Let us take care of you for once, okay?"

She smiled faintly. "Okay."

DANI SPENT most of the day on the couch watching movies with Niko and taking a late afternoon nap that left her feeling a bit out of sorts. She woke to the smell of something wonderful coming from the kitchen and slowly limped into the room to find out what it was. Niko was up on the counter, laughing with Sergei as they tossed a salad. Half of it was spilling out of the bowl but she couldn't help a fond smile as she watched. There was no doubt they were father and son, both blond and blue-eyed with dimples. She'd seen pictures of Tatiana, who'd also been blond and blue-eyed, so it was hard to tell exactly who Niko would look like as he got older but the resemblance was already visible. With their heads close together, they were adorable, Sergei trying to toss the salad as Niko attempted to snatch pieces of cucumber to eat.

"You two are making a mess," she said mildly.

"Hey." Sergei turned, his eyes warm as he smiled at her. "Did you have a good nap?"

"I did." She smiled back.

"Does your leg feel better?" Niko asked, wiggling to get down.

Sergei set him on the floor and he ran to her, carefully hugging the leg without the bandage.

"I feel much better. You and your daddy took good care of me."

"Does your boo-boo still hurt?" He put a tentative finger over the bandages.

"A little, but it'll be okay." She tousled his hair. "How about you wash your hands so we can eat?"

"Okay." He moved to the sink as Sergei brought a big bowl of pasta to the table.

"I used sauce from a jar," he explained wryly, as if embarrassed about the use of canned pasta sauce. "I added some grilled chicken, garlic, and mushrooms. It's probably not like what you make, but it's edible. And there's salad and garlic bread."

She grinned. "It sounds heavenly. Starting on the first of August, I'll cut way back on carbs, so I want to enjoy them now."

He grimaced. "I hear ya. Now that I'm thirty-three, I have to be a lot more conscious of what I eat, though I stay active enough not to limit myself too much."

"I'd like to get my body fat down to fifteen percent again," she said. "I think I'm at around nineteen now, so I have some work to do."

He glanced down, his eyes rolling over her like a surfboard riding a wave before settling on her face. "I can't even imagine you more cut than you are, but I'm looking forward to helping you get there."

She flushed, both happy and exasperated at the way he seemed to be paying a lot more attention to her. Was he actually interested or was he just taking advantage of their close proximity? He wasn't a jerk, she'd learned that about him by now, but he was still a hot single guy not looking to get serious. She'd originally made an unofficial deadline of losing her virginity before leaving for Colorado, but that had fallen by the wayside once she'd come to Alaska. Now she was thinking about it again, but he was a family friend, her boss, and the kind of guy she now knew could break her heart if she let him get too close. Maybe if she timed it to happen right before she left it wouldn't be too bad, but she had no idea how to approach a conversation like that. In the meantime, when he looked at her the way he just had, it was all she could do to not throw herself at him. Luckily, Niko's presence kept her from making a fool of herself. Especially today, when her injury had forced Sergei to be so attentive and solicitous.

11

They didn't do much of anything for a few days. Niko was a little bored but they kept him entertained with movies and board games, and Sergei interviewed two more nannies. Unfortunately, they didn't like either of them and he sat back in frustration after the second one left.

"I don't get it," he said in exasperation. "I'm using a top-rated agency. How can they not have any good matches?"

"It's Alaska," she said. "There may not be a lot of options, but I have a suggestion."

"I'm open to anything."

"My best friend, Sara, has been helping out in Vegas but she would probably be willing to come here for a year, give you a chance to meet people, get settled…"

"I take it you already asked her?"

"I mentioned it and she said she wouldn't stay forever, but she'd consider it for a season or two. She's getting her master's as well, but she can only afford a class at a time, so she takes them online."

He looked thoughtful. "I'd like to meet her first."

"She's good with Niko and she was with us when we went skating, so he was all about her being a girl hockey player."

Sergei winced, feeling guilty about the fact he'd only been on skates with his son twice. There was one time, his first year in Boston, when Niko was barely a year old. It had been his old team's Family Day, and Tatiana and Niko had come along with the other wives, girlfriends and children. Niko had been on skates, wearing a mini-version of Sergei's jersey, but it wasn't the same. They'd all gone as a family with Toli, Tessa and the kids while he'd been in Las Vegas but no one wanted to ice skate in the summer so that had been the only time. There were so many things he'd dropped the ball on in the time since Tatiana had passed away; he really needed to stop.

"You don't have to consider her if you'd rather not," Dani said, watching him intently.

"No, I was just thinking about the fact I've only taken my son skating once. And he'll be four this winter."

"My leg will be better in a few days and we can take him."

"Sounds good." He took a breath and suddenly came up with an idea. "How about I fly us to Vegas for your birthday? It's the first weekend in August, right? You'll be able to celebrate with family and it'll give me a chance to meet with Sara. If it works out, we won't have to worry about the nanny thing and can focus on Niko and both of us staying in shape for hockey season."

The smile that lit her face momentarily blinded him, it was so full of happiness and excitement. "That would be the best birthday present ever. Thank you!" She caught him off guard when she leaned over and brushed her lips across his cheek.

The area tingled from her touch and Sergei was fairly certain his cock took notice as well. They both seemed to have felt it because the air was suddenly charged with the electricity between them. There was an unspoken question in her eyes as she continued smiling at him.

"Would you like to go to a team party with me?" he asked slowly, wishing she would look at him the way she had just now more often.

"What?" She froze, staring at him as if she didn't understand what he'd said.

"I..." He cleared his throat and tried to formulate a sentence that wouldn't make him sound like the horndog he was. "Dani, this is stupid. The chemistry between us is off the charts. If I'm wrong, I'll apologize and stay at least ten feet away from you for the rest of the summer, but I know women, and I'm ninety-nine percent sure I'm not wrong. Am I?"

Her cheeks were pink and her eyes got a little glassy, but she shook her head. "No, you're not wrong about the chemistry."

"I sense a *but* coming."

She dipped her head. "I work for you, and even if I didn't, our brothers, our friends, there's Niko to think about... Everything would be really weird if we went there."

"You're right." His eyes never left her face. "But the alternative is walking around in heat for two more months. At some point, one of us is going to make a move and I'd be more comfortable if it was you."

Her cheeks burned pink. "That's *so* not going to happen. I already told you I'm not real experienced with this kind of thing, so if you're waiting for me to make some kind of sexual overture, forget it."

He took a step closer to her, one big hand cupping the side of her face. "Come to the team party with me. I want to spend time with you outside the house and it'll be good for you to meet everyone. The invitation said no kids, so we'll find a sitter for Niko and it'll be just the two of us."

"Are you asking me to go as your date?"

He hesitated. "I didn't really think that far ahead, but you're definitely not going as my nanny. You're my *friend*. Not my nanny, not my brother's best friend's little sister, not my employee. If I introduce you as my nanny, it'll start all kinds of gossip because anyone can see the spark between us the minute we're in the same room together and that's such a cliché. But if I simply introduce my friend Danielle, who's helping me with Niko before she goes to train for the Olympics, even if people jump to the friends-with-benefits conclusion, it nips gossip in the bud and you can still work for any team in the NHL without feeling like there was too much speculation about us."

"So you're taking a *friend* on a date?"

She had such a strange look on her face he cocked his head, a small smile playing on his lips. "Is that bad? Do you want it to be a real date? A not-just-my-friend date?"

"Like I told you, I don't do a lot of dating, so being on a date as your friend is a little confusing for me. Can't we just say we're going on a date and leave it at that?"

"Yeah, baby, we can." He leaned forward, his eyes trained on hers, hoping beyond hope she wouldn't turn away this time. She was watching him, too, and he moved closer. He brushed his lips across hers a few times, barely touching her, but when her eyes fluttered closed he knew he'd crossed the first threshold. The tips of their tongues touched almost tentatively, and he waited for her to give him some kind of signal she wanted more. There was something so beguiling about her he wasn't sure how to handle it. He'd originally thought someone so innocent would bore him; instead, she was like a sexual blossom ready to bloom and sprout wings.

When her mouth opened for him, he made sure to keep the pressure light and let her lead their progress. Niko was in the next room and he wasn't ready to take this to the bedroom yet anyway. A sweet but sensual kiss seemed like a good place to start, though, and the nearly undiscernible whimper of pleasure that escaped her told him he was right. Her inexperience was coupled with an almost tangible desire to experiment, but something in his gut told him to go slow. She wouldn't be one of those women who just jumped into bed with him, and though a tiny part of him was nervous about pursuing a woman who wanted more than sex, it would be silly to deny how right it felt now that he'd touched her.

"Mama D—*what* are you doing?" Niko came barreling into the room and skid to a stop as they jumped apart.

"Kissing." Sergei was unprepared to have this conversation with his toddler, but he wasn't going to allow it to be something his son thought was taboo either.

"Why?" Niko was frowning.

"Because we like each other," Dani responded with a soft smile. She held out her hand to him and Niko took it, climbing into her arms and firmly settling himself between her and his father.

Sergei smiled at the child's sneakiness, but sat back, wondering what she planned to say.

"You don't kiss me like that," the boy pointed out.

Dani threw her head back when she laughed. "No, of course not. That's how grown-ups kiss, not how we kiss friends or our children."

"Am I your children?" he asked solemnly.

Dani blinked rapidly, a tiny shimmer of tears glossing her eyes.

"Child," Sergei murmured. "You're one child."

"You're a child of my heart," Dani whispered, regaining her composure, and putting one of Niko's hands on her chest. "You'll always be right here with me, no matter where I am."

"When you're in 'rado for hockey?"

"Yes, when I'm in Colorado or Las Vegas or anywhere." She kissed the top of his head. "Now go find us a book to read. We've been watching too much TV."

"Okay." He took off up the stairs to find a book from his room and the adults looked at each other.

"Sorry about the interruption," Sergei said quietly, reaching for her hand. She twined her fingers with his and for a moment they were quiet.

"Did I say the right thing? To Niko?"

"Absolutely. It's hard to know exactly what to tell a three-year-old about kissing, you know? I thought I had a little time before I had to have that talk with him."

She chuckled. "Well, he caught us red-handed."

"Honey, are you going to be okay with casual?" He was intently aware of her closeness, the scent of her shampoo, everything about her, and it was enveloping him, making him think things he had no business thinking.

She was mulling over what he'd said, the look on her face a delightful mixture of mischief and determination.

"One date," she said finally. "Then we'll reassess. Is that fair?"

"More than fair."

"I just have one question."

"Sure."

"What am I supposed to wear?"

12

The day of the party was bright and sunny. Dani and Sergei had gone to the gym and she focused on her upper body to give her thigh time to heal while he did cardio. They kept it short so they had time to get home and get ready. The agency had sent a sitter they both liked, and though the woman wasn't available for overnight or long-term stays, she was happy to come for afternoons or evenings.

As Sergei got her settled with Niko, Dani looked in the mirror skeptically. She didn't wear dresses very often, and though she didn't consider herself a hardcore tomboy, her lifestyle had never really included dressing up like this. She'd called Tiff to ask for advice since Tiff had been the wife of a coach and was now engaged to a player. Tiff had sent her pictures of what to look for and Dani had texted her photos of herself as she'd been trying on different outfits. They'd agreed on a beige, cold-shoulder dress made of eyelet lace. Her slender neck and shapely shoulders were on display without the dress itself being overly tight around her torso.

The loose fabric flowed around her trim waist while still showing off her nice figure. It covered the muscular thighs she was self-conscious about while accentuating her shapely calves, and the outfit was finished with high-heeled strappy beige sandals that were a shade darker than the dress. The heels would make her the same height as Sergei, but as a tall woman herself, Tiff had assured her that any man worth his salt wouldn't mind.

The look on Sergei's face when Dani descended the stairs filled her with warmth. She sent a mental thank-you to her brother's fiancée for steering her in the right direction and closed her eyes when he leaned in to kiss her cheek.

"Absolutely stunning," he whispered against her ear.

"Thank you."

"That's a beautiful dress," Marj, the babysitter, said warmly. "I wouldn't have thought a blonde could pull off beige, but I would've been wrong!"

"Mama D, you look pretty!" Niko gushed, his mouth full of Cheerios.

"Thank you." She hugged him. "You be good for Marj, okay?"

"We're going to watch *Doc McStuffins*."

"You'll tell me all about it tomorrow?"

"Okay."

"See you later, buddy." Sergei kissed his son's head.

"Bye, Daddy!"

THE DRIVE to Gage Caldwell's house was quiet. Dani seemed preoccupied and Sergei was simply in a lust-filled haze. He wanted to turn around and go right back to the house, tell Marj to keep Niko downstairs and then lock the door of his bedroom—with Dani naked in his bed. That was probably a little too Neanderthal even for him, but he was beginning to second-guess this idea of taking her to the team party. He wasn't worried she would embarrass him or that he would have to answer difficult questions about what she was to him—he was more concerned with the single guys on the team going after her. She had no idea how gorgeous she was and a group of randy hockey players would be pushing each other out of the way to get to her. If he didn't stake some kind of claim on her, she would have a dozen dates set up by the end of the day.

The problem was he didn't understand why he cared. She wasn't going to be around for anything long-term, so he should've been happy she might get involved with someone else. Except he wasn't. Not even a little bit. He wasn't sure what he wanted but the idea of someone else being with her made him a little crazy. A casual fuck definitely wasn't in the cards, but if he didn't want a relationship, what else was there? He didn't want to start a relationship with a woman who could not only hurt him, but Niko too. Did he? Technically, they were already involved. What else could he call what they'd built over the last two months? They'd become friends gradually, and since moving to Alaska, she'd become an integral part of his life. Even without sex, he was as happy as he'd ever been when spending this much time with a woman. Except for the lack of sex, it was very much like being married.

Wait. *What?*

He shook his head, as if trying to shake the thought away. Where had that come from? He wasn't interested in getting married again, and definitely not to a woman leaving in less than two months. This was just fun, a casual reintroduction into dating life as a widower. Right? God, he hoped so.

"Are you nervous?" Dani's voice brought him out of his reverie.

"No." He frowned. "Well, maybe a little. Not nervous exactly, but I've played on quite a few teams in my career, and the seven weeks I played with this one were...different."

"In what way?"

"The guys are kind of uptight. I can't put my finger on it, but it's like everyone walks on eggshells. The only guy I've met so far who's been laid-back is Aaron, and he was out with a broken hand for the end of the season. The team captain, Jake Carruthers, is okay but everyone seems out of sorts, as if they're constantly worried about something. It's a strange vibe. I'm hoping with the new owner—"

"New owner?" Dani frowned. "I know the original owner passed away in December, but I thought it had been taken over by his corporation or something?"

"Not exactly. He willed everything to his nephew, but this guy's young, around my age, with no experience in hockey. There was a lot of talk in the locker room about him. I don't really know him, so I was a little surprised when he called to invite me to this."

"He called you personally?" Dani glanced at him. "Wouldn't he normally have his assistant do that?"

"You'd think so."

They glanced at each other and chuckled. "So today should be interesting, right?"

"For both of us. You're going to meet everyone and maybe you'll get a different vibe than I did. I'll be interested to hear your thoughts."

"I'm intrigued."

He reached for her hand. "Every guy on the team is going to be intrigued with you."

She flushed, lightly squeezing his fingers. "Don't be silly. I'm sure they're all married to supermodels and stuff."

"Is your brother married to a supermodel?"

"They're not married yet, but Tiff's beautiful enough to be a supermodel."

"She has a Ph.D., though, right? Did he fall for her because she's a wonderful woman or because she's pretty?"

"Point taken, but even if they think I'm great, they'll find out who my older brother is and run."

He laughed. "I can't argue with that because it would certainly be a deterrent for me."

She glanced over at him. "Actually, since we're out on a date, I don't think it is."

"Your brother and I are friends, so he knows I would never disrespect you. Those other guys don't have that relationship with him."

"True, I guess." She sucked in a breath as they pulled up to the gate of a huge, sprawling estate. The gate was open, with a security guard checking the names of the passengers in each car as they pulled up.

"This is something." Sergei whistled through his teeth. "I've been to some swanky houses for parties, but this is...*wow*."

"Wow is right."

There was valet service available, so Sergei turned over the keys to his car and he and Dani walked through the massive entranceway into what looked like a palace. Everything was gilded, overstated, decorated to scream extreme wealth. There wasn't time to see much, however, as a uniformed butler led them out back to where the party was in full swing.

"Sergei! Dani!" Aaron was the first to greet them, his curly blond hair blowing in the breeze as he approached.

"Hey, man." Sergei shook his hand, watching as Aaron leaned over to kiss Dani's cheek.

"Sergei." Gage Caldwell approached with his hand extended. "Welcome to my home."

"Thank you for having us." Sergei shook his hand, a little taken aback at the handsome man who was not only his boss but who owned the entire organization and this ostentatious house. "This is Danielle Cloutier."

"What a pleasant surprise." Gage turned assessing gray eyes to her, a smile creasing his features before he kissed her on each cheek. "I've heard a lot about you. Lonnie Finch is quite fond of you."

She smiled back. "I know he was close to your uncle. I didn't realize you were friends as well."

"I grew up watching Uncle Mac and Lonnie playing golf. I've known Lonnie all my life, but please, we can talk later. Help yourself to something to drink, the first round of steaks is coming off the grill now, and feel free to use the facilities."

He strode off, leaving Sergei, Dani and Aaron staring after him.

"Force of nature, eh?" Aaron chuckled under his breath.

"Interesting," Sergei nodded.

"Hot," Dani murmured, staring after him.

Aaron laughed. "Yeah, and he's single from what I understand."

"That won't last long," Dani grinned. She nudged Sergei. "Come on, I'm ready for a drink."

"Sure." Sergei put his hand on the small of her back as they walked and was gratified to see almost every guy that saw her do a double take. Though he was a little possessive of her, he hoped she noticed and stopped thinking something was wrong with her because she was tall, strong and athletic. She was fucking sexy as hell and the only person who didn't realize that was her. These guys were real men, not insecure college boys who couldn't appreciate a woman like Dani, and the looks on their faces told him they all wanted to know who she was.

Mine.

The thought was a tiny whisper of a word through his subconscious and though he tried to ignore it, he found himself unwittingly sliding his arm around her waist and pulling her to his side as one after the other of his teammates nudged each other. Oh yeah, these guys wanted to know more and since he'd been unabashedly single at the end of the season, they had to be wondering if she was a friend, a one-time date or someone more important.

13

Sergei got her a glass of wine and grabbed a beer for himself as they walked towards a group of people. The tallest of the group, a ruggedly handsome man of about thirty, turned with a grin.

"Hey, Sergei!" He held out his hand and they did a complicated handshake that made her want to roll her eyes. Did all guys do this shit?

"Hey, Jake. Good to see you." Sergei pulled Dani forward. "This is Danielle Cloutier. Dani, Jake Carruthers is our team captain."

"Nice to meet you. This is my wife, Adrianna." Jake gripped the hand of a pale blonde with hair so light it was almost white. She had bright blue eyes and a sweet smile as she shook Dani's hand.

Dani was introduced to half a dozen other players as well as a few wives and girlfriends, and she hoped she would remember at least some of their names. She wished she'd studied the team roster beforehand so the names would be familiar, but other than Jake, Aaron and the team's star forward, Kane Hatcher, she didn't recognize any of the names.

"Cloutier?" Kane looked at her. "You're Zakk's sister, right? You played for UND."

"Yes." She nodded. "Do you know my brother?"

"We hung out during the All-Star weekend a couple years ago. He bragged about you nonstop."

"That was the year we won the Frozen Four. He's my biggest fan."

"You're a hockey player?" Adrianna's eyes lit up. "That's so exciting. Do you still play?"

"Dani's been chosen for the Olympic team," Sergei interjected when Dani hesitated.

"Fuckin' A, that's awesome. High five!" Colt Matthews held up his hand and Dani slapped it with hers.

"The Olympics." Jake was nodding. "That's incredible, Dani. Congratulations."

"Thank you."

"When do you leave?" Adrianna asked. "I assume you have to be in some central location to practice with the rest of the team?"

"Yes. We'll be at the main facility in Colorado Springs. I leave the first of September."

"For how long?"

"Until the Olympics."

"That's a long time," the other woman responded quietly.

"It is, but it's a once-in-a-lifetime thing, so it's a worthwhile sacrifice."

"How do you feel about losing your girl for such a long time?" Kane asked Sergei.

"Oh, we're—" Dani began.

"This is new between us," Sergei interjected smoothly. "We're taking things one day at a time and we'll see what happens when she's gone."

"How does Zakk Cloutier feel about you bangin' his sister?" The vaguely familiar voice of Matt Forbes nearly made Sergei wince. Matt had played for the Sidewinders and had just been traded to Alaska. Sergei had heard the news but hadn't had time to process it since it had only been a couple of days.

"Last time I checked," Dani spoke before Sergei had a chance, "I was a grown woman free to make her own choices about who she *bangs*." She met his gaze unflinchingly, cocking her head slightly.

"Dude, don't be a prick." Jake gave him a hard stare. "I've heard all about your bullshit in Vegas and that's not gonna fly here in Anchorage; knock it the fuck off."

Matt snorted. "You gonna get me kicked off the team, Carruthers? You don't have to like me but my record on the ice speaks for itself."

"If your record on the ice was that important, you'd have been traded to somewhere like New York or Chicago, somewhere with clout instead of the team that finished last in the league."

Matt winced. "Whatever." He turned and slid his arm around a lean brunette.

"Hello, Sergei. Donna." Veronika gave them both a sinister smile.

"Hey, Victoria!" Dani shot back, her smile warm and genuine despite her veiled insult.

"It's Veronika," the other woman responded tightly.

"Sorry! Donna, Victoria...all the same, you know?"

Dani took a long sip from her wineglass and felt Sergei's warm breath against her ear as he whispered, "It's kind of hot when you put her in her place like that."

She turned with a mischievous smile. "Is it? Shall I do it some more?"

"Absolutely." They laughed together and he lightly kissed her cheek.

The crowd dispersed at that point, with Matt and Veronika moving off by themselves and Aaron, Jake and Adrianna staying with Sergei and Dani.

"That's the nanny I told you about," Sergei told Aaron.

"The one who was hitting on you?" He shook his head. "How the hell did she hook up with Forbes? He literally got here yesterday."

"Women like that will do anything to hook up with a player," Adrianna murmured. "Makes the rest of us look bad."

"She was gross," Dani muttered. "I would've killed him if he'd hired her to take care of Niko."

Adrianna shuddered. "Gross is right. I'm assuming he made a better decision?"

"As of right now I don't have a nanny," Sergei admitted. "Dani's leaving in September and the women the agency has sent haven't been a good fit at all. But one of Dani's friends from college is willing to come if we don't find anyone."

"If you're ever in a bind," Adrianna said softly, "please don't hesitate to call me. I don't go to all the games so I'd be happy to help."

"Thank you," Sergei nodded. "I may have to take you up on that."

MORE PEOPLE STARTED to arrive and Jake wandered off to talk to everyone while Aaron hung back chatting with Adrianna, Sergei and Dani. They grabbed plates of food and talked, enjoying the warm day and good company. Sergei was beginning to feel better about the team now that he was spending quality time with some of them. The arrival of Matt Forbes was a big disappointment —the guys on the Sidewinders hated him for some of the things he'd said and done while in Las Vegas—but Sergei planned to keep their relationship purely professional. Matt wasn't the kind of guy he would ever get close to. Seeing him with a woman like Veronika just reinforced everything he'd already heard about him.

On the plus side, as they sat and socialized, he found himself unable to stop touching Dani. Every time she laughed, he wanted to bask in her glow, and so did every other guy around them, even the married ones. She, Aaron, and Kane had been talking about hockey nonstop, and to everyone's surprise, Gage joined them as well, asking about her training regimen in Colorado and what preparation for the Olympics would entail. It was hard to give it a name but Dani was the kind of woman who made men wonder. Who she was, what made her tick, what it would take to get in her pants. In college, that had probably been more of a turn-off than her muscles, though he figured that might've played into it too since guys that age weren't mature enough to handle a woman like her.

Oh, this wasn't good. He had a thousand other things to think about, but Dani was the only thing on his mind and he couldn't seem to help it. Bringing her to this party had definitely been a mistake, but he wouldn't have changed his decision regardless. He was in so much trouble.

THEY DRANK and ate until well after the sun went down and someone started a fire in the fire pit. Supplies were brought out to make s'mores and Sergei couldn't remember the last time he'd had so much fun. Not since Tatiana had died, for sure. If he was honest, it was because of Dani. She was so damn easy to be with. There was no drama, no clinginess, not even the typical boredom with hockey talk. Tatiana had inevitably gotten bored at these types of events and wandered off with the other wives and girlfriends. Unfortunately, they had bored her, too, because she rarely found anyone who could talk medicine with her and she'd never been the type for mindless chatter. She'd been an intellectual snob, even with Sergei, and it was relaxing to be with someone who didn't demand anything of him, who didn't exhaust him far more often than she enthralled him.

When had he started thinking that way about Tatiana? Part of him was mortified, but when Dani shifted closer to him, her lean body pressed against his, it was hard to focus on why. For the first time since Tatiana's death, he was aware of the stirrings of...*something*. Life. Desire. Fun. He wanted those things again, and it was because of the beautiful blonde beside him. She was laughing at one of Jake's stories, interjecting her own take, making everyone else laugh too.

Watching her out of the corner of his eye, something shifted within him. He was so tired of fighting his attraction to her, keeping her at a slight distance. If he was honest with himself, the real reason he'd asked her to come as his date today was as a kind of test, to see how she would interact in his world. In retrospect, it had been a dick move. She deserved better from him and had never done anything to warrant being tested; she was a hell of a lot more honest than he was.

He absently stroked his hand over her thigh until he caught her peeking at him from under her lashes. He paused, wondering if he'd been reading her signals wrong, so he was surprised when she put her hand on his and moved it back to where it had been.

"Are you teasing me, Ms. Cloutier?" he murmured in her ear.

"Not at all, Mr. Petrov. I'm merely encouraging you to continue."

14

He bent his head and kissed her, lightly at first, until her mouth opened and her tongue sought his. *Shit.* This wasn't the time or place for a make out session, but he'd been dying to kiss her again. He pulled away reluctantly, his eyes trained on hers.

"I've wanted to kiss you all night," he breathed against her mouth.

"Canonball!" Out of nowhere, one of the younger guys on the team, Logan Pelletier, jumped into the pool fully clothed.

"Here we go," Jake chuckled, shaking his head.

"The water's great!" Logan yelled, coming to the surface. "Come on in!"

"Woo-hoo! Skinny-dipping!" Veronika started shedding her clothes, Matt encouraging her.

"Oh shit," Aaron whispered.

"Take it off, baby!" Matt held up his beer bottle in a lopsided salute.

Veronika jumped in the pool followed by Matt and someone Sergei didn't recognize. Tugging Dani by the hand, he led her away from the pool and into the pool house. There were changing rooms, restrooms and cupboards filled with towels, sunscreen and every pool amenity imaginable. Hopefully, they could be alone for a few minutes before anyone came looking for towels.

"Now that everyone's distracted, I can kiss you in private." He found her mouth with purpose this time, hauling her against him and sliding one hand under her dress. Sweet Jesus, she was wearing a thong. He ran his hand along the soft swell of her ass, wondering what made her so special. Every time he reminded himself she was leaving soon, he was gripped by the strangest need to ask her to stay. It was entirely irrational, and he tried to brush it off, but now that he had her in his arms it was perfect. *She* was perfect.

His fingers drifted to the silky strip of fabric along her hip and he slid along

the edge until he cupped the warm, damp V between her legs. "Damn, baby...
are you wet for me?"

"Is there someone else kissing me and touching me and whispering in
my ear?"

"There better not be." He let out a grunt of disapproval. "You're killin' me,
baby. Tell me what to do next."

"Keep kissing me?" She cocked her head, her eyes burning with intensity.

He sighed, tracing her full lower lip with his finger. "I'm not afraid of your
brother, per se, but I'm going to make damn sure I know what you want before
I touch Zakk Cloutier's little sister."

"You're already touching me, but if you want a formal proclamation, fine."
Her eyes twinkled with mirth. "I, Danielle Maryanne—"

"Maryanne?" he interrupted. "Did I know this?"

"I don't know but shut up and let me finish."

"Sorry." He tried to keep a straight face.

"I, Danielle Maryanne Cloutier, do formally proclaim that I want you to
make mad passionate love to me. Though maybe not here at your boss's
house." Her smile was impish. "What about you?"

"Jesus." He took a breath. "Well, then... I, Sergei Wayne Petrov—"

"Wayne? Your one-hundred-percent-Russian parents named you Sergei
Wayne?" She was gaping at him.

He rolled his eyes. "My hockey-obsessed father was one of Gretzky's
biggest fans. May I continue?"

"Sorry." She bit her lip in an obvious attempt to stop her laughter.

"I, Sergei Wayne Petrov, do formally proclaim that I will make you come at
least four times tonight. Against my fingers, all over my face, and at least twice
on my cock."

A flicker of nervousness shadowed her face but then she dipped her head
and pressed it against the hollow of his shoulder. "Did we just make sexual
vows to each other?"

"Seems like we did." He wrapped his arms around her. "And I'm going to
make good on one of those vows right now." He nudged her into the adjacent
bathroom and locked the door behind them.

"Sergei, wait..." She swallowed nervously. "I really don't think we should
be having sex in the bathroom at your boss's house..."

"Of course not." He was kissing the side of her neck. "You'll be making
way too much noise when I fuck you to do that anywhere but at home. I have
something else in mind right now. Think you can orgasm quietly?"

"Uhhh..." She grimaced. "Maybe?"

He laughed, leaning down to kiss her. This time his lips weren't gentle or
tentative. He slid his tongue into her mouth and kissed her hard, one hand
sliding back to cup her ass again. She moved against him, their bodies fitting
together easily. His mouth was soft but demanding, urging her to open
wider and kiss him back. He backed her against the wall, lips traveling to

the curve of her neck and nibbling the skin until she was covered in gooseflesh.

"Sergei..." Her voice was breathy, eyes closing as he licked her skin.

He rubbed his thumb along her nipple, feeling it harden at his touch. As he brushed his lips across the soft spot just behind her ear, her head fell back and she sighed lightly.

"You're so beautiful," he whispered, cupping her breast with one hand. "I love the way you respond to the lightest touch." He found her mouth again, seeking out her tongue and coaxing it into dueling with his until they were both breathing hard.

He pulled away, running his hands down the sides of her body before tugging her away from the wall and gently turning her away from him.

"Hands on the counter," he said softly.

"Sergei?" She looked at him over her shoulder, a hint of apprehension on her face. "I'm not protected."

"And I don't have any condoms with me. Don't worry, baby, just oral. Do you trust me?"

"Of course."

"Then spread your legs and keep your hands on the counter." He slid to his knees and lifted her dress, bunching it up around her waist. He moved his mouth south, pressing kisses along the bumps of her spine, the backs of her hips, the curve of her ass. She was hard and soft at the same time, so lean and muscular beneath the silkiest skin he'd ever had the pleasure of exploring.

Lightly fingering the edge of her thong, she whimpered when he slid two fingers underneath the lace between her legs. He toyed with the fabric, inching the panties down her legs until she stepped out of them. He wasn't in a hurry, taking in her beautiful ass, pale skin, and the glistening lips of her pussy. God, she was sexy bent over like this. Her thighs were trembling slightly and he suddenly remembered her saying she wasn't very experienced—was it possible no one had ever gone down on her before? Just the thought got him so hard it was almost painful and he was gentle as he spread her open with his fingers. Oh, hell, this was going to be fantastic. Her pussy was as gorgeous as the rest of her, pink and so fucking wet. If she was any hotter, he might blow his load without even touching her and he couldn't wait another second.

Instead of slow and gentle like he'd been planning, he just went for it. Doing it from behind like this was trickier than if she was on her back, but it was perfect for their current situation and a lot more sensual for her. He swiped his tongue right down the middle of her slit and chuckled as she let out a gasp, her ass rocking back against him.

He held her fast and used his tongue to collect some of the delicious nectar that was all but pouring out of her, licking it with long, firm strokes that had her making garbled sounds deep in her chest. She started breathing hard, her fingers white as she grasped the counter for all she was worth. When he found her clit and sucked it erect, he was gratified she started humping his mouth.

"Sergei…" Her heated whisper was full of need.

"I know, baby, just relax and enjoy." He kept up a steady rhythm with his mouth and tongue, discovering she responded better to rough than gentle. When he started to fuck her with his tongue she began writhing and grinding against him urgently.

"Oh!"

"That's right, honey." He sucked on her clit again and slid a finger inside of her. She was fluttering against his mouth, her tight, heated flesh aroused and ready to fuck. It was killing him that he'd have to wait, but without a condom there was no way they could do it.

He continued to feast on her sweetness, finding all the places that made her throbbing nub come alive. She tasted like candlelight and romantic walks in the park, if there was such a thing, and he had no idea where that came from. He'd never wanted a woman like this before. Maybe it was her innocence, or some combination of her sassy attitude and shyness behind the scenes that turned him on, but whatever it was he would have died if he had to stop now.

He put two fingers inside of her and curved them up until he found the spot that made her moan. That was all it took; her pussy clenched and shuddered against his mouth and she hissed out his name, moaning as she struggled to stay quiet. She bucked so hard he had to use his hands to hold her in place while his tongue kept up the steady pace on her clit. Watching her come was un-fucking-believable.

DANI COULDN'T STOP WHISPERING his name as the waves of her orgasm rocked her body back and forth, over and over. She was spinning out of control, sensations she'd never imagined shooting through her as she thrashed against him. The room momentarily faded to black, making her lose her breath and gasp for air. His tongue was still wrapped around her clit giving her more pleasure than she'd known was possible. Finally, he loosened his grip and softened his touch to a gentle flicking that made her mewl like a kitten. Her first experience with oral sex had been nothing like what she'd been expecting and now the beginnings of an uncomfortable aftermath had taken root, embarrassment at how she'd come undone in front of him washing over her. What had she just done?

He'd grabbed some toilet paper and was gently wiping her wet, sticky thighs. She nearly cringed, but then he was helping her slide her panties back up and had pulled her close.

"You're so fucking beautiful," he whispered. "I could feast on you for days."

She turned bright red and he cocked his head curiously. "Why are you blushing? Am I the first guy to go down on you?"

She nodded miserably, but he surprised her, yanking her against him so his erection was pressed against her belly. "That's so fucking hot. You feel that?

That's what being the first guy to eat your pussy does to me—and now I have to wait until we get home to take care of it."

"Sorry?" She wrinkled her nose but he was laughing.

"You're not sorry and I'm not, either—that was fucking *hot.*" He bent his head and kissed her.

She tasted her own musty flavor on his lips and found it mildly pleasant, but not nearly as good as the feeling of his hands on her, gripping her possessively.

"I can't wait to get you home," he whispered against her mouth.

"Me too."

"Let me wash my face and hands and we'll get back to the party." He paused, looking into her eyes. "You okay, honey? You're looking awfully uncomfortable."

"I've never done anything like this before... Where people might have heard us or whatever." She worried her lower lip with her teeth. "I don't want people to think I'm a bimbo or something."

He gently lifted her chin. "I'll beat the shit out of anyone who calls you a name like that."

She nodded slowly. "I know. I'm okay. It's just really intense between us, isn't it?"

"Oh yeah, and you ain't seen nothin' yet."

THEY LEFT SOON AFTER, and Dani stared out the window as Sergei drove home. He was holding her hand and she tried to wrap her head around where the evening had gone. Their casual date had turned into...so much more than a casual date. What they'd done in the bathroom had been amazing, but now she wasn't sure how to explain she was a virgin. Did she just blurt it out or wait until they were home and getting ready to do it? She wanted to tell him but part of her was afraid he wouldn't want to continue, that it would be disappointing for him. She didn't know how it worked. Sara said it was still good for the guy even though it would probably suck for her, but Dani couldn't bring herself to ask him. Maybe he'd never been with a virgin so he wouldn't know either.

"Are you having regrets?" His deep voice in the darkness made her jump and she turned in surprise.

"No, of course not."

"Then why are you sitting way over there all quiet and moody?"

"I've never done anything like what we did in the pool house, much less on what's technically our first date."

"I've discovered firsthand that life is short," he said gently. "Live it to the fullest, because in a flash it can be gone. I'd hate to think you have regrets about anything we did."

"Not regrets, just second thoughts, because I really like you."

"I really like you, too." He glanced at her. "I thought we agreed to try things out?"

"We did. And we did."

"Didn't you like it?"

"I did, but I don't know what to do next."

His voice was warm and a little bit raspy as he said, "You know exactly what we're going to do next. I'm going to pay Marj, send her home, and then I'm going to make mad, passionate love to you. Isn't that what you asked for in that sex vow you made?"

She smiled. "It is."

"I have lots of condoms, so we can go all night..."

Tell him! She had the perfect opening, but the words wouldn't come out and she stared at the big hand wrapped around hers instead. This was a mistake. She was too embarrassed to admit she was a virgin and he would undoubtedly run for the hills if she told him.

"By the way, I booked our flight to Vegas this morning."

"You did?"

"We're leaving on the second and coming back on the ninth."

"Thank you. That means so much to me. You're a really good guy, Sergei."

"You're pretty great yourself."

They didn't talk any more until they got home and Dani hurried up to her room while Sergei paid Marj and sent her on her way. Dani tugged the dress over her head and hung it in the closet, thinking she'd looked pretty tonight. Sergei had certainly thought so. No matter what else happened between them, he was attracted to her. The memory of the way he'd touched her made her squirm with an unfamiliar ache and she rested her forehead against the closet door. She needed to tell him but if she did, there was a chance he wouldn't want to be responsible for such an important event in her life. Especially when this was all supposed to be casual. Being honest could result in missing out on the best chance she'd had at losing her virginity since high school.

"Babe." Sergei's voice, with his barely discernible accent, washed over her as if he'd touched her, and she lifted her head despite her embarrassment at him finding her in nothing but her thong.

"Hi."

"You're not okay."

"I am. I'm just trying to find my inner vixen. If she even exists."

"Why? You're fine without her."

"I'm actually kind of shy about my body, Sergei. I'm not ashamed of it— I've worked hard to be the athlete I am and I'm proud of that, but it's been at the expense of my sexuality. I have none. Guys have said some really unkind things about my body."

"That's so wrong." He drew her against him, hands at her waist, looking deep into her eyes. "You're beautiful. I can't speak for other men. I don't know what they see, or what they like, but what I see is perfect."

She swallowed hard, suddenly overwhelmed and insecure. She'd always felt more masculine than her friends. Her thighs were muscular and her boobs fairly small, both of which were big turn-offs to the guys she'd gone out with in the past.

"What's going on in your head?" he asked softly, watching her face.

"You're out of my league—"

He gaped at her. "Are you kidding?" He yanked off his shirt and shorts before turning her so she was facing away from him, her back pressed to his front.

"Sergei, what—"

"Look at us." He'd turned them so they were facing the mirror, their naked bodies pressed together, with hers in the front.

She looked away and he leaned forward. "Look," he said firmly. He looked down at her breasts and slowly ran his hands over them. "You have the most perfect fucking tits—and they're real. When I touch you here—" He softly pinched her nipples between his fingers until she moaned. "You're so sensitive your whole body comes alive and it's fucking amazing." He moved her hands to his shoulders. "Don't move," he instructed lightly. He used his fingers to trace lines around the muscles that rippled in her abdomen. "What percentage of body fat did you say you have?" he whispered.

"About eighteen or nineteen percent right now," she said, trying to breathe as he touched her. "It was closer to fifteen in college."

"Uh-huh." He licked her neck as he used his thumbs to rub her hip bones. "You know how many women have that little body fat? Other than a serious athlete like you? None. And I think that's hot as hell." He splayed his hands over her incredibly flat stomach before inching them down until he could finger the silky curls between her legs. "You're a natural blonde—do you see how hard that makes me?" He reached back to take his cock in his hand and gave it a slow stroke, his eyes meeting hers as he did it. "Do you see what your body does to me? You're out of *my* league, baby."

She nodded slowly, fascinated as he continued to stroke himself. His chest was rising and falling with long, heavy breaths as she watched, and he gradually nudged her until she was facing him again.

"Come to bed with me, Dani."

"Yes."

15

She let him lead her to his room and watched as he locked the door behind them. Her insides always did a little dance when he touched her, and this was no exception. Staring into the depths of his dark blue eyes left her tongue-tied and aroused. He was captivating—and she wanted him to capture her in every way imaginable. His eyes turned molten as he moved in to kiss her. Their mouths linked with familiarity as their fingers slowly twined together. He kissed her until she whimpered, the fingers of one hand digging into his chest, exploring the light hair that curled there. Every flick of his tongue was pure heaven and she moaned, low, deep and needy. Her insecurities fell away as he continued to touch and kiss her, making her want to be as close to him as possible. She was enthralled by the way he moved, the way he sounded, and the way he tasted in her mouth. He was exactly the kind of man she'd fantasized about but never imagined existed.

He reached down to palm her breasts with his hands. "These are truly perfect," he murmured, bending his head to take one aching nipple in his mouth. She moaned as it went taut between his lips. The things he did with his mouth made her tremble all over, and any embarrassment over her inexperience faded away. His touch was all-encompassing, leaving her helpless to do anything but go along for the ride.

He moved to the other breast, taking his time and teasing her nipple until she was straining against him. Her breath came in short gasps, anxious for more but unable to tell him.

"I want you, *Maryanne*."

She giggled despite her arousal. "I want you too…*Wayne*."

SERGEI GRINNED as he lifted her in his arms. He carried her to his bed and gently set her down. He dug condoms out of his nightstand and dropped them beside her. She was on her back, her hair fanned out behind her. Sergei moved over her, kissing the side of her face as he gently toyed with a lock of her hair. It was soft and silky; he loved how it felt between his fingers. He wanted to feel all of her, under him and completely surrounding him when he buried himself deep inside of her. Just thinking about it made his cock ache painfully. Tearing open the package, he rolled the condom down his throbbing dick and looked at her. He moved his legs between hers, his cock pressed against her thigh as he lay on her.

She seemed nervous, so he caught her hands with his, bringing them to his lips. He kissed her fingers, one at a time, until he moved back to her mouth. Though he didn't believe in love anymore, he'd been drawn to her from the first time he laid eyes on her and something told him this was going to change everything; he was taking a huge risk getting this intimate with her, but he couldn't deny himself. It had been a long time since he'd wanted a woman like this and her shyness enthralled him. He wanted to show her how beautiful he thought she was and how sexy it would be when they made love.

He found her breathtaking, with soft, rippling muscles and a body that was a wet dream for him. Now that she was stretched out beneath him, he was a little mesmerized. Nothing had prepared him for the emotions of being naked with her. This was somehow much more intense than he'd anticipated but he was powerless to stop. He moved his finger to her clit and smiled, loving the way her body seemed to ignite the instant he touched her. He'd made her wet just stroking her thigh earlier tonight, so he was excited to see what she would do now that their bodies were entwined. He used his mouth and hands to tease and coax her into a frenzy, loving her raw reactions to his touch. He was so immersed in the pleasure she gave him he didn't pay attention to how tight it was when he pressed his cock against her throbbing entrance. All he was thinking about was being inside of her, and with one firm thrust, he sheathed himself. It was only then, as he pushed past the barrier of her virginity at the same time she cried out, that he realized what had happened.

His eyes met hers and he froze. "Dani..."

"Please..." Though she tried desperately to stop them, tears squeezed out of her eyes.

"Sweet Jesus, Dani, why didn't you..." He dropped his forehead to hers, myriad emotions whipping through him. While part of him wanted to stop and make her explain why she'd tricked him like this, the logical part of him knew it was too late. If he stopped now, not only would he have hurt her physically, his rejection would only reinforce her feelings of inadequacy. He wasn't a super intuitive guy, but no one had to tell him he needed to handle this carefully. Besides, pulling away now would be like amputating one of his limbs; he couldn't remember the last time a woman was this tight and wet.

"I'm sorry," she whispered. "I was afraid you wouldn't want to if I told you…"

"But I hurt you…" He sighed, bringing up his hands and placing them on either side of her face, his thumbs wiping away the tears leaking out the sides.

"I'm okay," she choked out, though her eyes told him something else.

"I should've taken it slower…" He sought her eyes. "Are you sure you want to keep going?"

"Yes." She nodded emphatically.

"I'm sorry I hurt you," he said against her mouth, his lips grazing hers softly. "Do you want me to wait so you can get used to how it feels?"

She nodded, biting her lip against the obvious discomfort.

He lay perfectly still, giving her time to breathe through the pain. He was fighting a thousand emotions, including an almost debilitating need to move, as he tried to remember what to do to make a woman's first time more bearable. She was tighter than he remembered anyone ever being, and he took a long, steadying breath so he wouldn't hurt her. She felt so damn good his cock was pulsing with the need for release, but he would wait until she was ready. Her eyes had closed, long pale lashes fluttering on her cheeks. He bent and kissed them, one chaste peck at a time, waiting for her to give him the signal she was ready.

"Honey, talk to me. What do you want to do?" He waited until her eyes opened.

"I want you to…make love to me. Like we agreed." Her voice cracked a little but her gaze never wavered.

"It's going to be uncomfortable."

"I know."

"I'm so fucking hard for you, sweetheart. But I don't want to hurt you anymore." He shifted a tad, sliding out a tiny bit. She winced, but her eyes remained locked with his.

"I'm okay. Really."

He moved a little more, and she wrapped her arms around his neck. When she lifted her hips slightly, he carefully pulled back, watching her face. He slid back in, as gently as he could, and this time it was her lips seeking his. Their tongues tangled, and as the kisses got hotter and more sensual, he felt her getting aroused again, moisture gathering around his already straining cock.

"Better?" he asked against her mouth, moving experimentally.

"Yes." She was trembling now, but there was an excitement in her eyes that nearly sent him over the edge.

"Easy." He started a slow rhythm, closing his eyes against the warm wetness enveloping him. He pulled out and carefully plunged deep again. She moved with him, a whimper escaping her.

"Ohhh." Her voice held wonder and an unmistakable curiosity.

"Yeah?" He licked her lips before gripping her firm, round ass and pulling her tighter against him; she already wanted more and he prayed he would last long enough to give it to her.

EACH STROKE of his cock inside her left Dani fighting the unfamiliar sensations of a faint burning coupled with a distinct need for something more. She didn't know how to tell him but the ache was almost more than she could bear.

"Sergei, I need—"

"I know." He kissed her before sliding his finger between them and seeking out the throbbing little pearl she wanted him to touch. He stroked it erect as she arched up against him. "Like that?" he whispered, moving with purpose now that she was pulsing with desire.

"Yes." She clutched at him, fingers digging into his shoulders as the ache between her legs turned to liquid fire. Her aroused state coupled with his expert fingers left her oblivious to the soreness, chasing another orgasm like the one he'd given her earlier.

With her hips meeting his, Sergei couldn't hold back anymore. Though he kept his thrusts gentle, he was moving with ease now, sliding in and out to the sound of whimpered cries that had to be a combination of pain and pleasure. He kept his finger on her clit, rubbing it in perfect rhythm with the movement of his cock, and there was no better feeling than that of her tightening around him.

"Sergei!" Her voice shuddered with frustration. "I don't know what to do. It hurts but it feels good—I'm so confused!"

"I know, baby, I'm sorry—next time will be better."

He kept his strokes smooth and easy, until Dani couldn't tell what hurt and what felt good. She was impossibly aroused, but the pleasure was tempered with a throbbing soreness that wouldn't relent. Her body moved of its own volition, bringing her right to the edge of ecstasy. Sergei picked up speed, his mouth fastened to hers, his body in complete control as she moved beneath him. He plunged into her one last time, the vibrations making them cry out together. His sheer bulk kept her pinned to the bed as the waves of their mutual orgasms drove them to the brink, barely able to breathe as they clutched each other.

UNABLE TO MOVE, with Sergei resting on her heavily, his lips still pressed to her neck, Dani wasn't sure what to do.

"You okay?" he whispered at last, his heartbeat getting back to normal.

"I'm wonderful," she whispered back. "Thank you for making my first time amazing."

"I wish you would have told me," he said softly, his fingers curled in her hair. "I would have made sure you were ready... I feel bad I was so rough in the beginning."

"It was going to hurt no matter what. And the end made up for it."

"Yeah?" He nuzzled her shoulder, his eyes finding hers in the darkness.

"Next time will be better, right?"

"You're probably going to be sore for a few days, so don't go rushing into anything." He cleared his throat slightly.

She gazed at him, a slight frown creasing her brows as she watched his face. "Sergei, you don't have to be uncomfortable. I don't expect anything because we did this. I was ready to lose my virginity and I wanted it to be you."

He sighed and rubbed a hand down her arm, obviously struggling to articulate what he wanted to say. "I don't want to hurt you, honey." He stroked her cheek. "What you gave me tonight was a beautiful gift but—"

"I'll be moving to Colorado Springs soon, far away from you and our life this summer. Once I leave, you'll never have to see me again."

He scowled. "That's not what I said—I wouldn't have slept with you at all if I never wanted to see you again. I just need you to understand that I can only give you sex and friendship—that's why I wouldn't have wanted to be your first. It usually evokes a lot of feelings I'm simply not capable of returning anymore."

"I'm not looking for anything." She spoke the words though her entire being screamed something else.

Neither of them seemed to know what else to say, so she was quiet when he rolled onto his back and pulled her onto his chest.

"Are you sure you're okay?" he asked finally. "Are you sore?"

"A little," she admitted.

"Want to go sit in the tub with me? There's a lot of blood."

"Oh, shit, I'm sorry."

"Don't worry about it. We'll throw everything in the washer." He pulled her to her feet, hauling her against him as he paused to capture her mouth again. This wouldn't end well, no matter how many times she told herself it didn't mean anything, but she was powerless to move away.

As he ran the bath and she did her best to clean up, the intimacy was tangible. Damn, she was going to fall hard. Everything about losing her virginity had been perfect. Despite the pain and discomfort, being that close to Sergei was unlike anything else she'd ever experienced. He was equal parts sexy and tender, as concerned about her pleasure as her safety, and it made her yearn for more.

"Promise you're okay?" he asked softly, lifting her chin so he could look into her eyes.

"Promise." She gave him a sweet smile and stepped into the tub behind him.

DANI WOKE UP FIRST. It was early, and Sergei was snoring softly beside her. She took a moment to look at him, take in his gorgeous face, the beautiful torso that was bare for her enjoyment, even the long fingers that had brought her so much pleasure. God, she was an idiot of a girl, letting a man who didn't return her feelings take her virginity. Now she was feeling weepy and sad, instead of reveling in the memories of last night.

With a mental sigh of disgust, she slid out of bed as quietly as possible and hurried down the hall to her own room. She pulled on running shorts, a sports bra and a tank top before using the restroom and brushing her teeth. After pulling her hair into a ponytail, she grabbed a pair of socks out of the drawer and padded down the stairs to the kitchen. She'd have a protein shake and then go for a run. She was sore and out of sorts, but that wouldn't keep her from getting in a few miles.

Memories of last night rushed back and forth across her mind like a DVD alternating between fast forward and rewind. She let out a huff, trying to clear her head. Breathing in deeply, she spread her arms, rested her hands on the edge of the counter and let her head fall forward. She desperately needed to let go of some of these overwhelming emotions or she would never be able to face him.

Strong arms wrapped around her waist from behind and Sergei's breath was warm against her ear as he whispered, "You're *so* not okay."

"I am." She squeezed her eyes shut, trying to keep unexpected tears from falling.

"You're crying," he said, gently turning her to face him. "Aw, baby, I'm sorry."

"It's not... You didn't... I'm..." She burst into tears, burying her face in his shoulder, mortified to break down like this.

"I hurt you, didn't I?" he moaned, stroking her hair with one hand as the other circled her waist and kept her close to him.

"No." She tried to shake her head but was nestled too firmly against him. "It's just... I never... And I thought... But it wasn't..."

"It wasn't very good, I know." He pressed light kisses to her temple. "But if you want to try again, it'll be better. I promise."

She sniffled for a few minutes and finally broke free, reaching for a napkin to blow her nose.

"I'm sorry," she said quietly, not meeting his eyes. "I don't know what's wrong with me."

"All normal, hon. Losing your virginity is supposed to be a little emotional, a life-changing event you'll never forget, full of romance and intimacy and love...and I didn't give you any of that. I'm sure you have regrets and I wish—"

"No, stop." She put a finger on his lips. "That's not what this is about."

"No?" He arched a brow, watching her intently. "Then what is it?"

"It was..." She took a deep breath. She refused to lie, to make a mockery out of her first time. No matter what happened, she wanted to look back on this without regrets. "Wonderful. Everything about yesterday was wonderful. I felt beautiful—sexy even—and the way you got all jealous at the party made me excited, happy, like I finally found the right guy, the one who gets me, appreciates me in all the ways I need." She took a shaky breath. "But this morning I realized it was all that stuff you talked about... The life-changing event, the romance, all of it. Except it's not. You don't love me. You're not interested in romancing me or even dating me and I'm frustrated because I want more of all of it. The excitement, the sex...you. I want more of *you*, Sergei."

His mouth crashed onto hers with passion she hadn't been expecting, but she opened to him greedily, anxious to take anything he was willing to give. Despite his rough movements, his kisses were tender, far gentler than she'd been expecting, and the sigh of pleasure that escaped her was almost inadvertent.

He pulled away abruptly, his blue eyes dark with passion and a need that mirrored her own.

"I want more of you, too," he said softly. "But you need to know, if we're going to keep sleeping together, you're mine. I'm very much an alpha male and I won't share while we're together. I don't do love, but I do possessive and faithful—as long as we're doing this, you're not to be with anyone else."

She glanced at him in confusion, a crease forming between her eyebrows. "But if we're not in a relationship—"

"We are," he grunted. "It's a sexual relationship, but as long as it lasts, you're mine. No one touches you but me."

"You won't make a commitment to me but I have to be faithful to you?" She folded her arms and took a step back. "Like hell!"

16

Sergei hadn't battled feelings like this since college and didn't know what to do about any of it, so he went with what worked. He pushed her against the wall, his lips finding hers again. Her mouth was lush and soft, so fucking sexy his dick was hard as stone. He grabbed a fistful of her hair and wrapped it around his hand as he kissed her, his mouth grinding against hers, lips and tongue punishing in their attack. To his surprise and delight, she didn't hesitate to respond. Her mouth opened and her tongue met his fervently, one hand grabbing his left butt cheek and squeezing hard. He growled, a low rumble in his chest that let her know he liked it before pulling away.

"Mine," he grunted. "You gave me your cherry and I'll be damned if I let another man have what's only been touched by me before I'm ready to give it up. It's not forever, but it's definitely for now, and it's exclusive—for both of us."

"But you said you don't do relationships."

"I said I didn't want to get married again. Not the same thing."

"O-okay." Her eyes were wide and confused but the way she looked at him told him she wanted him. *Now. Again.* Even as uncomfortable as it had been for her. Damn if that didn't make him even harder.

"God, you're fucking amazing," he murmured, holding her close. "I'm going to show you a whole new world, baby. I'm hard and edgy in bed and going to spend the rest of the summer making you want things you never knew existed."

Her eyes were sparkling with excitement. "I like the sound of that," she admitted, her breath a little raspy.

He chuckled. "Hearing you say shit like that is hot as hell, but not yet, not today. You're definitely sore and I want you to enjoy it next time. Okay?"

She licked her lips and nodded. "Yes."

"I don't think you have any idea what's to come in the bedroom."

She nodded. "I haven't done a lot of stuff, but I've read a lot and I want to experience it all. *Everything.*"

"Yeah?" His eyes glittered as he wondered how far she would let him go. "You going to let me put my cock here?" He pressed his forefinger between her cheeks, right through the thin fabric of her shorts, and felt her jump.

"I, um, I guess," she whispered.

He smiled, impressed with her openness. "When the time is right, you'll really like it."

"Okay." She swallowed hard but met his gaze without wavering.

"Come on, let's have breakfast and when Niko wakes up we can go to the gym together. You can't want to get away from me already." He tried to be playful, keeping his gaze warm so she wouldn't see the lust burning up inside of him.

"No." She rested against him, her head falling on his shoulder.

He wrapped his arms around her, content to have her close. Last night had thrown him for a loop. In retrospect, all the signs had been there, but she'd masked them with her sweet demeanor and fierce independence. She'd been so open about her insecurities it hadn't occurred to him she was that innocent. Inexperienced yes, but not a virgin. He wasn't angry about it—she'd wanted him and told him so. She hadn't tried to back out or even asked him to stop when he was hurting her, so she'd been ready and willing to make love with him. He just didn't understand why she'd wanted a man who didn't have romantic feelings for her to be her first.

He gently pushed her away, reaching down to take her chin in his fingers. "Will you tell me the truth about something?" he asked softly.

"About what?" There she went blinking those green eyes at him.

"Why me? Why would you want a broken shell of a man so much older than you to be your first?"

"Because no one else ever appreciated me or made me feel sexy or made me want it so bad. That first day, when you yelled at me about Niko calling me *Mama D,* there was something so raw and masculine about you, I knew instantly you were the one."

"You knew you wanted me to be your first while I was being an asshole?" He quirked a smile at her.

"Okay, I knew instantly I wanted *something* because you made my heart beat faster, but by the time we got here to Alaska, I was already fantasizing about being with you."

"Shit, baby." He slid his hands around her waist, a little disconcerted she'd felt about him exactly what he'd felt about her. Right from the beginning, no less. Now what was he going to do?

"Look, it's all good," she said, turning to the counter and starting to make coffee. "There's no reason we can't enjoy the summer and each other while taking care of Niko and getting ready for hockey season. We're friends, aren't we?"

"At the very least." He kissed the back of her neck.

"We can have fun while I'm here and shake hands before I go, right?" She turned to look at him, whatever she was thinking masked behind inscrutable green eyes.

"Is that what you want?"

"It's what we both want, right? Let's not overthink it, okay? I appreciate your sensitivity about it being my first time, but I'm okay. I got a little overwhelmed this morning because I've never had a morning after before. Now that I know we're okay, I won't break down like that again."

Her eyes were practically pleading with him to agree, so he did, nodding easily and following her lead in starting to get breakfast ready. It didn't sit well with him, though, and he wasn't sure why. She was going out of her way to convince both of them that the loss of her virginity hadn't changed anything, but he knew better. Those tears this morning hadn't been because of mere discomfort; she'd been emotional, experiencing intense feelings that were new to her but for whatever reason didn't want him to know it. Whether she was protecting him or herself, he couldn't be sure, but later, when he had her in his bed again, he'd find out.

THAT AFTERNOON they gave in to Niko's repeated pleas and took him ice skating. Dani had taken him a couple of times in Las Vegas, along with Tiff's twins and Toli's stepdaughter, and Niko had been a natural. She'd tried to play it down since Sergei seemed to feel so guilty about not teaching him to skate, but it was obvious the moment they set him on the ice at the local rink. Sergei had a wool cap over his head and kept his head down to stay under the radar, but Niko took off like a bat out of hell.

"Holy shit," Sergei laughed. "You weren't kidding. He can barely stand up and he's practically lighting it up."

"He's going to be fast, like his father and uncles."

Sergei cut his eyes to her. "You know about Vlad?"

She smiled. "Zakk and Toli are best friends; Zakk's my big brother. There's no way I could live in that house and not know. And yes, I understand Vlad being your half-brother isn't public knowledge because of your father's enemies."

"So you know what happened in Russia."

"When your wife died?" She nodded, moving her feet across the ice slowly, her eyes never leaving Niko.

"Her father was mafia," he said, even though she hadn't asked. "For whatever reason, even though we were both in the NHL, both wealthy, both healthy and successful, he wanted her to marry Toli. That was the plan. When she and I foiled it by falling in love, he was furious. That's why she agreed to leave her career as a physician and come to the U.S., even though she didn't want to. It was the only way to get away from whatever bullshit he had in store for us."

"She loved you."

"I'd like to think so." He gazed at his son, slipping and sliding across the ice as fast as his awkward strokes would allow.

"It's okay. You don't have to talk about it."

"I want to," he said slowly. "I never have before. I mean, Toli, Dom and Zakk were there and we've told Vlad, but I've never actually talked about it to anyone else."

"About which part?"

"The way she died."

"You can tell me anything." Dani slid her hand into his, matching his paces as they moved together, his gaze now focused on nothing in particular while she kept an eye on Niko.

"The details are complicated and go back to when she and Toli were teenagers—he's five years older than I am and she was three."

"I didn't know she was older than you."

"Did you know my father was KGB and is still loosely involved in whatever faction of that organization is active?"

She nodded. "Zakk has only ever talked about the basics, saying the less Tiff and I know the better, but he told us you and Toli don't ever plan to set foot in Russia again because of it."

"Which is why no one outside the family can ever know that Vlad is our half-brother. That would put him in danger as well."

"I certainly would never tell anyone and Zakk only told me because I spent so much time at Toli and Tessa's, it was hard *not* to put together parts of the story."

"What it all boiled down to was her father wanting an alliance with our father to link the mob with the KGB, but for reasons we'll probably never understand, it had to be *Toli*, not me. We didn't know that, so when Tanya and I fell in love, we figured her father would have the alliance he wanted regardless, especially since at the time I wanted to stay in Russia. But he was furious, told her he would kill me to keep us apart. She was pregnant, though, and her mother was still alive, so she had some control over him. We got married and moved to the U.S. For a while, it seemed like everything would be okay."

"Couldn't the Russian mob or the KGB or whoever get to you in Boston almost as easily as they could in Russia?"

He nodded. "It's a lot harder here, and if they were caught, they'd go to jail, unlike over there, where shit like that happens every day."

"That must've been scary."

"I was busy with hockey," he said after a minute, his jaw working in irritation. "Tanya took care of everything—Niko, the house, and apparently the situation in Russia, though I didn't know it then. She kept her father at bay, kept our home together, and took care of our son, all while being threatened and badgered." He let out a ragged breath before he continued.

"The night she died, they'd kidnapped Anton, and Toli had gone after him. He was fully prepared to die in exchange for the safe return of his son. Tanya was pissed, and she got on the phone, trying to call in favors, do anything she could to help. I refused to let my brother go in alone, you know? I mean, he's my big brother and he needed backup. Zakk and Dom had flown in, anxious to help, but at that point no one knew what was going on. Toli said his goodbyes to us, to our parents and to Tessa, and he went to get his son. I was hiding under a blanket on the floor of the back seat of the car—"

"I can't even imagine how scared you all were," she murmured, reaching out to lift Niko to his feet after he wiped out in front of them.

"I know," he replied, unconsciously reaching for her hand again. "I don't know what Tanya did while Toli and I were heading to the meeting point, but she showed up about fifteen minutes after we did. I was lurking outside the building, so I saw her go in but couldn't get to her in time to stop her." He paused, a dark shadow covering his face as he slowed to a stop, leaning against the boards of the rink. "That's when I knew it was all about me, that her father was only going to give Anton back in exchange for me, not Toli. The old bastard knew I'd never let Toli go alone and he was right. I walked into that warehouse and announced myself, told him to take me... Tanya pulled a fucking gun out of her pocket and shot her father at the same time he shot at me. Except she stepped between us and took the bullet."

"Oh, Sergei." Dani squeezed his arm, moving close to his side. "I'm so sorry."

"She killed her father and took a bullet to protect me, but I couldn't protect her. How fucked up is that?"

"None of it was your fault, Sergei. You couldn't help that her father was an asshole or that yours was KGB."

"My dad sacrificed a lot to protect us boys—even Vlad, who grew up in an orphanage—and then my wife made the ultimate sacrifice to protect me. What kind of man does that make me?"

"A survivor," she whispered, leaning up against him, forcing him to look at her. "A strong, loving man who knows life isn't always fair. A devoted father who's going to make sure his son has a better future. Those things make you better, Sergei, not weaker."

"I couldn't defend my own wife. I stood there and let her jump in front of a bullet." The pain and shame in his eyes was so poignant it was like someone was squeezing her heart from the inside.

"Oh, Sergei." Dani moved up against him so they were almost eye-to-eye. "You had no way of knowing what her father was going to do—you're a hockey player, not some kind of mafia thug. She grew up with that life, and probably knew her father better than most people. There's no shame for you in her sacrifice. She was prepared to defend you and she did. Feeling guilty about it makes a mockery out of what she did. She didn't do that to make you suffer; she did it so you and her son would be free."

"It sure doesn't feel that way when—" He snaked out an arm to catch Niko as he tripped. "Easy, buddy, you need to slow down."

"Skate with me, Daddy." Niko's eyes shone with excitement. "Can we go fast? Mama D can go really fast!"

She gave them a little nod of her head and Sergei only hesitated a second before gripping Niko's hands and then turning backwards so he could pull the little boy. He paused to lean over and brush his lips across hers before moving off with his son. Dani watched them with a grin, Niko's excited laughter echoing off the walls. Sergei's face was relaxed now too, the dark shadows of his memories fading with the light provided by his son's happiness.

She'd known most of that story, but not the details, not that Tatiana's father had hated him or that she'd gone in most likely knowing she would die to save her husband. She had to have been a remarkable woman and for a moment Dani wondered how Sergei could ever get involved with anyone else after having a woman that had loved him enough to die for him. She'd never been truly in love so that concept was foreign to her. It made her a little sad, too, because she liked him a lot. There was a tiny part of her that wished they could explore something beyond sex and friendship. He was handsome, sexy, rich, athletic, gentle, loving and brave—what else could any woman ask for?

Sighing, she pushed off, picking up speed to catch up to Sergei and Niko, who were speeding around the ice as fast as was safe. She matched Sergei's stride, grinning as he winked at her.

"Mama D, it's so fast!" Niko squealed.

"I know." She laughed, losing herself in the moment and determined to enjoy what time she had with them. They weren't her family but they were her friends and that should be enough.

17

After three hours of skating, they were all tired and Niko fell asleep the moment they put him in the car.

"That was fun," Sergei said as he turned the car towards home. "I'm glad you talked me into doing this. And thanks for listening earlier."

"Any time. Thank you for trusting me with something so personal."

"I think you trusted me with something far more personal." He reached for her hand and she let him take it.

"That was just sex. This was—"

"That wasn't *just* anything. It was intimate and beautiful...something I'm honored you shared with me."

"Have you ever been with a virgin before?"

"A long, long time ago," he admitted. "I think I was seventeen. I'd only ever been with one girl before her, so I was terrified I'd done something wrong."

"I wasn't worried about that."

"No?"

"I trusted you."

"But I didn't know you were a virgin," he protested.

"I trusted you knew what you were doing in general. It was going to hurt no matter what, right?"

He grimaced. "That's what I hear... It did, right?"

"Oh, yeah."

"But you still want to do it again?"

"Well, yeah." She cocked her head. "Don't you?"

"You have no idea how much."

"Good thing." She nudged him playfully. "You owe me a huge do-over."

"Oh really?" He nudged her back. "It's not *my* fault you were a virgin."

"But you had more fun than I did."

"You had more fun than I did when I went down on you in the bathroom."

She flushed. "So then we both owe each other do-overs."

"Niko's going to bed early tonight."

AFTER DINNER, a bath, and one episode of *Doc McStuffins*, Dani put Niko to bed. Still tired from his day of ice skating, he fell asleep almost instantly and Dani softly shut his door behind her when she stepped out. Sergei had monitors in several rooms of the house that were always on, so they shut his door at night to keep his room quieter.

With the evening ahead promising an intimacy she'd been thinking about since last night, her entire body buzzed with nervous excitement as she padded down the hall to her room. She didn't know if Sergei would come to her or if he expected her to go to him, but their routine at night varied. Sometimes they'd watch a movie or talk; other times she'd go to her room to read and she wasn't sure what he did. Most nights they were together, though, even if she was on her laptop and he turned on a baseball game.

Slipping into her bathroom, she brushed her teeth and brushed out her hair. It had gotten long in the last year, nearly to her waist now, and she'd debated cutting it. Not too short, but maybe six inches or so, where it would still be long enough for a ponytail or braid when she played hockey but not so much to take care of. Not that she did much with it lately anyway, between taking care of Niko and working out. She fluffed it out a little, letting it cascade down around her shoulders and chest. It looked nice that way. She wished she thought about doing more with it, but it never seemed like a priority. Why had her looks never been a priority?

Sergei likes your looks. The thought made her smile and she stepped out of the bathroom feeling better. She paused in the hallway when she heard his footsteps on the stairs and he came into sight. His eyes raked over her in a way that made her insides flutter with sheer desire and she took a shaky step towards him.

"Hi," she whispered, unable to find her voice amidst the nervousness coursing through her.

"Hi." He smiled down at her, rubbing the knuckles of one hand lightly across her cheek. "Your hair looks pretty like that."

"Thank you."

"Can I take you to bed, Maryanne?" His eyes were twinkling, teasing her, and she cocked her head.

"Is using my middle name code for being horny?"

"Maybe?"

"Okay, Wayne." She slid her arms around his neck. "Take me to bed."

He backed her into his room and his mouth was on hers the moment the bedroom door closed behind them. His tongue slowly teased the seam of her lips until she parted for him and then she was lost. She'd kissed a few guys in college, but nothing compared to Sergei. His touch was simply magical and the connection between them was impossibly potent. She'd had girlfriends who'd told her about having intense chemistry with a man, but hearing about it from others was nothing like experiencing it personally. His touch brought her alive, as if she was someone special—even if she wasn't necessarily special to him.

When his hands cupped both sides of her face, pulling her closer and holding her head, it was like being devoured. She couldn't move but she didn't want to; she just wanted more of everything Sergei.

"I want to touch you this time," she breathed against his mouth. She forced her eyes up, to focus on his, instead of on the slant of the hip bones poking up from his waistband; if his abs were any more chiseled she could bounce a quarter off them.

"Take my shorts off," he commanded gently.

She ran her hands along his strong, hard stomach. The thick but light-colored hair on his chest was beautiful, accenting his pecs and solid shoulders. She dug her fingers into them before pressing her chest against him. The heat of his skin moved through her like lightning and the ache between her legs made her squirm with need.

"Sergei, I want—"

"I know what you want," he whispered, moving her hand to his shorts. "And I'm going to make you come so hard, you're not going to remember your name. But first, you're going to undress me."

"But—"

"Shh." He put a finger on her lips and brought her hands to the elastic of his shorts, guiding her in sliding them down. He was naked underneath and she gazed at his erection in fascination. His cock was bigger than she'd imagined, long and incredibly hard. Tiny drops of pre-cum leaked from the head and she instinctively reached out to touch it.

"I didn't realize it was so...*big*," she murmured, unable to stop her smirk.

"I haven't had any complaints."

"I honestly don't know what to do with it."

"Rub your thumb over the tip."

She did as he instructed; it was both soft and hard. The skin was velvety, and she wondered why she'd always thought it would be rough. When she hesitated again, his hand closed around hers and guided her, showing her how to touch him.

"Touch me, baby. It's all good." He was breathing hard and his eyes closed as she continued to stroke him. "Yeah, that's it."

Her inexperience made her feel ridiculous, but his gentle coaching and words of encouragement emboldened her. When she started to move her hand faster, he groaned, making her even braver. She picked up the pace, the way he'd shown her, and figured she was doing okay since he gripped her hair and let out a hiss.

"Enough," he whispered. "I'm not ready to get off yet, and you're driving me wild. The first orgasm always goes to my woman."

My woman.

The words hit her square in the gut and she dropped to her knees more from the impact of what he'd said than any plan to seduce him, but as soon as she did, his hands were in her hair.

"Not yet, honey."

"I want to," she whispered, slowly licking her lips. "I need...to touch you. The way you touched me."

"Not on your knees. Come to the bed."

"Why?" She cocked her head.

He hesitated. "Do you like being on your knees for me?"

"My friend Sara once told me she loved being on her knees when she gave a blow job because the whole experience empowered her. Something about the strength in a human being's jaws and the vulnerability and trust the man gives her by letting her take control like that. I know a lot of girls think it's demeaning but... The way Sara talks about it, when you really enjoy being with that person, sounds really hot."

"I can't speak to what a woman feels in that position," he said softly, lifting her chin with his finger. "But if you want to do it this way, I'd love it. I just don't want you to feel pressured."

"I don't." She leaned over, pressing a chaste kiss right on the tip. "I want to taste you like you tasted me the other night." She tentatively nibbled on the head. "Except all I know about doing it is what Sara showed me with a banana."

He snorted with laughter. "That's actually pretty close. How about you pretend this is a banana and I'll let you know if you need to adjust a little."

She grinned. "Okay. Promise you won't laugh?"

"Laugh?" His eyes glittered as he shook his head. "Not in a million years. The idea you've never done this before makes me want to go all caveman and beat my chest and shit."

She took a deep breath and opened her mouth, gripping his length with one hand and using the other to guide him into her. It was more pleasant than she'd imagined and as she closed her lips around him, she lifted her eyes to search out his. He was staring at her with a look she'd never seen before: adoration and lust, tempered with...respect? Did he respect her for sucking him off? She was so confused she momentarily forgot what she was doing.

"Suck a little harder," he encouraged. "Take as much as you can, but you don't have to try to impress me by choking yourself."

"I don't think I'm ready to deep throat," she acknowledged, "but I'll do my best."

She drew him into her mouth in earnest this time, licking and sucking the way Sara had shown her that one Sunday morning over breakfast. They'd laughed and laughed, but now she was grateful for the introduction. And Sergei definitely wasn't laughing. He was thrusting his hips forward in a slow, gentle motion, letting her get used to the sensation of him fucking her mouth. He didn't rush or try to go too deep, keeping his strokes shallow even when his breath quickened and he began shaking with exertion as he tried to stay in control.

He abruptly pulled away, making her gasp as he yanked her to her feet and tossed her on the bed. "I told you the first orgasm goes to you," he growled against her mouth. "But that was un-fucking-believable. I'd never have believed that was your first blow job if I didn't know you."

She flushed, inexplicably proud to know she'd pleasured him.

"Now shimmy out of those panties for me."

She pulled them off with two quick tugs, looking up at him expectantly.

His strong, powerful body was poised above her, his eyes on hers as he dropped his mouth to hers again. There was so much passion between them it left her breathless, even as she felt a moment of trepidation, the memory of last night's painful coupling making her tense.

"Easy." His voice was tender, fingers on her cheek as he paused. "We'll go nice and slow this time."

She was vaguely aware of him sheathing himself with the condom before settling between her legs, but where there had been pain last time now there was only a gradual build-up of pressure as he slid into her one delicious inch at a time. Until there was nothing between them. No pain, no space, not even air. As she adjusted to the feeling of him filling her, stretching her until she was sure she would burst with need, she dug her fingers into his scalp. He was refusing to let her rush him, holding back and forcing her to return his kisses with slow, languid strokes of deliciousness. Even as lightning strikes of energy began coiling low in her belly, she could only focus on the man above her. Watching him glide in and out of her was the sexiest thing she'd ever seen. He'd changed positions, holding himself up with his arms, and she watched the muscles in his stomach ripple with each stroke; that alone was enough to push her towards the edge.

"Sergei." This time she wouldn't let him slow down, yanking at his arms and tugging his mouth back to hers so she could fasten her lips to his greedily. "Fuck me," she whispered urgently.

"Oh, my beautiful Maryanne..." He let out a groan. "I don't want to hurt you."

"You won't. I want you, Wayne. Harder. Faster. *Please.*"

"You have me, baby." He snapped his hips forward, sheathing himself completely and Dani let out a grunt of surprise.

"Oh..." Her eyes rolled back as he picked up speed and trapped her hands above her head with his. "Sergei!"

"That's it, baby... Let me make you feel good."

Everything blurred and her body took on a life of its own. When her orgasm crashed over her, the heat was unlike anything else. Sergei's followed right on her heels, his grunt of pleasure practically ripping out of him before his lips pressed to hers again.

They stopped moving gradually, slowly coming back to reality. The air sizzled with urgency, as if once wasn't enough, even as they tried to catch their breath.

"What do you think?" he whispered against her mouth. "Better than last time?"

"Fuuuuuckkk..." she moaned, throwing an arm over her eyes. "That was amaze-balls."

"I thought so." He rolled onto his back, reaching out to twine the fingers of his left hand with those of her right.

"Can we do it again?"

"As many times as you want."

"Can I be on top?"

He chuckled. "Sure."

"Will you, um, do what you did at the party again sometime?"

"Go down on you?" He turned onto his side, smiling into her face. "Sure, babe. Anything else?"

"I'm not sure." She gnawed on her lip thoughtfully. "What else haven't we done?"

He laughed heartily. "Oh, honey..."

"Oh, that other thing you mentioned!"

"Which...thing?"

"You know... The butt stuff."

"You want to try anal?" He looked surprised. "We just figured out missionary, babe."

"You said it feels good, right?"

"That's what I've been told, but it's not like vaginal sex. You have to work up to it."

"What do you mean?"

He pulled her on top of him, shaking his head. "One step at a time, Maryanne. We'll start with a finger, work up to a plug... But you're not ready for that, and frankly, neither am I."

"Why not?"

"'Cause it's way more intense than this and I want you to be comfortable with all of this before we get to all of that."

"Okay." She nestled against his chest. "I'm liking all of this, though."

"Me, too, Maryanne. Me, too."

18

———

Dani woke up to find herself alone in Sergei's bed. Fumbling for her phone, she realized she'd left it in her room so she had no idea what time it was. She sat up, listening for signs of life, and heard the faintest sounds of laughter coming from downstairs. The door of the bedroom was closed so she eased it open and tiptoed out, even though she wasn't sure why, slipping into her own room.

Her phone told her it was after ten, which was late for her, but they'd had a long night. They'd made love again and then lay together talking for what must have been hours. They'd started relatively early since Niko had been in bed by eight, but it had to have been well after midnight before they'd fallen asleep. It had been wonderful, too, lying there together, talking and laughing. Her body was still humming from how thoroughly he'd loved her and she smiled as she cleaned up, dressing for the day. She hadn't had much in the way of expectations, but Sergei had far surpassed them.

She padded down the stairs and found Sergei and Niko cleaning up the kitchen.

"Mama D, are you sick?" Niko turned to her, his blue eyes narrowed worriedly.

"No, silly, I just couldn't sleep last night so I was tired this morning."

"Did you get enough rest?" Sergei asked softly, one hand resting lightly on her waist.

"I did. Thank you for letting me sleep in."

"It's summer. You should be doing a lot of resting."

"So should you."

"I'm fine." He turned to Niko. "So, Niko wants to go hiking today. You in?"

"Sure." Since the boys had eaten, she pulled out the blender to make her protein shake, smiling to herself as Sergei sent Niko to go play and then pressed himself up against her back. He dropped a light kiss on her bare shoulder before resting his chin there.

"You sure you're okay? Not too sore?"

She nudged him with her elbow. "I'm fine. My friend Wayne is very good at this bedroom stuff."

His gruff laugh against her ear gave her goose bumps. "He told me he's looking forward to more quality time with Maryanne."

"She's looking forward to it, too." She turned on the blender and turned to face him, sliding her arms around his neck. "Sergei, what are we doing about Niko?"

"Putting him to bed?"

She laughed. "I mean, right now, during the day. Are we going to touch and kiss like this? It might confuse him."

"Yeah, maybe. I don't know. I guess we shouldn't be overt about it, but at the same time, I'm not going to pretend you're some kind of casual fuck. That's not what this is, Dani. For as long as we're together, we're together. I'm not going to teach my son to be a prick."

"He's three. He has no idea that there's a correlation between the way we touch in front of him and other things that go on."

"No, but it becomes part of his subconscious and as he gets older, there will be a part of him that puts two and two together. I never want him to think I'll touch a woman I don't care about like that in front of him. And a woman like you, whom I'm intimate with, who's also part of his life? Yes, he's going to see the appropriate parts of it."

"And when he asks…whatever a three-year-old might ask?"

"I tell him you're part of my life. When you go to Colorado, it's not like we won't be friends anymore, and I'll explain you're playing hockey for the Olympics. Because we're going to be your two biggest fans."

"You will?" For some reason that almost made her tear up.

"Of course." He kissed her lightly, reaching behind her to turn off the blender. "Every exhibition, every televised anything, and it will be all Olympic hockey, all the time, come February."

"My only regret is that none of you will be there." She sighed. "You, my brother, Sara… Although I think my parents are going. Zakk said he's getting them flights and tickets to the hockey events, but he's surprising them in October for their anniversary."

"I'd be there if I could. I wish it lined up with the All-Star weekend."

"I know." She made a face. "But knowing Zakk and the other Sidewinders will be watching helps, even if it adds a little pressure."

"What am I? Chopped liver?" he teased.

"I didn't know you were interested until just recently."

"I'm interested." He slid his hands down to cup her backside. "But today, we're going hiking, so get some nutrition into you while I get Niko ready."

"Okay." She nodded, turning to pour the protein shake into a glass, her butt still tingling from where he'd touched her. God, she hoped she didn't react to him like this every time he touched her outside the bedroom—it was a little overwhelming. Of course, he was overwhelming. How the hell had she gotten so involved with Sergei Petrov? She desperately needed to talk to Sara.

THEY HIKED in a place not far from Anchorage called Flattop Mountain. It was a bit touristy, but only about a fifteen-minute drive from the city and not terribly steep since they had Niko with them. After Sergei had told her where they were going, she'd done a little research online, finding that the Arapaho and Ute Indians had traveled the area to reach hunting grounds of the Great Plains. The peak was just over 12,000 feet and the round-trip hike was almost nine miles. Sergei had said he didn't think they could do the whole thing with Niko, so they would go as far as they could and turn back.

While the beginning of the path wasn't bad, it got steeper, but the spectacular views made it worthwhile. Sergei carried Niko in the beginning, putting him down when it got more difficult, he and Dani taking turns holding his hand. Dani stopped often to take pictures, which allowed Niko to rest, and she found herself so caught up in the beauty surrounding them she didn't think much about the climb itself.

"Selfie time!" she called out, lifting Niko into her arms and turning her back on the gorgeous background so it would be in the picture.

Sergei stepped in, sliding an arm around her waist and smiling.

Looking down at the picture, Dani felt a surge of emotion; they looked like a family, like they belonged together. She hated feeling like a romantic ninny, but being with Sergei and Niko was so natural.

"I think we can make it," Sergei said as they continued to climb. "According to the information I have, it starts to level out here so the last third of a mile shouldn't be too bad. If you want, we can take turns going up while the other stays here with Niko."

"How do you feel, buddy?" Dani asked him, kneeling in front of him. "You think you can hike a little more?"

Niko seemed amenable since they'd been sitting for a while and he'd had a good snack, so he nodded.

"We'll take it slow," Sergei said. "If anyone gets too tired, we'll turn around. We've already seen some beautiful stuff."

"At this point, we're too close not to go all the way," Dani said. "I want to do it."

"Okay. I can carry Niko if I need to; this is pretty flat."

"I'm hiking, Daddy," Niko protested mildly, grinning up from under his Alaska Blizzard baseball cap.

"You just tell us if you're too tired, okay?"

When they got to the top, Dani took a deep breath, looking around in fascination. "Wow. Just wow. This is gorgeous."

There was rocky terrain, snow-covered peaks and the Tyndall Glacier in the distance. They'd decided not to actually approach the glacier since they'd been warned it was dangerous, but it was still beautiful.

They sat on the ground enjoying the beauty around them and Dani wondered for the first time if she would be happy living here. She wasn't sure what made her think about that, but it undoubtedly had to do with the gorgeous man and sweet little boy on either side of her. She didn't want to articulate anything in particular, but there was no universe where leaving them would be easy.

"Ready to start heading back?" Sergei asked. "People I talked to said we shouldn't be up here much past noon and it's getting there."

"Yeah, let's go. We definitely don't want to get caught in those thunderstorms they talked about."

With a few final pictures and one last look at the view, they started back down.

It was three days before Dani had any time alone. Sergei went to meet up with Jake and Aaron for a beer and she was home with Niko. She'd just gotten him to bed and sank onto the couch, ready for some girl talk. It had been too long since she and Sara had talked. Though they texted regularly and kept in touch, they hadn't had a real conversation in weeks. The truth was, she and Sergei were together constantly. Even tonight, he'd acted almost guilty as he'd told her he was going out with the guys. She'd laughed, telling him it was fine and reminding him he needed to bond with his new teammates. He'd kissed her before he left, whispering that she should be naked and waiting for him in bed when he got home. Something she was totally on board for. Their sex life was out of control but more fun than she wanted to admit.

"Hey!" Sara answered immediately.

"Hi. What's goin' on?"

"Same shit, different day. You?"

Dani chuckled. "Definitely not the same shit as the last time we talked."

"You did it," Sara squealed. "Oh my god, you lost your virginity."

"And then some."

"And then some? Tell me everything."

Sara's excitement was contagious and Dani gave her an abridged version of the sexcapades that had been going on for the last five days or so.

"I'm so jealous." Sara sighed. "I haven't gotten any in ages."

"You were getting more than your share all through college while I got none," Dani pointed out. "It's my turn."

"Okay," she conceded. "You get your share now."

"I think there are quite a few single guys on the team," Dani mused. "Maybe Sergei can introduce you when you get here?"

"I hope so." Sara paused. "So…how's the rest of it?"

"The rest of what?"

"Your relationship."

"Um, fine?"

"Come on, Dani, this is me and I know you. If you were a casual-lay kind of girl, you'd have given up your cherry to that football player in our freshman biology class."

Dani hesitated. "Honestly, I don't know. Since I've never been in a sexual relationship before, I don't know how it works when you're this intimate with someone. I've spent the last four nights sleeping with him. For all intents and purposes, we live together since I'm now sharing his bed. I take care of his house to a degree, we do things as a family and for the last four nights, the minute we put Niko to bed we were naked and all over each other. Is that normal?"

Sara let out a long, put-upon sigh. "Oh, honey."

"What?"

"No, okay? No, that's not normal. Most people go out on dates and, whether it's the first date or later, have sex but then go home to their own beds. They certainly don't live together, take care of a child together, and spend 24/7 together. This has every element of a serious relationship except one thing."

"What?" Dani asked warily.

"Commitment?"

"Um, well, that's not entirely accurate. We agreed that we would only be with each other for as long as we're together. At least until I leave for Colorado."

"It's exclusive?" Sara sounded startled.

"Is that bad?"

"Not for him, but it could be very bad for you."

"Why?"

"Don't even try to tell me you're not having feelings."

Dani didn't say anything.

"Dani?"

"Well, yeah, some, I guess. But we're friends—I have feelings for you, too. That doesn't mean I'm in love with you."

"No, but if I were to tell you I didn't want to be friends anymore, wouldn't it hurt?"

Once again, Dani fell silent for a while. "So you're saying I'm going to get hurt, because once it's time to go he won't be my exclusive live-in lover anymore."

"Pretty much. What does he say?"

"We haven't talked about it beyond the no-fucking-anyone-else conversation. But he says he's not capable of falling in love again, that he's broken."

"And you don't believe it."

"It's not possible. He's amazing. Maybe he's not capable of loving *me*, but he's definitely capable of loving. I feel it every time he touches me. I may not have a lot of sex experience, but I have life experience, and there was a lot more than sex going on when he did everything he could to make the first time better. When he dragged me to sit in the bathtub with him afterwards. When he got up with Niko the other morning to let me sleep in. When he got all up in arms about not showing affection around Niko, how he's not going to teach his son to take advantage of women. Even though said child is a toddler who probably doesn't even notice. Oh, no, that's not a man incapable of love. Maybe it's just me."

"Would you stop that?" Sara hissed, the annoyance in her voice vibrating through the phone. "Did you ever think it's because you're leaving, so he knows there's no future? You're going to the Olympics, which isn't optional, and then to your dream job working for an NHL team. None of that includes him or Alaska, so why would he open himself up to that?"

"I guess you're right," Dani mumbled.

"Dani, maybe you need to think twice about this friends-with-benefits arrangement. Your whole voice lights up when you talk about him. And those pictures you posted online the other day while the three of you were hiking? Honey, do you have any idea how much you look like a family? You could be Niko's mom, and while it maybe wasn't obvious to others, anyone who knows you could see the intimacy in those selfies of you and Sergei."

"You think my brother saw them?"

"Your brother definitely saw them."

"How do you know?" Dani asked in alarm.

"Because I was over there helping Tiff with the boys and she and Zakk were arguing."

"About me?"

"Well, Zakk wanted to call Sergei and ask him flat out if he's sleeping with his sister. Tiff forbade him."

Despite the seriousness of the conversation, Dani chuckled. Her brother was physically formidable, but his fiancée was a force to be reckoned with. "So what happened?" she asked after a moment.

"Tiff told him he wasn't getting any for a year if he did anything and he backed off, but then she got in the shower and he called Toli."

"Oh, fuck me loud!" Dani hissed. "Seriously?"

"Oh yeah. Obviously I couldn't hear Toli's end of the conversation, but he seemed to talk him off the ledge. Your brother was saying stuff like, 'If he hurts her...' and, 'You think they're getting married?' but by the end, he mumbled something about minding his own business for now and bringing it up when you come home for your birthday."

"Great." Dani scowled. "Way to ruin my trip for me."

"Sorry. But the point is, everyone sees there's something between you just from some innocent pictures with Niko. I can't imagine what it's like being you."

"We've only been sleeping together a week or so."

"The sex is an intense bonus, but if that's all it was, there wouldn't be the electricity you can see in pictures. I think you're falling hard and don't even know it."

"Well, even if that's true, it's too late to stop it. So why not enjoy it while it lasts and deal with the aftermath later? Besides, when I get to Colorado, I'm going to be way too busy with hockey to worry about a broken heart. Everyone has them, right? I'm probably way past due."

Sara groaned. "Dani, I don't think—"

"Come on, don't. I just want to giggle about how big his dick is and have you tell me about some cool thing I can do in bed to surprise him. Let me enjoy this, Sara. Please?"

Sara was quiet for a bit before saying, "Ice cubes."

"What?"

"Put an ice cube in your mouth before you blow him."

"Oh my god! For real?" Dani tucked her legs under her as Sara explained what to do.

19

The days ran into each other as Sergei and Dani kept busy exploring Anchorage, taking Niko ice skating and keeping a strict workout regimen. Sergei was in the best shape he'd been in during the summer for as long as he could remember and he felt great. Of course, it probably had something to do with the stunning blonde gracing his bed every night, too. She was beautiful, smart, curious, and fun. Everything they did turned into an adventure, whether it was finding a new book to read to Niko or some touristy excursion outside the city. A handful of teenage romances, two marriages, and umpteen one-night stands had never provided the overall satisfaction he got from Dani. How some other guy hadn't snatched her up was beyond him. It was a bit of a cliché, but she was truly perfect. Maybe not for everyone, but for him? Absolutely. Looks, personality, and heaven help him, their sex life. Not just quantity, but quality. She wanted to try everything, trusted him implicitly and so far had enjoyed it all, too. He'd never had a sexual partner like her, and outside the bedroom she was even more delightful.

Because of her, he'd been warring with a lot of different emotions lately. They'd settled into their life together seamlessly, as though they were a long-time couple, and the idea that she was leaving him—them—was messing with his head. While he couldn't even fathom saying the words "I love you" to another woman ever again, he also couldn't comprehend the enormity of watching her just move to Colorado and then make a permanent home in Las Vegas. It bothered him more than he was willing to admit, and as he buttoned up the dress shirt he was putting on for their date tonight, he wondered what to do next.

They were going to dinner with Jake, Adrianna, and Aaron. The three of them were close—they'd gone to college together—and they'd asked Sergei to join them. It had been almost second nature to tell them he'd be bringing Dani, and then he'd had a moment of discomfiture when he'd had to *ask* her if she wanted to go. After he'd already told Jake she was. It had been so long since he'd been involved with a woman other than Tatiana, he'd forgotten about little things like asking a woman out. Hell, now that he was thinking about it, he felt like a real shit. He'd never taken Dani out on a proper date, bought her flowers, or even told her she looked pretty outside of a sexual context. He needed to fix that immediately. He was many things, but an asshole wasn't one of them.

"Hey, which shoes do you like?" Dani's voice made him turn and his breath caught in his throat.

"Wow..." he breathed. "You look absolutely gorgeous. Is that new?"

She flushed, giving him a shy smile. "Tiff has been my online fashion consultant. I send her pictures and she tells me what to buy. I figured they've already seen my only dress, so I needed another one. Which meant more shoes...and then I found two pairs in my size, which is really hard since I wear a women's eleven."

He glanced at the two different shoes in her hand. One was red, with a skinny high heel and had an opening for her toes. The other was a nude color, with a thick, chunky heel he thought was called a wedge. The dress she was wearing was a pale pink and both shoes would match in color. However, the red ones were sexier and although they would make her his height or possibly a bit taller, he didn't care.

"The red," he said in a husky voice. "They're almost as gorgeous as you."

She dipped her head. "Thank you. I'll be ready to go in a couple of minutes."

"No rush." He watched her disappear down the hall and wished she was getting dressed here in his room with him, instead of hurrying off to her own room all the time. Things had definitely gotten complicated since they'd started sleeping together, but the odd thing was he had no regrets.

Pulling on his sport coat, he headed down the hall in the direction she'd gone and stood in the doorway of her room, watching her slide on the sexy red heels. He let out a low whistle.

"You sure you want to go out to dinner, Maryanne?"

She grinned up at him. "Keep your pants on, Wayne. We'll be naked in a few hours, but I need you to feed me first."

"I suppose I can wait for us to eat."

She picked a small black handbag up off the bed and met his eyes. "If I was better at being girlie, I'd have a purse that matched my shoes, but I guess it's too late to worry about that."

"You know guys don't care about that stuff, right?"

"Yeah, but other women do."

"Don't worry about Adrianna. I can't imagine Jake's wife is going to be bitchy to you."

"I hope not."

THEY TALKED ALL the way to the restaurant and when she stepped out of the SUV, he watched the young man at the valet stand almost trip over his own feet trying to talk to her. Another restaurant patron rushed to open the door for her and Sergei barely had time to slide his arm around her waist before the maître d' hurried over to greet her.

"Am I going to have to beat the men off of you tonight?" he whispered in her ear.

She cut her eyes to him, a beautiful smile on her lips. "Not necessary. I don't see anyone but you."

Damn. She'd done it again. Six little words and his chest was doing all kinds of funny things.

"Hey, guys." Jake was on his feet, shaking Sergei's hand and pulling out a chair for Dani.

Everyone exchanged pleasantries and Jake ordered a bottle of wine. By the time they'd ordered and settled in with wine and a basket of delicious bread, the ice had been broken and the five of them were like old friends. Adrianna was quiet and a bit shy, but sweet and easygoing. Aaron was his usual relaxed self so Jake and Sergei seemed to lead most of the conversation. Dani appeared to be taking it all in, so Sergei occasionally drew her in but mostly let her do what was most comfortable for her.

"Dani, I looked you up online," Adrianna said during a lull. "How exciting to be chosen for the Olympic team. Jake and I enjoyed watching you in the Frozen Four."

"You watched?" Surprise shone on Dani's face.

"Last night." Jake rumbled out a laugh. "After we realized you'd be at dinner tonight. I felt a little foolish that I'd never seen you play."

"That seems to be a theme with women's hockey," she said lightly. "But it's okay. My brother and his friends always watch, and that means the world to me."

"You must be bummed you won't be able to go watch her in Seattle," Aaron said to Sergei. "Pain in the ass the NHL isn't shutting down for the Olympics."

"Yeah, it's disappointing for sure." Sergei nodded. "But you can bet I'll be losing a lot of sleep staying up to watch every minute of every game."

"How does it work?" Adrianna asked, her blue eyes guileless as she looked at Dani. "If the team is made up of players from all over the U.S., how do you practice?"

Dani raised a finger, indicating she should wait as she took a sip of wine. "I'll be moving to the training facility in Colorado Springs the first of September. We'll train together until we leave for Seattle in February."

"And you'll be here in Anchorage?" Adrianna turned to Sergei.

He nodded, though he picked up his glass of wine to avoid saying anything.

"But then you'll be back, right? I mean, five months isn't a huge sacrifice for something as cool as the Olympics."

Dani bit her lower lip. "Oh, well, actually I won't. I've been offered a job with the Sidewinders as an assistant trainer and I'll be moving to Vegas after the Olympics."

There was an awkward silence as everyone looked from Sergei to Dani and back again.

"These plans were in place before we met," Sergei said after a slight hesitation. He had to give some kind of explanation, because a generic friends-with-benefits response wouldn't cut it, but he didn't have anything that sounded much better. "We've only been together a short time and we knew from the beginning that she was leaving. Everything between us is casual."

"You're a stronger woman than I am," Adrianna said to Dani. "I've followed Jake around since the first day I met him. I don't know what I'd do without him."

There was another strange silence as Adrianna looked sad, Jake looked embarrassed and Aaron looked...angry? There it was, that strange dynamic he'd felt since the beginning here in Anchorage, but right now, all he cared about was Dani. He'd clasped her hand under the table and her fingers were icy; the conversation about leaving had upset her even though she'd handled it with aplomb. Hell, he was upset and he didn't even know why.

Luckily, Jake shifted the conversation and soon they were laughing about something that happened on the road last season. Dani was quieter, though, smiling politely but not engaging like before. The food was delicious but she picked at it, clearly not herself. When the waiter came to take their plates, Dani excused herself to the ladies' room and Adrianna went with her.

"I'm sorry Addy put you on the spot like that," Jake said once it was just the guys. "It's obvious we upset Dani and I'm sure that wasn't her intention. She doesn't always think before she says stuff like that."

"It's okay," Sergei shrugged. "I'll talk to her when we get home."

"You're gonna let her go?" Aaron asked mildly. "Seems to me you're crazy about her."

"Dani's amazing," Sergei responded, looking away. "But I'm a widowed single dad with a shit-ton of baggage. She needs someone younger, who can help her follow her dreams, not hold her back. I'd be a true asshole if I let her know how I feel about her."

"Shouldn't that be her decision?" Jake asked, his green eyes sympathetic.

"You think I should make her decide between her future of working on an NHL team and giving it all up because I have some confusing feelings for her? So I can go play hockey while she stays home taking care of a kid that isn't even hers?" He made a face. "No. Not gonna happen. I care for her enough to let her go."

"Makes sense," Jake nodded.

"No, it doesn't." Aaron scowled at both of them. "Instead of giving a grown, intelligent woman the respect of making her own decision, you're deciding what's best for the little lady. What is this? The 1800s? You're both Neanderthals."

Sergei was taken aback by his black scowl.

"Aaron's divorce has been ugly," Jake said. "He wants someone else to have the happily-ever-after he didn't."

"Bullshit," Aaron muttered. "I happen to think Dani's great. Shit, if she didn't only have eyes for you, I'd ask her out in a heartbeat. If she wanted me to leave Alaska, I totally would."

Blood rushed to Sergei's head and he had to take a deep breath not to say something he might regret. Who the hell did Aaron think he was? This was bullshit. Before he could open his mouth, Jake put a restraining hand on Sergei's forearm and laughed.

"Okay, you win," Jake said to Aaron, digging a twenty-dollar bill out of his wallet and handing it to him. "You were right—jealous as hell."

"Sorry," Aaron gave him an apologetic grin. "Jake said you two were just fuck buddies. I bet him twenty bucks it was more. Don't worry. I'm not that kind of guy—I'd never ask out your girl."

Sergei huffed out a little laugh. "You guys suck."

"You're really gonna let her go?" The disbelief in Aaron's eyes was obvious. "I think you're crazy."

"I have to," Sergei said simply. "Anything else would be selfish as hell."

"Sometimes selfish isn't a bad thing."

"I've already done selfish and it didn't end well," Sergei muttered, turning his head as he caught sight of Dani coming back towards the table. She took his breath away in that tight pink dress and those red heels. Every other man in the place saw it, too, following her with their eyes. Except instead of her usual sweet, sexy smile, she didn't make eye contact and sank into her chair, continuing her conversation with Adrianna.

All through dessert and after-dinner cocktails, Dani kept an emotional distance from him, and by the time they left he was frustrated. He understood why she might be upset, but Adrianna had put them both on the spot. What was he supposed to say? They hadn't talked about it beyond their exclusivity agreement for the time being so he'd done the best he could without any warning. He hated that he'd upset her, but what choice had he had?

20

Dani went straight to her room when they got home. Sergei was taking care of Marj and she needed a few minutes to recover from their evening. On the surface it had been fun, but Adrianna's question had made it abundantly clear she was getting involved. Hearing him refer to what they had as *casual* had hurt, even though it was accurate. Sara had been right about her getting attached and she'd been foolish to think anything with Sergei could be casual at this point.

Frustrated, she yanked off the pink dress and kicked it across the room. The dress and the shoes were going in the back of her closet until she left. Maybe she'd take them to Vegas and leave them with Tiff. She certainly wouldn't need them in Colorado. She was done with dating. Once she left Sergei, she would go back to being a tomboy who was too athletic for regular guys.

She sprawled across her bed in frustration, realizing how used to Sergei's bigger bed she'd gotten and how much harder it was going to be to walk away from him than she'd initially thought.

The knock on her door made her sigh but she called for him to come in.

"Hey." He walked in slowly, sitting on the edge of her bed. "I, uh, I guess you're mad at me."

"Nope." She stared up at the ceiling. "I'm mad at myself."

"Yourself? Why?"

"For letting myself care about you. For letting myself be a *girl*. Maybe that's why I was always bad at it, because I knew it would suck. Maybe being all tomboy-tough was how I protected myself."

"Oh, Dani. Honey, you were always a girl."

"No. No, I wasn't. I was that weird, arm-wrestling tomboy who played better hockey than all the guys and couldn't get laid 'cause guys were scared of her."

"There were a dozen guys at that restaurant tonight who would've been happy to sleep with you."

"Because I was being a *girl*." She glanced at him in exasperation. "If I just go back to being awkward, tomboy Dani, they won't want me anymore."

"Dani?"

"What?" She made a face at him.

"I'll still want you."

She pointed her finger at him. "Stop it! That right there is what got me into this mess. Why would a gorgeous hunk like you want something beyond a casual lay with me? I knew better but I needed to experience it... Ugh." She threw her arm over her eyes.

The mattress tilted a little as he leaned over, slowly pulling her arm away and forcing her to look at him. "You can do so much better than me, but one thing you need to get straight is there's nothing casual about what's going on between us. I don't look at other women, I don't think about other women—hell, I can't even remember the last time I thought about my wife, Dani. You've become part of my life. And Niko's."

She stared at him, something inside her tightening almost painfully. "But?"

"All we have is now. You're leaving and I have to stay. You've got this exciting new career and the Olympics... Niko and I would just hold you back." His eyes sought hers as he leaned closer. "Don't you see? I have so much baggage..."

"I guess I don't."

"I know." He scooted up to stretch out beside her and they lay on their backs, side by side, without talking.

"Tanya kept pulling me back to the life I'd tried so hard to leave," he said after a slight hesitation. "I wanted to be American. I came to the U.S. and went to college in Boston, both because of hockey, but also so that I had options in case of an injury—where I could get a real job and stay in the States."

"What's your degree in?" she asked curiously.

"International finance."

"Definitely something you could get work in."

"I married an American woman, my college sweetheart, but damn, when my best friend in college was killed, everything fell apart. I couldn't focus, I couldn't get past it, and for a short time it felt like going back to Russia would be the best way to stop obsessing about it. Instead, my wife divorced me and I fell in love with my brother's girlfriend. The thing is, she had so much drama it was impossible to think about myself, my career, anything but her. I loved her, but she sucked me into a life I'd worked so hard to avoid because of my father."

"And now?"

"Now I waffle between excitement that I'm back in the States—for good, I hope—and guilt that she had to die for it to happen."

Dani was quiet for a bit before she spoke. "Obviously I didn't know her and wasn't there to see the way she died, but it sounds like she loved you and Niko enough to sacrifice herself for you two to have exactly this—the life you always wanted, a childhood without fear for her child, and the freedom for you to never look back at the mob and all those horrible people. Her sacrifice was for you, and even if you take what you and I have out of the equation, wouldn't she have loved you enough to want you to be happy again? I know that's not with me, but—"

"Wait." He frowned at her. "Don't say it like that. There's nothing wrong with you or what we have. It's just that we're at different places in life, sweetheart. I'm a lot older than you, and my kid has to be my priority. You have your whole life in front of you and shouldn't be tied down to a family that's not even yours. It would be different if I was able to love again, to truly give myself to someone and start over with marriage, more children... I just don't think I can. I'm broken, Dani."

"I wish you wouldn't say things like that." She turned onto her side, resting on one elbow so she could look into his handsome face. "There's nothing broken about you. You're sweet, tender, gentle. Both with me and with Niko. What else is there?"

"I don't know." His face was a mask of pain and uncertainty.

"You could say I'm broken, too, you know? I never felt like a woman until you. You did that. You made me feel sexy. I know I'm pretty and there's nothing wrong with my body, that it's just not for everyone. But when I'm with other guys, something happens and I scare them away. Maybe it's because they're immature, but maybe it's because they weren't *you*. And maybe I don't see you as broken because when you're with me, you're not."

"Jesus, Dani." He lifted his head to kiss her, his lips claiming hers so sweetly it was like she'd never been kissed before. He rested one big hand on her hip, his touch gentle but also possessive; he claimed her every time he touched her.

When he finally pulled away his eyes were hooded with desire but there was something else there too: *Need.*

"Let's go to my room," he whispered, his eyes never leaving hers. "This bed is too small for us."

"Sergei..."

He brushed a lock of hair off her forehead. "We have six weeks. How do you want to spend them? Together like we've been the last few weeks, or as just friends?"

She nearly laughed. Like going back to being just friends was even an option at this point. The smart thing to do would be to go back to Vegas until she had to leave for Colorado, but that wasn't happening. She needed him as much as he obviously needed her. "You think we're capable of going back to being nothing but friends?" she whispered against his mouth.

"If you ask it of me, absolutely."

"I can't, Sergei. I'm—" She broke off, unwilling to use words like "invested" or "attached." She was, but it didn't need to be said. He knew.

"I know, baby. I don't know what's going to happen or what we're going to do come September, but you're right—when I'm with you I don't feel broken anymore."

"Let's go to bed." She slid off the bed and held out her hand.

THEY TOOK Niko skating the next day. They were going every few days because he enjoyed it so much, and though Sergei and Dani had begun to get tired of the monotony of skating in a circle surrounded by little kids, Niko was improving in leaps and bounds. Luckily, no one seemed to recognize Sergei or realize he played on the local NHL team, so they were often some of the only adults out there. There was a morning session that ran from ten until noon, so it was perfect. They would skate for two hours, have lunch and then Niko would nap for a few hours. It gave them time to get their own things done, but this afternoon they had Marj coming over. Sergei was planning to take Dani to a movie and then an early dinner. He'd never taken her out on a date with just the two of them, and it was time. No matter what happened in September, he wanted her to enjoy their time together. Hell, if he was being honest, he wanted to enjoy it.

The things she'd said last night had resonated deeply. He'd been through a lot in his life, one crisis after another tempered by his success as an athlete. Losing Tatiana had felt like the end, like all he could hope for was to make enough to take care of himself so he could be a good father. He didn't need nor deserve any other happiness, especially not in the form of a sweet, sexy blonde whose spunk and bright green eyes had consumed him from the moment they'd met. How the hell had he gotten this lucky? She was remarkable in every way and her innocence had had him under a spell since the first time he'd touched her. With so much beauty both inside and out, he could touch her all day and never stop. Maybe she was right; maybe they were so good together because they were right for each other. He didn't know how to keep her, how to make her want to stay with him, but he was starting to want to try.

A high-pitched cry made him turn in confusion. Dani was skating full-speed toward the other side of the ice, where Niko was sprawled on his back screaming.

"Niko!" Sergei took off after Dani, watching as she dropped to her knees beside the little boy.

"What happened?" he panted, dropping beside her and freezing. There was blood coming from somewhere, seeping onto the ice in a dark red puddle.

Dani had her hands on his upper arm, applying pressure as she yelled for someone to call 9-1-1.

"Blade of a skate cut through his wrist," she said over her shoulder. "We need to get him medical attention immediately."

"I can drive him—"

"No!" She barked out the word. "If I move my hands and the pressure, he could bleed out. I need a pen. Does anyone have a pen?"

A crowd had gathered and people began calling out until someone pulled a pen from their jacket, tossing it on the ground by Dani.

"Pull the hair tie out of my hair," she said to Sergei.

He pulled the black elastic band that had been holding her ponytail and held it out.

"Slide it up his arm," she instructed.

Sergei's hands were shaking as he did it.

"Now grab the pen and hang on to it until I tell you." Dani kept pressure on Niko's arm as she moved the hair tie above his elbow and snatched the pen from Sergei. Sliding it between the tie and his arm, she started to twist it, creating a tourniquet of sorts.

"Paramedics are here," someone yelled.

"They need to hurry," Dani panted. "I don't know how long this will hold."

There was movement as the crowd parted to get out of the way and paramedics dropped to the ice and took over for Dani. She sat back, her face pale and hands shaking, though she turned to the paramedic closest to her.

"Blade of a skate cut deep; I think it might've hit an artery."

"Good job with the tourniquet. You probably saved his life." The paramedics were working swiftly and Sergei slid his arm around her shoulder.

"Mommy…" Niko's voice wafted over the hushed whispers around them.

"I'm here, buddy." Sergei reached over to pat his head.

"I want Mommy…" His voice cracked a little.

"Son…" Sergei's voice cracked, too.

"Mama D!" Niko twisted away from the paramedic but Dani was instantly there, one hand on his cheek as she slid to her stomach so she could be eye level with him.

"I'm here, sweetie. Right here."

"I'm scared."

"Daddy and I are right here," she spoke in a soft, soothing voice. "You need to lie still so the paramedics can help you, okay? Otherwise you're going to have a really bad boo-boo."

"It hurts."

"I know, but you're going to be okay. They're going to give you medicine so it doesn't hurt so much."

"We need to move him," someone called out.

"Can I go with him in the ambulance?" Sergei asked one of the medics.

"Mommy," Niko cried. "I want Mommy to come in the 'bulance!"

"Sergei…" Dani turned wide, anxious eyes to him.

"Go," he said brusquely. "I'll meet you there."

"You sure?"

"Go." He pressed a light kiss on the top of his son's head and headed off ice to take off his skates.

"I need sixty seconds to take off my skates," Dani called to the paramedics, skating behind Sergei and sinking onto the ground as soon as they were off the ice. As she unlaced one skate, Sergei did the other, not saying a word. She grabbed her sneakers off the bench where she'd left them, paused to squeeze his arm and then ran to catch up to the stretcher in her socks. Sergei watched her go and let out a long, deep sigh. What the hell had just happened?

21

It was hours before they got home. Niko had been given pain medicine and something to help him relax while the doctor stitched his wrist and he cried pitifully. Sergei had been a little hurt that Niko only wanted Dani, but he hadn't allowed either of them to see it because she'd been uncomfortable about it, constantly looking to him for the assurance it was okay to be the one holding Niko through all of it. Even on the drive home, Niko had cried until she'd agreed to sit in the back with his car seat and hold his hand. But this was about Niko's comfort, not his insecurities, so Sergei had shut his mouth and done what was best for his son.

Now Niko was sleeping and Dani was showering off the blood she'd been covered in. He wandered up to his room, since she was in his shower, and merely leaned against the wall watching. Her eyes were closed as the water sluiced over her, but when she spotted him she held out her hand. He hesitated for barely a second before yanking off his clothes and joining her under the hot spray. She moved so he could wet his hair and then she reached for his shampoo, putting it in her hand and gently massaging it into his hair and scalp.

His eyes closed of their own volition and it wasn't until this moment he understood how much the ordeal had shaken him.

"It's extremely fortuitous your wife has medical training," the doctor had said. "The blade nicked an artery and several veins—the bleeding could have been much more significant. She probably saved his life."

Sergei hadn't corrected him that she wasn't his wife, nor had he dared to look at Dani. He'd simply shaken the doctor's hand before picking up his son and holding him tightly.

She probably saved his life.

This amazing, sweet, sexy woman not only had brought Sergei's blackened soul back to life, she'd saved his son. His priority in life was Niko and without Dani he might have lost him. The very idea made him a little queasy and he had to lean against the wall to catch his breath.

"It's okay." Dani's voice was as warm as her hands as she washed him. "He's going to be okay."

"If you hadn't been there…"

"It was an accident. Little kids get hurt all the time. I'm sure you would've thought about a tourniquet to stop the bleeding."

He met her eyes. "I was frozen. I responded when you told me what to do, but I was staring at the blood and trying to remember my name."

"If I hadn't been there, you would have jumped into action. You're his father. It would've been instinct."

"You're not his mother but it was still instinct."

"This is what I studied, what I want to do with my life. It's a lot more natural for me." She slid her hands down his stomach, along the crease of his thigh and then to where she lightly cupped his balls. His cock instantly sprang to life, hardening at her featherlight caresses.

"Thank you," he said in a rough voice, one hand resting lightly on her waist. "There are no words for what you did."

She kissed her way down his chest, dropping to her knees. "Let's see what you have to say about what I'm about to do."

"Mommy!" The high-pitched wail startled both Sergei and Dani out of a deep sleep.

She swung her legs over the side of the bed without thinking. "He's probably in pain."

"You get his meds." Sergei was up too. "I'll get him."

"Maybe we should bring him in here for the rest of the night," Dani said, pulling on shorts and a T-shirt. "It's after four, so he probably won't sleep past seven anyway."

"That's a good idea."

She padded down to the kitchen to grab the prescription they'd had filled and some watered-down juice. Taking care of Niko was second nature now and the intimacy between her and Sergei tonight had been noticeably more intense. His need for her had been over-the-top, greedy in the way he'd taken her over and over. Something had shifted, but she couldn't help but wonder if it was because of the trauma of seeing Niko get hurt and then receiving stitches. Sergei had done his best to stay strong, but she'd seen him turn his head while the doctor had been sewing up the little boy's wrist. It had bothered her a little too, but only because she adored Niko and it was almost like watching her own child in distress. She had a strong stomach and didn't have a problem with blood and the like, but Niko was different.

Going back upstairs, she found Sergei and Niko cuddled on the bed, Sergei whispering softly to him in Russian.

"Hey, buddy. How about you take your medicine so you feel better?" Dani slid onto the bed next to them.

"Yuck." He wrinkled his nose at the little cup of pink liquid.

"I know, but because you're not feeling well, you can have juice to wash it down." She held up the sippy cup.

Niko sighed, but nodded wearily, drinking down the medicine and then practically snatching the cup from Dani's hand. After he'd drained it, he nestled into Dani's side and she pulled him close while Sergei reached over to turn out the lights. He'd moved around the bed and was now behind her, one arm draped across her waist, his hand resting on Niko's side.

THE THREE OF them dozed off and when Dani opened her eyes again, Sergei was on his back, texting someone on his phone. Their eyes met and he leaned over to kiss her.

"Good morning," he whispered.

"Good morning."

Niko was still asleep so they quietly got out of bed and went to separate bathrooms to freshen up. A few minutes later they met up in the kitchen and began their usual morning routine. If she was going for a run, she made herself a protein shake and he made breakfast for himself and Niko. If she wasn't running, like today, she made breakfast for all of them while he made coffee.

"Who were you talking to so early in the morning?" she asked as she began mixing up pancake batter; it was Niko's favorite and she wanted to surprise him.

"Toli. Wanted to catch him up on what happened yesterday."

"Ah." She heated up the griddle.

"He says, 'Thank you.'"

She shook her head, though she was smiling. "You guys are acting like I did something out of the ordinary. Anyone with even a little medical training would have jumped in to help."

"But they didn't. You did. And the doctor said things could have gone really, really wrong if you hadn't."

"He's okay and I'm happy I was able to help him. I adore that little guy."

"I know. He adores you, too."

"I'm hungry." Niko wandered into the room looking sleepy and Sergei immediately scooped him up, kissing the side of his face.

"Good morning, big guy. Mama D's making pancakes for you."

"Yay!" Niko's eyes lit up and he grinned.

THE NEXT FEW days were low-key since Niko didn't have his usual energy.

Though their nights were filled with more passion than ever, they weren't able to spend much quality time together during the day because Niko was so needy. Dani had gone to the gym by herself twice, since they didn't want to bring Niko to the on-site daycare center just yet, and Sergei had met up with Aaron again tonight for a few beers. It had been nice to get out and talk to another guy, but knowing she was waiting in bed for him made it much better because he couldn't wait to get home to her. In just under a month, their sex life had gone from cautious but passionate to constant and sensual as hell. She wanted to do everything, all the time, and he couldn't get enough, either. Their chemistry was off the charts and every time he thought he might start getting bored, either she suggested something she'd heard about or asked him to try something new.

The thing was, there was no way to get bored with her. It went way beyond sex and he wasn't naïve enough to think this was about getting his dick sucked every night. She made him happy in ways he hadn't allowed himself to think about since even before Tatiana had died. With Tatiana, he'd loved her enough to put up with her crazy life and the constant worry that someone might come after them, but it had been exhausting. With Dani, everything was easy. Too easy sometimes. Which was why the strangely intense feelings he was beginning to have for her were unsettling. They were involved in every way and he would be lying if he said he wasn't happy. He was relaxed, in great shape, and so well-fucked he felt nineteen again in that department. His son was happy and thriving, they had a great home, and if hockey season started tomorrow, he'd be ready to go. Well, that would be the case if Dani wasn't leaving and about to throw his entire world off-kilter. Because it would.

Dani wasn't downstairs when he got home, so he checked on Niko before heading to his room. He was surprised to see his own bed empty when he got there and he sighed, unsure what to do next. Maybe it would be best if he left it alone, left her alone. Maybe putting a little emotional distance between them was the right thing to do.

He pulled off his shirt and tossed it in the hamper, followed by his jeans and socks. He brushed his teeth and padded towards the bed, wondering if he would sleep without Dani by his side. He'd gotten used to it. Gotten used to her. *Dammit.*

Something on the bed caught his eye and he reached for it in confusion. It was a book covered with plain brown paper, as though he wasn't supposed to see the book's actual cover. He opened it slowly and the inside cover had a note.

Sergei—

We have thirty-seven days to try sixty-four positions. Do you think we can make it before I leave for Colorado?

Dani

P.S. I covered the book so Niko wouldn't be tempted to open it if he ever found it.

He flipped a few more pages and laughed. She'd bought them a copy of some modernized version of the Kama Sutra. And left it on his bed for him. A trickle of guilt wound its way through his subconscious because this was her way of saying she wanted him to go to her, that she was losing faith in him. In them. That she wasn't secure enough in what they had to wait for him in his bed. *Fuck.*

He put the book down and padded down the hall in his boxers. Her door was still closed but she had to be awake, knowing he'd found the gift she'd left him. He hesitated outside for a second, trying to decide what to say, how to talk about what was going on between them.

"Come in," she called when he finally got up the nerve to knock.

"Can we talk on my bed?" he asked with a faint smile.

"We won't do much talking once we go to your bed."

"Says the woman who left a book of sexual positions for me."

"Not interested?" Her lips twitched.

"I'm interested, you little minx." He held out his hands and she took them.

"What do we have to talk about?" she asked as he tugged her back to his room.

"Vegas."

"Huh?"

He pulled her T-shirt off, anxious to have his mouth all over her as soon as possible. "There is no way in hell I'm going seven days without making love to you while we're in Vegas, but there's an even smaller chance I'll be able to do it in either of our brothers' guest rooms."

She frowned. "I didn't think about it."

"And now you've given me this damn challenge."

"Not up to the task, Wayne?"

"Maryanne, you have no idea how up to the task I am, but we're going to lose seven days in Vegas if we don't come up with a solution."

She licked her lips as he backed her towards the bed.

"There are three choices," he said slowly before wrapping his mouth around one pert, pink nipple and biting down until she moaned. He'd discovered she liked him to be a little rough with her and it was so damn good to hear the sounds she made.

"Wh-what are they?" she gasped, as he drew her breasts together and licked the line between them.

"We can go seven days without making love." He moved back to her nipple.

"Th-th-that sounds like a...t-terrible idea." Her breath was getting choppy.

"I agree." He pushed her onto her back and pinched both nipples with his fingers. "The other option is to sneak around. We meet in a bathroom, get a

hotel room for a few hours, shit like that." He yanked at her panties, acciden-
tally ripping the strings at the sides. "Sorry—I'll buy you new ones."

"Sergei!" She let out a squeak as he nipped the inside of her thigh. "I don't
want to...sneak around."

He figured he'd better tell her about option number three before he licked
her into oblivion, because he already knew which position they were going to
start with. "Then we have to be open about the fact we're sleeping together,
and you stay with me in Toli's guest room." He wasn't sure how she would
feel about that, so he pried her open and licked long and slow along her slit.

"Ohhh..." Her voice dropped and she arched into his face.

He kept his touch light, but she was sensitive and already fluttering with
need. "Door number one, two, or three, baby."

"Three..." she moaned. "Oh, Sergei, please, more..."

"So you're going to tell your brother we're sleeping together."

"No..." She was panting harder now, tugging at his hair. "You are."

He chuckled against her quivering pussy, sucking her clit between his lips.
"That's what you want?"

"I want you to stop talking!" she cried.

He pulled away and flopped onto his back. "Then climb over here and
drop that sweet pussy of yours over my face while you suck my cock."

She scrambled to comply but paused just before she sucked him deep. "Just
to clarify—you're going to have a talk with my brother about the fact that I
suck your cock?"

"Oh hell no," he groaned as she practically swallowed him. "I'm...*fuck*...
going to...*Jesus, baby*...tell him...we're...*oh god*...dating."

22

S tepping off the plane in Las Vegas, Dani was so excited she could barely contain it. She gathered her carry-on and Niko's backpack as Sergei carried his laptop bag and Niko. The stroller was waiting right as they got off the plane and he strapped Niko in as they headed through the jetway and into the building.

"This is the best present ever," she whispered, squeezing Sergei's arm. "I hadn't realized how much I've missed everyone."

"I know." He leaned over to lightly kiss her lips. "You sure you're ready for all the crazy between the two families?"

She rolled her eyes. "I'm an adult. You're an adult. We're having fun until I leave for Colorado. Zakk, especially, needs to chill."

"Dani." Sergei stopped walking and slid his fingers through hers. "I didn't tell him."

"You didn't…" Her voice trailed off and she frowned. "But you promised."

"I know. I'm sorry. I just—there was no way to say it. If I had a sister and Zakk called to tell me he was sleeping with her—"

"You were going to tell him we were dating, not screwing."

"We're guys. All he's going to hear is that we're screwing."

"So no sex or touching or *anything* for a whole week?" Her eyes rounded with dismay.

He laughed. "Relax, Maryanne. Wayne isn't down with that plan, either. We're just going to let them see. We're going to hold hands as we come out of the terminal and everyone will know and there won't be any weird one-on-one conversations."

She snorted. "Until my brother corners you somewhere and demands to know what your intentions are."

"I can handle that but calling him out of the blue just didn't sit right with me. I needed to talk to him about it in person, but there isn't time now, so are you okay with the new plan?"

"It's all good for me." She grinned. "I'm so happy and excited to see everyone, I'm not letting anything bother me."

He patted her behind and gave it a little squeeze. "Get ready. You know this is going to go south quickly."

"Oh, it'll be fine. We're consenting adults having fun." She leaned over to peer into the stroller. "And you're going to show everyone your boo-boo, aren't you, Niko?"

"Boo-boo!" He held up his bandaged arm proudly.

TOLI WAS the only one waiting when they got past the security area. There was no mistaking the way his eyes immediately narrowed in on where their hands were linked, but he didn't say anything and instead threw his arms around his brother. He hugged Dani next and then reached down to scoop Niko out of the stroller, rubbing his head against the boy's tummy until they were both squealing with laughter.

They walked towards baggage claim and Sergei got their suitcases while Toli and Dani watched Niko.

"We figured there was no reason for Zakk and me to both come," Toli was saying. "You said you'd have a ton of luggage and the stroller and car seat, so I brought my SUV since that's where his seat will be while you're here."

"Is my brother going to have a heart attack?" Dani's eyes met Toli's warily.

He chuckled. "Not a heart attack, per se, but perhaps a mild coronary episode that will end with shots of tequila out by the pool."

"Ugh."

"It'll be fine," Toli said softly. "He knows Sergei's a good guy and would never do anything to hurt you."

"He *is* a good guy," she murmured.

"Mommy, I'm hungry," Niko tugged at her hand impatiently.

She caught the look of surprise on Toli's face but it was exhausting trying to explain everything to everyone. She adored Niko and if he wanted to call her *Mommy*, what could she do? Even Sergei had stopped trying to redirect him. Once she left, he would undoubtedly forget about her. He was three, for heaven's sake. At least that's what she told herself every time she thought about not being with them anymore. She had wonderful, exciting plans in her future, but in her heart, all of her plans included Sergei and Niko, which made no sense whatsoever.

"As soon as we get the suitcases," Toli was saying to him. "Aunt Tessa has dinner waiting for us."

"Sketti?" he asked hopefully.

"As a matter of fact—" Toli laughed, "—spaghetti is on the menu. And meatballs and garlic bread and Caesar salad."

Dani groaned. "I'm starting to cut back on carbs."

"After your birthday tomorrow," Toli said firmly. "There will be way too many carbs between now and tomorrow night."

She smiled. "You're right. Carb-palooza until day after tomorrow."

"Carb-palooza?" Sergei frowned as he joined them.

"Approximately twenty-four hours of carbs, carbs, and more carbs. Then we get serious."

He nodded. "Sounds good to me."

"We need to talk about sleeping arrangements," Sergei said as they walked towards Toli's SUV.

"That's between you and Dani," he said amiably. "But you're welcome to share the guest room. Niko will be on the daybed in Alex's room since we've got both a crib and a daybed in there now. What Zakk's going to say, well, that's a different story."

"It'll be fine," Dani said quietly. "I'll talk to him when we get home."

"Everyone's at our house," Toli said, opening the trunk and loading the luggage while Sergei installed the car seat in the second row. "So you'll find out soon enough."

They drove home chatting amiably, but Dani was more nervous than she let on. No, Zakk wouldn't be a big jerk about it, but he'd definitely have something to say to Sergei, which was why she'd wanted him to let Zakk know ahead of time. She didn't want her birthday trip to be tarnished by this, especially when Sergei made her so happy. Tiff would calm Zakk down, and he wouldn't make a scene in front of everyone, but behind the scenes he could be way overprotective.

"Don't worry," Sergei whispered in her ear as they pulled into Toli's garage. "I'll talk to him. I'll make sure he's good with it."

She nodded absently because Sara had already come out and had wrapped her in a big hug as soon as Dani got out of the SUV. "I missed you so much!" she gushed.

"Me, too!" Dani hugged her tightly, the excitement of being back with her friends and family rushing back.

"You girls take Niko inside," Toli called out. "Sergei and I will bring in the suitcases."

Dani picked up Niko and Sara grabbed Dani's purse as they walked inside.

Zakk was the first one to greet Dani as she walked in, lifting her in a big bear hug, Niko squished between them.

"Hey, kiddo." He kissed the top of her head. "You look great. Alaska's been good for you."

"Thanks." She grinned up at him. "You're looking very tan."

"Just spent a week in Hawaii," he said, "so yeah."

"Let's eat," Tessa was calling.

A buffet of sorts had been set out on the island so everyone filled plates and headed out to the covered portion of the patio to eat. It was a veritable feast, with three types of pasta, red sauce with meatballs and alfredo sauce with vegetables, garlic bread with cheese and without, and three types of salads with every available dressing.

Dani got a plate for Niko and settled him outside next to Sergei before going back inside to fill her own plate.

"So what did Zakk say?" Sara whispered once the men were all outside.

"About what?" Tiff asked, her hazel eyes twinkling.

Dani dragged her lower lip between her teeth before blurting out, "Sergei and I are dating."

Tessa let out a little whoop of glee while Tiff made a fist and pumped it in the air, saying, "I knew it!"

"Holy shit," Vlad's wife, Rachel, said. "He's so hot."

"And hung." Sara giggled.

"Well he's a Petrov," Tessa reasoned. "If he's anything at all like Toli, it's probably huge."

"Is he the biggest you've been with?" Tiff was teasing her.

Dani blushed. "I, uh…" She hung her head. "Sergei's the…only."

"He was your first?" Tessa's eyes widened.

"Can you imagine having Sergei as your first?" Sara sighed dreamily. "Mine was Norman Richter, when I was fifteen, and he was covered in zits. His dick was so small he had to do it like ten times before he broke through. It was miserable."

"I was sixteen," Tessa said. "It wasn't terrible, but it was my high school sweetheart and it was pretty awkward. Neither of us had any idea what we were doing."

"I was seventeen," Tiff said. "My first time was…interesting. A much older man my mom set me up with so—"

"Your mom set up your first time?" Dani gaped at her.

Tiff chuckled. "My mom wasn't like other moms, but yeah, so my first time was with someone really experienced and it was honestly pretty good. It hurt but he made up for it with other stuff."

"It hurt," Dani said, still blushing furiously, "but it was still good. Really good."

"And now you're dating." Tessa clapped her hands. "A new sister-in-law. Yay!"

"It's not serious." Dani back-pedaled as lightly as she could. "I mean, I'm leaving for Colorado in four weeks and then I have a job here."

The room fell silent and Tiff cocked her head. "You gave up your virginity to him and you're just going to leave?"

"That was always the plan," Dani protested. "I mean, I like him, but he has to be in Alaska and I have all kinds of things going on. We're close friends and I really like him, but it's still pretty new. We're figuring stuff out as we go."

"Sergei's a great guy," Tessa said, "but losing Tatiana broke him. Be careful with your heart, honey. I don't know that he'll chase you if you go follow your dreams."

"I know," Dani sighed. "But it's okay. I couldn't have asked for a better guy to be my first everything. He's handsome, gentle, funny and oh my god, the sex."

"We're going to need a girls' night out to talk about all that, but we better get out there or the guys are going to know we're talking about them." Rachel laughed.

"And Zakk suspects but doesn't know," Tiff mused. "Are you planning to tell him?"

"We're staying here together," Dani said. "So he's going to figure it out pretty quickly."

Tiff grimaced. "You should talk to him, Dani. He loves you and wants you to be happy, but when he finds out it's not serious and you two are just having fun until you leave, he's going to go into big-brother overdrive."

"I'll talk to him." Dani stared out at the patio where the guys were all laughing and having a good time. "Can we keep it under wraps until after we eat, guys? Please? Let me enjoy dinner and then I'll pull Zakk aside."

"Absolutely." Tessa picked up her plate. "Let's go."

23

When almost everyone had finished eating, most of the women got up to help Tessa clean up the kitchen but told Dani to relax. Vlad and Toli disappeared and before he realized what had happened, Sergei and Dani were alone with Zakk, except for a few of the kids, who were in the pool.

Zakk narrowed his gaze on Sergei and then cut over to Dani. He let out a huff and shook his head. "This feels like a set-up," he muttered.

"Sergei and I are dating," Dani said quickly.

"And I'm the last to know?" Zakk scowled. "I thought we were closer than that, Dani."

"We are. But you're overprotective sometimes and, honestly, I'm not a child. Sergei is your best friend's brother and I didn't want everything to go to hell."

"I wanted to tell you in person," Sergei added. "I told Dani I'd call you but it felt too high school-ish, so I thought I'd wait until I could tell you face-to-face."

"So you're in love with my sister?"

A muscle in Sergei's jaw twitched as he struggled to come up with a response.

"We're not in love, Zakk. We're dating. It's barely been a month." Dani wouldn't look at him and Sergei felt like a jerk.

Zakk turned assessing green eyes, exactly like his sister's, to Sergei. "My sister is your summer hook-up then?"

"No!" Sergei grunted in frustration.

"What? No!" Dani spoke at the same time, folding her arms across her chest. "Stop it, Zakk. We don't know what we're going to do; we're just taking it one day at a time. It's *new*."

"I'm crazy about Dani," Sergei interjected quietly, though his heart was racing and his stomach was threatening to revolt. "But she's got big plans that are going to take her far away from Alaska, so we're not rushing into anything. Down the road, when she's done the things she wants to do, we'll reassess."

Where the hell had that come from? Jesus, he was losing his mind over this girl and her brother's unrelenting stare had reduced him to a nervous teenager. *What. The. Fuck.*

"I know you're a grown woman," Zakk said, looking at Dani. "But you'll always be my little sister and there will never be any guy, any relationship, any situation where I'm not concerned about your well-being."

"And I love you for that, but you have to trust that Sergei and I know what we're doing. Please don't embarrass me, Zakk. All of our friends and family are in there probably tripping over themselves to see what's happening and that's not fair—no one did that to you when you got your late coach's widow pregnant before you were even in a relationship."

Zakk scowled but grudgingly nodded. "You're right, and you have my word I won't embarrass you." He turned to Sergei. "But I need your word that you're going to take care of my sister, in whatever way works for the two of you."

"Of course." Sergei held out his hand and Zakk shook it.

"So, you don't need my word on anything?" Dani asked dryly, eyeing them. "I mean, I'm in this relationship, not the two of you."

Sergei chuckled as he leaned over to kiss her. "Sorry. You have my word I won't piss your brother off."

She smiled but her good mood had been spoiled; she suddenly wanted to just go back to their easy life in Anchorage.

DANI CAME awake to warm lips nuzzling her neck and Sergei's erection pressed against her back. She smiled in her sleep, wiggling closer to him and basking in his warmth. To her surprise, he pulled away after lightly squeezing her breast.

"Rise and shine, birthday girl."

She opened one eye. "It's my birthday and I have to get up at..." She frowned at the clock on the nightstand. "Eight twenty in the morning?"

"Birthday shenanigans begin now." He slid off the bed. "Put on workout clothes."

"Not only do I have to get up early, I have to work out?" she gave him a dirty look. "You're not very good at this birthday stuff."

He laughed. "Actually, this isn't my doing—this is Toli and Zakk's gift."

She frowned, but he'd already pulled on shorts and slipped out of the room. She couldn't imagine what surprise they had for her that included exercise but knowing her brother, it was epic. He'd given her an SUV for her twenty-first birthday and last year had flown her and Sara to a resort in

Hawaii for a week. Excitement built up as she brushed her teeth and pulled on bike shorts, a sports bra, and a T-shirt. Zakk had to have something big up his sleeve if he'd enlisted Toli's help, so she grabbed her purse and hurried downstairs.

Toli and Tessa were making waffles, Raina, Alex and Niko were eating, and Sergei had just poured a cup of coffee for her. He put a little cream in it and handed it to her, since he knew exactly how she liked it.

"Happy birthday!" Tessa sang out.

"Happy birthday!" Toli echoed.

"Happy birthday, Auntie Dani." Raina grinned at her with a mouth full of waffle.

"Haffybirdy," Alex chortled, waving.

"Happy birthday, Mommy." Niko gave her such a sweet smile her eyes grew a little misty.

"Thank you, everyone," she replied, walking over to kiss all three of the kids on the tops of their heads.

"Sit down and eat," Tessa said with a grin. "They have quite a morning in store for you."

"Do I get to know what it is?"

"Not till we get there." Sergei gently pushed her into a chair. "It's your birthday, and one of my gifts to you is to spoil you."

She smiled up at him. "Okay. Can I help Niko cut his waffles?"

"Nope." Tessa winked at her. "I'll do it."

"Fine." Dani sat back and sipped her coffee, chuckling as Sergei got a plate of waffles for her and Toli topped off her coffee. "I could get used to this," she said.

"Eat up," Toli encouraged. "We have to get going soon."

WITHIN TWENTY MINUTES they were on their way to whatever the surprise was. Dani knew right away they were headed to the Sidewinders' arena but she wasn't sure what that could mean. Even if Zakk had booked ice time for them, she didn't have equipment or anything, so it had to be something else.

Toli nodded at Sergei as they parked. "Take her inside. You know where to go."

"Yup." Sergei took Dani by the hand and they went in through the players' entrance as the security guard waved them by.

"Happy birthday, Ms. Cloutier."

"Thanks, Ralph." She waved back and followed Sergei. "Sergei, tell me what's up."

"No." He squeezed her hand. "You're going to love it, so just go with it."

He led her back towards the locker rooms and she frowned. It was eerily quiet, and even though it was summer, she'd expected her brother to be here. She paused in the hallway, looking at Sergei. "I'm not being pranked, am I?"

He shook his head. "No chance in hell, honey. I'm all about a good prank as long as it isn't something hurtful, but not on your birthday. Promise."

"Okay." She let him pull her forward and he stopped in front of the team's locker room.

"Happy birthday, sweetheart." He stepped aside and she walked into the room. She'd only taken two steps before she faltered and then stopped completely. Her vision blurred with tears and she couldn't manage a single word as she stared at the scene before her.

At least half of the Sidewinders were in the room, standing in front of their usual lockers, even though the team cleaned everything out at the end of every season and they wouldn't officially come back to work for more than a month. Sara was there, too, also wearing a jersey, using the locker next to Zakk's.

Lonnie Finch came out from the back holding a jersey with the back facing out. It had "D. CLOUTIER" printed across the top. "Happy birthday and welcome to the Sidewinders, Dani." He handed her the jersey. "And to officially welcome you to the team, your brother and Toli asked if they could borrow my arena, my team and my staff." He made a face, as if annoyed, but she knew better. If he'd been annoyed, this wouldn't be happening, so she merely waited for him to continue. "Today you'll play as a Sidewinder in a private charity exhibition game for a group of underprivileged children. I'll need you to sign this one-day contract to play for the team."

Dani's mouth fell open.

"I already signed mine," Sara said lightly, grinning at her. "Hurry up so we can play!"

"I, um, okay." Dani took the pen someone handed her and blindly signed the contract.

"It's time to rock and roll." Head Coach Brad Barnett came into the room and looked around. "You all look pathetic and tired. Except Dani. Happy birthday, sweetheart—why are you crying? Okay, are we gonna play some hockey or what?"

Dani still hadn't moved, except to sign the contract, and was staring at everyone.

"Since it's not appropriate for me to wear another team's jersey," Sergei came up behind her, "I'm going to coach the second team, and Coach Barnett and I are going to choose teams the old-fashioned way."

"I, um, okay." Dani nodded and looked at Coach Barnett. "I know it might throw things off balance, but I want my brother on my team—we've never played a real game together."

"Works for me." He nodded back.

Dani walked over to her brother and threw her arms around him. "Thank you."

"You're welcome." He hugged her tightly before looking at Toli. "This was actually Toli's idea—I came up with the charity game part."

"Thank you all." Dani turned to her brother's friends and teammates, many of whom were her friends, too. "You don't know how much this means to me."

She got a bunch of high fives and hugs while Sergei and Brad flipped a coin to decide who would choose for their team first.

"Let's do this!" Brad said with a grin. "I won the toss so I pick first and I take Dani and Zakk."

Sergei grinned back. "I'll take Toli and Vlad."

"The Russian connection!" Brad laughed.

"Hey, don't start without me!" Eighteen-year-old Anton Petrov came barreling into the room, a huge smile on his face.

"You're late, son!" Toli said to him.

"You left without me!" Anton shot back, sinking onto the nearest bench.

"I choose Anton," Brad said, looking right at Toli, who stuck his tongue out at him.

"Fine," Sergei interjected. "I take Karl. We'll leave you the old man."

"Hey!" Rob Rousseau, the team's thirty-nine-year-old back-up goalie gave Sergei a sour look but they both laughed.

Sergei and Brad made a show of choosing the perfect members for their teams.

"That's it, gang," Brad said, rubbing his hands together. "My team will wear home jerseys and Sergei's team will wear away jerseys. The away team can head over to the visitors' locker room and we'll get ready to rumble. Remember, this is modified rules—no checking, no roughing of any kind, especially you boys that like to goof around."

He eyed Toli and Zakk, who raised their eyebrows as if asking, "Who? Us?"

24

C oach Barnett split them up on different lines and the excitement building inside of Dani was almost more than she could stand. No, this wasn't the real thing and it was all for fun and charity, but the Sidewinders were real. They were professional hockey players and for today Dani was one of them. And she was actually playing a real game on the same team as her brother. Brad had them on a line together and she listened intently as he drew up a few plays on a dry-erase board.

She was excited to be playing with Anton as well. He'd been drafted by the Sidewinders this past summer and would be playing for the Boston College team in the fall, which was also Sergei's alma mater. Coach Barnett had been Sergei's coach back then and they all had a special bond. Sergei had gone to college with two other Sidewinders, Dom Gianni and Cody Armstrong, and the friend in college who'd died had been Coach Barnett's son, Brian, so they were a lot closer than other players and coaches. Even Sergei, who didn't play for them. Anton was the next generation and they were all so excited that he intended to play here after graduation.

"Mom and Dad are here," Zakk whispered as they walked down the hall to the tunnel leading to the ice.

"They are?" Her eyes widened. "Aw, Zakk, this is amazing. Thank you so much. I love you." She hugged him again.

"Love you, too, kiddo." He gave her a nudge. "You're the birthday girl, so you lead the team out onto the ice."

"Isn't it always the goalie?" she asked, frowning.

"Not today." He winked. "Go on."

She skated out onto the ice and was shocked to see a fairly large crowd filling almost all the lower level seats. Her parents were against the glass holding a big sign that said, "Happy Birthday, Danielle!" and next to them were Tiff, the twins and Savannah. On the other side were Tessa, Rachel and a few of the other wives and children. Everyone was waving and cheering, while music blasted through the loud speakers.

She skated out to warm up, waving to her parents and friends. Glancing over at the other side of the ice where the "visiting" team was warming up, she couldn't help but smile. Toli and Vlad weren't really warming up but were standing by the bench talking to Sergei. Anton skated over to them and said something that made them all laugh, before skating back to his side of the ice.

"Sorry you're not with your dad," she called to him.

He waved her off. "It'll be more fun to play against him."

Sergei watched the game through the eyes of a stranger. Though he was right there, coaching from the bench, laughing and goofing off with his team, his eyes never really left Dani. Not only was she strong and beautiful on the ice, she was in her element. Though she hadn't played in about a month, she was leaner, stronger, and tougher than she'd been five or six weeks ago. Seeing her skate alongside Zakk was eerie because they played with such a similar style. They were both tall and fast, and when he passed a backhand shot to her that she promptly put in the net over the right shoulder of one of the best goalies in the NHL, Sergei's heart swelled with pride. Damn, she amazed him every time she was on the ice and for the first time he understood her reality as a female hockey player. She would never have what he had, or what she was experiencing right now. She could play professionally, but the women's league wasn't big, wasn't widespread and no one could afford to live on the salaries they paid.

It was a serious issue. Making an average of ten grand a year, with all the teams located in the northeast where the cost of living was astronomical, who could afford to play? With a master's degree under her belt, Dani deserved to make a good living and the Sidewinders were offering her that opportunity after the Olympics. Watching her with her friends and future coworkers, Sergei realized this was exactly where she needed to be. This was her future and it would be good for her. Not only would it pay well, it would keep her around the game she loved so much and close to her brother and friends to boot.

"She's amazing, eh?" Toli stood beside him as they watched Dani score yet again.

"She is."

"I can't wait to see her in the Olympics."

Sergei's chest tightened painfully but he nodded. "She's going to kick ass."

"Do you think she's happy? With her birthday present?"

Sergei forced a smile. "She's ecstatic. Look at her out there. She's played almost every shift and doesn't get tired."

Toli followed his gaze. "She makes you happy, doesn't she?"

"Yeah." Sergei turned away and tapped Vlad on the shoulder. "Get out there, lazy!"

Vlad laughed and lumbered to his feet. "Relax, Coach. I'm going."

THE HOME SIDEWINDERS team beat the visitors 6-4 and Dani was thrilled as she skated off the ice, Zakk's arm around her shoulder and Sara on her other side; she'd never had so much fun. Even playing against guys who were bigger and faster than she was, she was exhilarated and excited. If the Olympics was half this much fun, it would rock her world. She was so ready for Colorado Springs she could taste it. She hadn't realized how much she'd missed a competitive level of hockey until now.

"Today rocked," Sara was saying as she pulled off her jersey.

"It did."

"I think you're supposed to go to lunch with your parents and Zakk and Tiff. Are you going to invite Sergei?"

Dani hesitated. She'd been prepared to tell her brother about Sergei, but she hadn't known her parents would be here and that added a level of complexity to the situation.

"You don't want your parents to meet him?" Sara looked puzzled.

"It's just... My dad isn't as overprotective as Zakk, but he'll be more focused on the future, like wanting to know what Sergei's intentions are. Zakk mostly understands keeping things casual, but I don't think my parents will. They'll think it's serious."

"It's not?" Sara was frowning at her.

"It's complicated," Dani muttered, tugging on a T-shirt. She desperately needed a shower but she hadn't brought clean clothes since she hadn't known about this.

Dani hurriedly gathered her things and went to find her parents since most of the Sidewinders were signing autographs now. She ran into Sergei in the hallway and instead of the usual warmth at seeing him, all she felt was frustration.

"You were incredible out there," he said softly, pulling her against him. "I'm so proud of you, baby. No one watching would ever know you aren't actually a member of the Sidewinders."

She flushed with pride. "Thank you. It felt really good to play at that level."

"Zakk and Tiff planned a big family lunch for you guys, so we should get going. I'm sure you want to shower. I'll drop you off at home and then come back to hang out."

"Aren't you coming to lunch?" she faltered, feeling a little confused and foolish. Why was this suddenly so hard? In Alaska it had been stupidly easy.

"I wasn't invited," he said simply.

"Of course you're invited." She took a breath. "But I don't know what we'll tell my parents."

"The truth, honey. We're dating but it's not that serious because you're leaving. If we need to say more than that, you'll have to guide me because I don't want to lie to your parents but I also don't want to cheapen what we have by insinuating it's a friends-with-benefits arrangement."

She wanted to ask him what, exactly, they had but this was neither the time nor the place.

"Okay," she said. "Let me say goodbye to Sara and the others and we'll get going."

DANI WAS NERVOUS. After all the time they'd spent together over the last few months, he knew every nuance of her body language, every expression that crossed her face, and she was nervous as hell. Introductions had been easy, though he'd seen the curiosity on both her parents' faces when she'd introduced him once they'd arrived at the restaurant, since they'd taken two cars. Tiff's sons, Derek and Duncan, had thrown fits about being the one to sit next to Dani, so they were on either side of her and Sergei was across from her. Zakk and Tiff were on either side of him, Savannah was in a high chair at the head of the table and Dani's parents, Joe and Jennifer, were across from each other at the other end. It was large but intimate, and once they were settled, her parents eyed Sergei with obvious interest.

"Is there something you want to tell us, dear?" Her mother's eyes gleamed with both curiosity and mischief.

Dani rolled her eyes, something Sergei rarely saw her do unless she was goofing around with Niko.

"Actually, no," she responded. "But since you're about to jump out of your skin trying to find out, yes, Sergei and I are dating."

"It's about time," Jennifer said smoothly. "I thought you were going to be single forever. Tell us about yourself, Sergei."

Dani opened her mouth but nothing came out and Sergei opted to spare her as much discomfort as he could. "You probably already know I'm widowed and have a three-year-old son, Nikolai. I was born and raised in Moscow, but I came to the U.S. to attend Boston College fifteen years ago and have mostly played in the NHL since graduating, though I did go back to Russia for a few years. I play for the team in Anchorage now so Dani and I have been taking everything slow since she's going to be gone for the next six months."

"Long-distance relationships are hard," her father said thoughtfully. "Do you plan to be faithful while she's gone?"

"*Dad.*" Dani scowled.

"It's a fair question," Sergei interjected. "And the answer is I don't know. We haven't talked about the next step for us. Once we do, we'll make that decision."

There was an awkward silence but Zakk spoke up. "Well, Tiff and I have news."

"You're finally getting married!" his mother gushed.

Zakk sighed. "No, Ma. We're expecting another baby."

"Yay!" Dani grinned, jumping up to run around the table and hug both of them.

"I'm just finishing the first trimester," Tiff said softly. "We're expecting another little girl in February."

"That's wonderful." There was more hugging and kissing before they went back to their seats.

"I still want to know when you're getting married," Jennifer said firmly. "It's been long enough and now there will be four children to think about."

"Mom, the kids are fine," Zakk said as patiently as he could. "Tiff doesn't want to get married and I don't think a piece of paper makes a difference."

"But why?"

His mother obviously wasn't going to let it go and though Sergei felt bad for Zakk and Tiff, he was grateful the focus was no longer on him and Dani.

"Mom." Zakk gave her a dirty look.

"It's okay." Tiff squeezed his hand and turned to her future mother-in-law. "Mom, I do want to marry Zakk, I just..." She hesitated, obviously trying to determine how to convey what she wanted to say. "I want it to be special, something different. And I definitely don't want to be pregnant. Maybe in another year. I don't know exactly, and I'm sorry if that's not a good answer. I want to, and we will, but not until the timing is right for me. Right now, I'm overwhelmed with the kids and trying to get my new practice off the ground... And now another baby. Please, can you forgive me for needing a little more time?"

"Oh, sweet girl, you're Zakk's wife and another daughter to us regardless of a piece of paper, but it feels unfinished somehow..." Jennifer flushed. "I realize I'm probably a little old-fashioned, but I can't help it."

"It's okay." Tiff smiled. "I love your son and there is absolutely no one else for me, forever. I would do anything for him—even marry him today if he said it was important to him."

"I can wait," Zakk said softly, kissing her cheek.

Conversation moved back to the upcoming baby and Sergei had the strangest pang of...envy? Jealousy? He couldn't quite articulate what he was feeling but watching the way Zakk looked at his fiancée made him miss being in a couple. It had taken him a little while to warm up to the idea of Tatiana being pregnant since she'd been three months along before she'd told him, but then he'd been beyond excited. Those had been good times, some of the happiest in his life, and he'd never expected to be that happy again. Yet he was. Dani made him that happy.

"Why didn't you bring Niko?" Jennifer was asking him.

Sergei smiled. "I figured three kids was enough and he tends to dominate Dani's time when he's with her. I know she wanted to spend some time with the twins and Savannah."

"There's plenty of love and attention to go around in this family," Jennifer said lightly. "I can't wait to meet him."

Sergei tried to swallow the lump in his throat. Niko didn't really have grandparents. Tatiana's parents were dead and he wouldn't have wanted Niko to have a relationship with her father anyway. His parents were alive, of course, and he sent pictures and videos regularly, but he didn't plan to ever go back to Russia and his father suspected the government would never let him and his wife come to the U.S. together. His mother, Anastasia, wasn't comfortable traveling alone, so he'd resigned himself to the fact Niko wouldn't have grandparents who were an active part of his life. With Dani, not only would he have a woman who truly made him happy, his son would also have grandparents, an extra aunt and uncle, and more cousins. How the fuck was he going to walk away from Dani three weeks from now?

25

Dinner that night was at Zakk and Tiff's house. Once again, the food was plentiful, varied, and delicious. Steaks and burgers came off the grill, plus scalloped potatoes, baked potatoes, four different salads, corn on the cob, broccoli casserole, and beverages that ranged from pitchers of homemade sangria to bottled water and everything in between. It was a family event, but here in Las Vegas family extended to a lot of close friends. The house was full, the back patio was full, and the kitchen bustled with activity.

Dani couldn't remember the last time she'd had such a fun birthday and if it wasn't for the strange undercurrent with Sergei, it would've been the best day of her life. Nothing was wrong between them, but the constant barrage of questions about their future weighed on her. She'd known leaving him would be hard and had tried to mentally prepare herself for the sadness that was inevitable, but her feelings for him grew stronger with each passing day, diminishing the excitement of the Olympics and her new job.

"You shouldn't be thinking about such serious stuff," Sergei whispered, coming up behind her and sliding his arms around her.

"How do you know what I was thinking about?" she laughed, leaning into him and soaking in his warmth.

"You always get that tiny little frown between your brows when you're thinking about something that makes you unhappy."

"You know me too well," she sighed.

"What were you thinking about?"

"What do you think?"

"Us."

"Yeah."

"Not today, okay?" He turned her around and pulled her close. "Enjoy your birthday. Enjoy your family. And presents… Did you see that stack of presents out there?"

She smiled at that, nodding. "Oh, yeah."

"Let's not ruin tonight with all that other stuff. Tomorrow, let's go out on a date, just the two of us, and we'll talk. Okay?"

"Okay."

DANI HADN'T BEEN EXPECTING MUCH in the way of gifts because of the incredible one she'd received this morning from Zakk and Toli. However, her parents got her new Under Armour to take with her to Colorado, Sara got her the new mystery novel she'd been wanting, and Tiff, Tessa, Sara, and Rachel had all chipped in for a spa day tomorrow. The last bag came from the Michael Kors store and she frowned slightly as she picked it up. There was no card, just a tag hanging from the handle that said "Love, Sergei." She dug through the paper and pulled out a gorgeous handbag and matching shoes. They were in a trendy blush-pink color, very similar to the dress she'd worn out to dinner with him, and she bit her lip to keep from crying. He'd remembered what she'd said about wanting shoes and purses that matched.

She met his eye and smiled, blinking away happy tears. "Thank you," she whispered. "You heard me say I wanted these…" Though she hadn't specified these exactly, he would know what she meant and no one else needed to know the details.

"I do listen," he said lightly, kissing her lips when she leaned over. "Sometimes."

"Time for cake!" Tiff called out.

Dani made a wish and blew out the candles, her eyes meeting Sergei's as she did. She usually wished for things like new sticks or skates for her birthdays. This year she wished for Sergei, in whatever capacity she could have him. It was getting close to the time she would have to leave him and her gut told her he was thinking about it too. Every time their eyes met she sensed a sadness in him she'd never felt before. It could only mean one thing, but she refused to think about it. Not tonight anyway. Maybe not even this week. If he was going to end things, it would have to be when they were back in Anchorage.

THE NEXT FEW days went by quickly between the spa day, visiting friends, and spending time with her parents, so it was the day before they were supposed to go home before they had a chance to go out and spend a little time alone. They were together in bed every night but, except for the night of her birthday, they were usually naked and all over each other immediately. Sergei had tried, starting the night of her birthday, to scale back their insatiable sexual appetites, but the following night she wasn't having it and had his dick in her mouth before he had a chance to say he was tired. There were no excuses after that and he didn't bother trying to hold back. In the back of his mind, he knew he had to let her go, and he was going to enjoy every moment they had left. Especially since this would be their last day together. He'd made the decision last night after a lovemaking marathon that left them both completely spent.

She was growing on him in ways he didn't want to accept, and if it was happening this fast—technically just over a month that they'd been sleeping together—he couldn't imagine what it would be like in another month, when she left. Niko was beyond attached to her, calling her *Mommy* and stuck like glue to her whenever she was around. Niko loved his father, but Dani was his go-to for everything, and the only reason it bothered Sergei was because she was leaving them. Well, he was going to send her away, even though she didn't know it yet.

"You're the one thinking about something serious today," she said as they settled into a booth at a local restaurant. "You were thinking about it last night, too. Well, after you turned me into a quivering puddle of orgasmic goo."

He chuckled. "I wasn't thinking about anything except that luscious body of yours," he said.

"Uh-huh." She cocked her head. "What's going on, Sergei?"

He took one of her hands between his and gently rubbed his thumbs across her skin.

"Sergei?" The worry in her eyes gutted him.

"I think..." He took a deep breath. "I think you should stay in Vegas."

"What?"

"This thing between us is intense. We're both getting attached and it's not a good idea."

"Because I'm leaving?"

"Niko is really attached, Dani, and we don't know what the future holds. It's not fair to let him think you're going to be his new mommy when that's probably not going to happen."

Dani looked like he'd punched her in the face and he tried to back-pedal. "I don't mean we're completely through, I just mean you should be able to focus on your dreams without worrying about the family you left behind. It's not fair to you and it's not fair to Niko. He's three. He doesn't understand the significance of the Olympics. All he's going to know is that you're gone."

"But I can come back," she whispered.

"Honey, you have a job waiting for you. How many NHL teams do you think are going to hire a woman who's just out of college to be the assistant team trainer? It's the chance of a lifetime and I'm not going to let you give it up."

"Shouldn't that be my choice?" Her green eyes were emerald lasers even though they'd filled with tears.

"You're going to choose between your first lover and your first job?" He shook his head. "That's unfair. And if things didn't work out with us, you'd hate me."

"But Sergei…"

"Listen to me." He gripped her chin with his fingers and stared deep into those emerald depths. "I'm not going anywhere. I'll be in Anchorage raising my son and playing hockey. You go do your thing. We'll keep in touch. I checked my team's schedule and we'll be in Denver in October, so I'll come see you. Maybe you'll have moved on or—"

"Stop it," she hissed under her breath. "I won't have moved on! Don't try to ease your guilt by putting it on me. I'm crazy about you, Sergei, and after the Olympics I'd be willing to do whatever it takes to make things work. All you have to do is say you want me to."

He hated himself for what he was about to do, but he had to do it. He'd already had one woman give up her dreams for him, and all that had gotten her was dead. He wasn't directly responsible for her death, but it boiled down to her making all the sacrifices for him. He'd asked the same of Maria and that had gone badly as well. No, the best thing for Dani was for him to let her go now, before he hurt her even worse.

"Honey, I can't make you promises for the future. I care for you, but I decided I wasn't going to get married again, and that hasn't changed. I know you, and after meeting your family, that would eventually be important to you."

"You don't think you could *ever* love me?"

Her eyes were so full of hurt he nearly cried himself.

I already do, he thought miserably, but what he said out loud was entirely different. "I don't think I can love anyone like that again. Tatiana took that with her when she died."

"Seriously?" She was staring at him, her eyes blazing despite the single tear that leaked out of the corner of one. "Did my family scare you off? Or were you just using me all along and felt like a big jerk when you had to pretend I meant something to you in front of others?"

"You do," he said quietly.

"Then why don't you want me?"

"Because I'm going to hurt you. That's what I do. Maria gave up her career to follow me to Russia and I broke her heart. Tatiana gave up everything for me—her medical career, her family, her country—and then she died for me, too. I won't ask another woman to sacrifice for me, no matter how much I want her."

Dani closed her eyes, her jaw working as she struggled to maintain control.

"Please don't cry." He tried to wipe the tears that were falling faster now, but she batted his hand away.

"You will not humiliate me," she hissed under her breath.

"No, of course not."

"The story will be that I broke up with you. That being here this week made me realize how much I missed my brother and friends here in Vegas. You will not tell anyone the truth, especially not your brothers, because they'll tell Zakk. Do you understand?"

He tried to reach for her again but she'd scooted away from him and he didn't pursue it. "Yes. I'll do anything you want to make this easier for you."

"And you're going to pay to ship my fucking car here."

"I can have it shipped to Colorado if you want," he said quietly. "That way you can fly and won't have to drive that far by yourself."

"Whatever. I don't care." She swiped at her eyes.

"Dani." He grabbed her hand, holding on even when she tried to pull away. "Please. Stop."

"What?" She met his eyes squarely, wearing the same expression she'd worn the day he'd snapped at her for letting Niko call her *Mama D*.

"We can do this any way you want, but please don't let Niko see you angry."

She wilted a little at the mention of his son. "I would never take it out on him."

"Taking it out on him and letting him see us at odds with each other is different."

"We won't be at odds. We'll go home and say I've decided to stay here and then I'll talk to Sara about trading places with me. I can take over what she's been doing for Tiff and Tessa and she can get settled in Anchorage."

"If that's what you want."

"It is."

"Sweetheart, I'm sorry." He put one of his big hands on the side of her face and nearly lost his resolve when her eyes fluttered closed and she leaned into his palm.

"I know. But you warned me. I thought maybe you'd want me now more than you'd want to hang on to the past. I guess I can't compete with her."

"You're not competing with anyone," he said quietly. "You're a treasure. That's why I can't take the chance I'll fuck up your life. Everything about this guts me."

She wouldn't look at him but finally asked, "Sergei, how do you do this?"

"Do what, sweetheart?"

"How do you breathe when your heart is broken?"

He swallowed. "You just put one foot in front of the other, day after day. One day you realize it stopped hurting at some point."

"That sounds awful."

"It is."

"And you're doing it to me anyway."

"I'm doing it to protect you, baby. Please believe that."

"I don't. I can't. 'Cause then my heart would be broken for you, too."

"I don't deserve your sympathy." He pulled her against him and she buried her face in the hollow of his shoulder. He waved away the waitress when she came by to get their order, keeping Dani close to him.

They sat at the restaurant for a long time, ordering drinks but neither of them had much appetite. Talking didn't seem necessary and Dani didn't move from where she'd had her head on his shoulder for a long time. Sergei kept one arm around her, wondering how stupid a man had to be to let a woman like her go. It would be better for her in the long run, but it sucked right now. Hopefully, hockey and her family would distract her.

26

Toli and Tessa had taken the kids somewhere and were still gone when they got home and Dani went up to their room. She stood in the doorway looking around sadly, memories of the last six days washing over her like a light summer breeze. She didn't know if she wanted to kiss him or smack him, but then his arms were around her and she squeezed her eyes shut tightly. As if that would somehow make the pain of leaving him less acute.

"What do you want to do?" he whispered.

"I have to move my shit across the street to my brother's, but I'd rather do that after you and Niko are gone."

"Okay. I think Toli is grilling tonight so everyone will be here and we can tell them what we've decided together."

"What you've decided."

He nodded. "Yes, but you said that's not our story."

"I don't even care about the story at this point," she muttered, running her hand through her hair.

"Would you rather I spent tonight at a hotel?"

"No." Her eyes puddled with tears.

"Ah, baby, this is what I was afraid of, that no matter how honest we were, I was going to hurt you."

"It's not hurt so much as...loneliness? I'm excited about my future, but without you and Niko, it feels a little empty."

"It won't for long." He rested his chin on her shoulder. "You're going to be busy, and within a few weeks, you won't have time to miss us. You'll be working harder than you've ever worked in your life as far as hockey is concerned, making new friends, and getting ready for the Olympics."

"Feelings don't just disappear because you're busy."

"I know, baby. Believe me, if anyone knows that, it's me."

They were quiet.

"Let's just get through tonight," she said at last.

"What do you want me to do?"

"I want you to make love to me," she said, slowly pulling her shirt over her head.

"Honey…"

"We're alone. You're leaving tomorrow. I need this. You asked what I wanted; that's what I want."

He pulled off his shirt as well. "Then I'm in."

THE NEXT MORNING, Sergei called the airline to delay his departure by a day and transfer Dani's ticket to Sara. Dani had been gone before he woke up and he hadn't heard from her yet today. Toli told him she was working out but it had been hours and there hadn't been any sign of her.

"You going to tell me the truth about what's going on?" Toli asked when the kids were taking their afternoon naps and Tessa was upstairs doing laundry.

"What do you mean?"

"Dani didn't decide she wanted to stay here because she missed her family. What did you do to make her not want to live with you in Anchorage anymore?"

"I told her we had no future, that I wasn't capable of loving anyone ever again."

Toli reached out and smacked him on the back of the head, cursing a blue streak in Russian, Italian, and German. "Are you fucking stupid?" he finally asked in English.

Sergei scowled. "Don't, okay? I'm doing what's best for *her*, not for myself. It would be easy to let her get caught up in the romance, the fun, all the presents I can buy her and let her give up her dreams to raise my kid while I fly off all over the continent playing hockey. In what universe is that fair to her?"

"The universe where you go home and love her back. The universe where she and your children are waiting at the door when you come in and their smiles light up your life. That universe."

"That's your universe, big brother, and Dani isn't Tessa. There's nothing wrong with Tessa, but she wanted a man to take care of, to make babies with… Dani's going to the Olympics and then she's going to work for the Sidewinders. I'm not taking that away from her the way I did both Maria and Tanya."

Toli shook his head. "You took nothing from them. They loved you and they chose to go. Maria was never good for you, and you know it. Moving her to Russia didn't end your marriage; the fact that she wasn't the right woman for you did. And Tanya made choices, Sergei. We've never talked about this because it seemed wrong to speak ill of the dead, but dammit, she made the choices she made. By the time she got caught up in her father's mob lifestyle, I was already in the NHL making a lot of money. I may not have been the perfect boyfriend, but she could have come to me. I would have taken her out of Russia and paid for her to go to medical school here. She chose to stay and get revenge on her father instead of walking away. It wasn't until she got pregnant that she put someone before herself and agreed to move to the U.S."

"What the hell are you trying to say?" Sergei furrowed his forehead in anger.

"I'm trying to say she did what she wanted and it had nothing to do with you. Not really."

"You're saying she didn't love me."

"On the contrary. I'm saying you and Niko were the *only* things she loved more than her need to get revenge on her father. She may not have ever realized it if you hadn't gotten her pregnant."

"That was an accident."

"I know."

"Dammit, Toli, I don't know what you want from me!" He got out of his chair and stalked outside even though it was a thousand degrees and he was already uncomfortable.

Toli followed him slowly, leaning against the wall of the house and folding his arms across his chest.

"All I want is for you to not make this mistake with Dani. She loves you. It's all over her face. I thought her skin was going to crack from how hard she was trying to convince us last night that her staying here was her idea."

"The convincing was her idea, not mine."

"So you're just going to leave her here?" Toli was shaking his head. "Sergei, I—"

"It's the right thing to do," Sergei said firmly. "I'm not going to make her choose. Not again. Both of the women I've loved in my life got hurt because of me and I love Dani enough—"

"So you do love her."

Sergei nearly growled at him. "Weren't you the one who let Tessa go back to her husband because she had to come to terms with her failed marriage before she could truly be with you? I have to let Dani go, and I'm tired of having to convince people I'm right."

"Who else have you had to convince? Dani?"

"Yes, Dani. And now Niko, although it'll be a different type of conversation with him."

"You're my kid brother and I love you," Toli said slowly, "but you're an idiot."

"Thanks." He made an impatient motion with his hand. "Maybe in a few years I'll retire from hockey, but until she's had a chance to live, I'm not tying her down to my life, my schedule."

"You're thirty-three. You're not retiring any time soon."

"Not all of us are you. I don't want to play until I'm forty."

"I love the game, I make a lot of money, and I'm healthy. Why would I stop?"

"I guess it's different because you have someone at home helping you. I'm doing this alone now and it's exhausting, even with a good nanny. Niko needs me, not a nanny."

"Which is why you need Dani."

"That's not going to happen, so let it go, okay? And please, don't mention this to Zakk. She'll kill me. She asked me to allow her to retain some dignity with her family, so she's not the girl who got dumped by her first and only boyfriend."

"Her first…" Toli narrowed his eyes. "You were her first boyfriend?"

Sergei pursed his lips, unwilling to say anything else so personal and intimate about Dani. "Guys were intimidated by her and she was picky, so yeah, first *adult* boyfriend."

"Indeed." Toli didn't say anything other than, "Of course I won't tell Zakk. I don't want him to kill you."

Dani took Sergei, Sara and Niko to the airport the following day. She'd kept her distance yesterday as he'd made arrangements for Sara and they sorted out the details, but she'd wanted to drive them today. She'd been too busy helping Sara pack and get organized to think much about what she would do when they were gone, but now that they were actually leaving, she wanted to be close to him for as long as possible. This wasn't what she'd thought a breakup would feel like, because he wasn't telling her he didn't care about her. He just didn't think he cared about her *enough*, which made no sense, because no matter how he tried to quantify his feelings, she always came to the same conclusion: Whatever he felt right now was enough to make her happy. Maybe he didn't have it in him to tell her he loved her in words, but she felt it every time he touched her, every time they were together.

"Why don't we drop Sara and Niko at the terminal with the luggage and then go park so we can talk for a minute?" she suggested lightly.

Sergei didn't respond but nodded. He unloaded the stroller and luggage, unhooked the car seat and then got back in the car as Sara and Niko waited on the sidewalk. Dani drove to the hourly parking area and pulled into a spot, putting the SUV in park but unable to look at him.

"What's on your mind, honey?" he asked softly.

"Is this it? We just go our separate ways like there was never anything between us?"

"I think that would be easier for you, but Niko is going to take it hard."

"I know." She sniffed, horrified she would cry in front of him. Again.

"Damn." He pulled her close.

"If this is the right thing to do, why does it feel so wrong?"

"Because I'm broken and I break everything around me."

"You're not broken," she whispered. "You're *not*."

"Ah, baby, you're too good for me."

When he kissed her she almost melted, her mouth opening under his and giving him everything she had. This was all that was left; he was really going back to Anchorage without her.

He pulled away slowly and their eyes locked.

"Don't stay," he whispered against her lips. "I'll walk to the terminal and tell Sara you said goodbye. I'll call you tonight so you can talk to Niko."

"Are we still letting him think I'm playing hockey now?"

He nodded.

"I can't stand the thought that we'll never see each other again," she admitted sadly.

"I know." He stroked her hair, gently pushing it away from her face. "God, you're beautiful, Maryanne."

She blinked away tears, managing a small smile. "You're not too bad yourself, Wayne."

"I'll call you tonight, see how you're doing, and let you talk to Niko."

"Fly safe," she whispered.

He pressed his lips to hers one last time, hard, and then he was gone, jogging through the parking garage towards the terminal.

27

Dani got up and ran with Toli and Zakk every morning at five. It was better to run before the sun was up or it got too hot, so they did it early. Toli and Zakk normally ran every other day, but since Dani had gone on her own on their off days, they'd started going every day. Hockey season would start for them in a month anyway, so they didn't mind ramping up their workout regimens. Dani worked harder, though, running every morning, weightlifting every other afternoon, and getting the old gang together to play hockey as often as they were available. Sometimes she ran at night, too, after the sun went down. Pushing herself physically was the only way to fight through the emotions she was dealing with and it was the easiest way to distract herself.

It also kept her out of the house. She loved Zakk, Tiff, and the kids, but they were their own family, one that she wasn't truly a part of. Zakk and Tiff often put the kids to bed and then went up to bed themselves, lost in whatever they did when they were alone together. She knew they had a great sex life because Tiff talked about it a lot, but she didn't like to think about her brother having sex. Hell, she didn't want to think about anyone else having sex right now because she missed it.

She missed sex, she missed Niko, she missed Sara, and she practically ached for Sergei. Her mind, her body, her very soul longed for his touch, and if she hadn't been living it, she would've laughed at anyone who said something like that aloud. She didn't, of course. She usually told Sara those types of things, but not in the current situation. She didn't dare tell Tessa or Tiff, because it would get back to Zakk, who thought she was fine and simply getting ready for hockey. No one knew how her heart broke a little more each day she didn't hear from Sergei. Though she often spoke to Niko, it was through Sara and her contact with Sergei had dwindled down to almost nothing in the two weeks since he'd been gone. Sara said he was quiet too, keeping to himself a lot except when he worked out with Aaron. Otherwise, he spent time with Niko and went to bed when he did.

Sara was lonely, too, but for different reasons. She said Sergei was polite but kept his distance unless it had to do with Niko, so she didn't have anyone to talk to either.

It sucked for all of them, Dani thought as she jogged home from her late-night run. She'd been restless tonight, so it was nearly ten o'clock and she was just getting back from a five-mile run. It probably wouldn't be a good idea to get up at five to run yet again, but she wasn't sure what else to do. Pushing her body was the only thing keeping her from losing her mind emotionally.

"Hey." Zakk's deep voice resonated through the kitchen as she came in through the garage and she stopped, still breathing hard.

"Hey. Why are you still up?"

"Came down for a drink and noticed your bedroom door open. Tiff said you've been running a lot at night. Are you running in the morning and again at night, Dani?"

She nodded. "Yeah, sometimes."

"You've been working out seven days a week for the last two weeks and you know as well as I do your body needs time to recover and heal."

"I'm heading into training," she said lightly, grabbing a bottle of water out of the fridge. "I'm fine."

"Don't bullshit me, Dani. What's going on?"

"Nothing. It's the Olympics, Zakk. I need to be in the shape of my life."

"You said you wanted to stay in Vegas because you missed everyone so much, yet we never see you unless we need help with the kids. Royce said he called to see if you wanted to go play pool with him and Tore and you said no." Royce and Tore were his teammates on the Sidewinders, and Dani was close to them.

"Tore wants to sleep with me and Royce uses me as a stand-in so girls leave him alone. I don't have time for either of those things right now."

"Other than working out, what else do you do? Didn't you stay so you could spend time with us? Your family and friends?"

"Yeah, of course, but—"

"Oh, just stop." He put up a hand, palm out. "What happened between you and Sergei?"

"Nothing."

He shook his head. "I don't believe he just randomly broke up with you, knowing you were leaving in a month anyway. A guy in his situation, where we're all friends and practically family, wouldn't do that. He would let you leave and then say the relationship fell apart because of the distance. Unless you cheated on him or something, but I'd bet my left nut you didn't, so tell me."

"Zakk, I'm an adult and this is my personal life. Please leave it alone."

"Either you tell me or I'll ask him," he called after her as she headed for the stairs.

"He'll tell you to mind your own business too," she called back.

As soon as she got upstairs, she texted Sergei:

My brother is fishing for info about what's going on with us, so if he really does call you (he threatened to), tell him to mind his own business. Thanks. D.

She got in the shower and let the lukewarm water course over her. It felt good. Her muscles were sore after going so hard the last two weeks. Zaak was right; she needed to give herself a day of rest, so she'd sleep in tomorrow and spend time in the pool with the kids. Maybe have a beer or two, watch a movie. It would be a good day to think of nothing. Especially not Sergei.

After pulling on an oversized T-shirt and clean panties, she sat cross-legged on her bed and grabbed her phone.

Three missed calls from Sergei and then a text:

If you don't pick up I'll call Zakk myself.

She called him back, shaking her head.

"Dani?"

"I was in the shower," she said mildly. "I'd gone for a run."

"Why does Zakk want to talk to me?"

"Because he thinks I'm working out too hard and you must've done something pretty bad for me not to want to go back to Anchorage with you."

He sighed.

"I told him you didn't and he wouldn't let it go."

Sergei chuckled. "Honey, he's your big brother. Either he's on the phone with Toli now or they'll be talking about it in the morning."

"Jesus, I'm a fucking adult. I wish everyone would stop mothering me!"

"Easy, honey. He cares about you. As do I."

"Yeah, well, you gave up that right."

"I did not. I can care about anyone I choose."

He was trying to be funny but she wasn't in the mood. "Honestly, I'm fine. Yeah, I'm a little bummed... I miss you. I won't lie about that, and I'm probably cranky because I'm late getting my—" She stopped abruptly.

"Getting your?" he prompted.

"Sleep," she said quickly. "I've been working out too much."

"Getting my sleep?" he repeated. "Or maybe getting your period?"

"That's not what I was going to say."

"Dani, could you be pregnant?"

"Not unless you forgot to use a condom. I just... I might be a little late."

"Are you usually?"

"No, but I don't usually run ten miles a day for two weeks or lift as much as I've been lifting, either."

He blew out a breath. "You should take a test."

"Yeah, I will."

"Dani, you have to tell me. This isn't something you should handle on your own."

"Again with the insinuation that I can't take care of myself!" she huffed. "I'm pretty sure I'm not; we were always careful, but I'll let you know. I have to go." She disconnected, feeling like a big baby, but this was the last thing she needed. *Fuck.* This was not part of her plan.

DANI SAT on the closed toilet seat taking long deep breaths. She'd been a little nauseated but it was starting to pass. One line. Negative. *Negative.* Negative. The test was fucking negative. She'd done the math, looked up the dates she would have been most fertile and how pregnant she could be. Technically, since a woman's body wasn't a machine, it was possible to have conceived the last time they'd made love, which had been exactly sixteen days ago. But it might be too soon to show up on a test. However, this one was negative and she breathed a huge sigh of relief.

Instead of calling, she took a picture of the test and texted it to Sergei with just one word:

Negative.

She'd wait a week and take one more if she still didn't get her period, but for now, everything was okay. She needed a beer and breakfast, in that order.

NEGATIVE.

Sergei stared at the phone for a long time when he got her message.

Negative.

She wasn't pregnant. She was going to take another test in a few days, she'd added in a subsequent text thirty minutes later, but she was confident they were okay.

So why didn't he feel relieved? All he'd felt when she'd slipped about not getting her period was excitement. What the fuck was that about? He didn't want another kid.

You love kids.

Shut up.

You and Dani would make beautiful babies.

Shut *the fuck* up.

He had to shake his head to stop talking to himself—and answering.

She'd been in his life for about two and a half months and gone for two and a half weeks but it was like someone had rolled over him with a boulder. He missed her so much it felt like there was a crater in his chest. This was different than anything he'd experienced with a woman before. When Tatiana had died he'd been grief-stricken and in shock; now he was just a zombie, going through the motions each day.

Sara was great, keeping the house tidy in between cleanings from the service, taking stellar care of Niko and even going to the gym with him because it seemed wasteful not to use Dani's membership. Other than that, though, they didn't interact a lot. She kept a respectful distance, making sure not to wear anything too skimpy to bed and always fully dressed when she came downstairs. He'd caught her in the freezer getting ice cream at two in the morning once, but though she was braless, her nightshirt covered her bottom and she'd had on little shorts underneath. She was cute, but not Dani, and she'd told him flat out she wasn't interested in any kind of booty call. That was fine with him because he had zero desire to even look at another woman, much less the best friend of the woman he loved.

Yeah, he'd come to that conclusion the moment she'd made the comment about her late period. The excitement that coursed through him had been immediate and he couldn't deny he would've been happy if she'd turned up pregnant. Even if it meant her Olympic dreams would be over. A baby would bring her back to him, which had been all he'd thought about since he'd left her in Vegas. He still believed he'd done the right thing in letting her go, but not if there was a baby. They'd been careful, though. Well, he'd been careful. She hadn't been involved in the protection department, but he couldn't think of a single time he'd forgotten or seen any visible breakages.

"Is she really okay?" he blurted out at lunch, catching Sara off guard as she cut Niko's grilled cheese into four diagonal pieces.

She looked up. "Don't put me in the middle, Sergei. She's my best friend and you're my boss."

"I'm not your boss," he said impatiently. "I mean, yes, you're taking care of Niko for me and I'm paying you, but I'm not your boss in a traditional sense. I trust you with my child, so that makes us almost family, or at the very least friends."

She smiled. "That's nice, and I feel that way, too, but I won't betray her to you."

"How is telling me if she's okay a betrayal?"

"Sergei. You were her first everything. You think she's just gone on her merry way without a second thought?" She sighed heavily. "You two are so freakin' stubborn, but that's not my business. Here's what I'll tell you: Overall, she's fine. She leaves for Colorado next week and is super excited about the Olympics. Is she a little sad? Sure. But that's to be expected. Just don't lead her on, Sergei. If you don't think you can love her, let her go. Please."

A prickle of shame made him drop his head because she was right. He'd been subconsciously hanging on to her, hoping to keep her thinking about him, so maybe someday... But there was no someday. She had a brilliant future ahead of her and he would only drag her down. He had to remember why he'd ended it in the first place and that was the right thing to do. It would suck, but he had to pull away even more. Unless a subsequent pregnancy test turned up positive, there couldn't be any more contact. Outside of Niko, of course, but Sara could handle that.

"You're right," he said aloud. "I won't contact her again."

She let out a huff of exasperation. "Don't be a jerk. If you go cold turkey it'll screw with her head during the first week of practice with the Olympic team! Dude, don't make it blatant."

He chuckled at her look of indignation. "You're right. Sorry, I'm just trying to navigate all these...feelings."

Sara arched a brow. "Feelings? Like guilt? Or feelings like...*feelings*."

"I don't know, but it doesn't matter. She's better off without me. You said so yourself."

"I said no such thing. I said not to lead her on if you don't love her. If you have feelings for her, that's a totally different thing."

"Do you know what happened to my first two wives?"

"I know Tatiana died. I don't know anything about your first wife."

He wasn't sure why he felt compelled to tell her about Maria and Tanya, but he did. She needed to understand how broken he was, so she would know he was doing the right thing. So someone would agree with him and the heaviness in his heart would lift. Maybe. *Hopefully.* Because he was in love with Danielle Cloutier and letting her go sucked ass.

28

The first week in Colorado was busy and exciting, for which Dani was grateful. She was far too busy getting to know her coach and teammates, and learning her way around Colorado Springs, to worry about Sergei or her broken heart. Her teammates were great and their head coach, Laurel Saunders, was fantastic. A gold medal Olympian herself, she was smart, tough and a lot younger than Dani would have imagined, just thirty-two. They worked hard but so far everyone got along and Dani was glad that the only time she thought about Sergei was late at night, after she dropped into bed. The rest of the time she was on the go, and usually so tired that when she lay down she fell right to sleep. So she was wholly unprepared for Coach Saunders's announcement the following day.

"I have news," the attractive woman said as they gathered for their pre-practice meeting. "Some really exciting things are coming up, so get ready. First, we're going to Las Vegas on the twenty-fifth for an exhibition game against the Sidewinders. It'll be mostly their rookies and prospects, but it'll still be NHL-level hockey in front of a huge crowd." She cut her eyes to Dani. "I believe there will be at least one veteran player on the team who's going to be on the ice."

Dani laughed. "My brother won't go easy on me just because I'm his sister."

Her new friend and roommate, Hailey Dobson, nudged her. "He can go hard on me, though."

"He's engaged, goofball."

"A girl can dream!"

"Okay, ladies." Coach Saunders was shaking her head. "We'll leave on the twenty-fourth, play on the twenty-fifth, come back the next day. Everyone up for a real game?"

Cheers went up and she smiled before continuing. "Good, but be ready to work your asses off. We don't want to embarrass ourselves in front of a very loyal Vegas crowd. Okay, second. It can't be all work and no play around here, so we're going to attend the season opener in Denver as a team. Colorado is playing the team from Anchorage—"

Dani didn't hear the rest of her sentence because of the roaring in her ears. *Damn.* They were going to the Colorado game against Alaska and Sergei would be there. Close. Close enough to touch. Touching him would be good. It would probably be bad in the long run, but short-term it would feel good. Too good. She tried not to think about him too much, but she missed the hell out of him. There was nothing wrong with a booty call, right? He'd already broken her heart and she was too busy with hockey to sulk, so a few good orgasms wouldn't hurt. *Right?*

"Are you paying attention?" Hailey nudged her.

"Sorry." Dani snapped back to the present, focusing on the rest of what Coach Saunders was saying.

"...along with Aaron Ferrar, from the Blizzard, flying in for the all-day goaltending clinic."

"Aaron's coming?" Dani spoke without thinking. "He's a great guy."

A few eyebrows raised around the room and someone said, "He just got divorced. How well do you know him, Dani?"

She flushed. "Just friends. I nannied for Sergei Petrov part of the summer and—"

"You were Sergei Petrov's nanny?" Petra Santini's eyes widened. "He's soooo hot."

The other girls snickered.

"Yeah, and we bought Aaron's house so—"

"We?" Petra asked, cocking her head.

Dani was blushing furiously but tried to laugh it off. "I helped him choose the house, buy furniture, get everything set up. You guys know what I mean."

"I think we all know what she means," someone chortled on the other side of the room.

The girls all laughed but there was no malice in it and Coach Saunders picked up where she'd left off, telling them about more additions to their schedule and a few other things she needed to mention.

AARON TOOK her to dinner on his last night in Colorado and though it wasn't a date, she wore her pink dress just to be able to wear the matching shoes and purse Sergei had bought her. Other than maybe Christmas, she wouldn't have many opportunities to wear a dress between now and February, so she took advantage of it.

"You look lovely tonight," Aaron said as they walked into the restaurant.

"Thank you." She let him pull out her chair and she sank into it with a smile at the waiter, who'd been eyeing her legs.

"So how's it going?" he asked after they'd ordered.

"It's busy. I'm pretty much on the ice or in the gym, all day, every day."

"Sounds familiar," he nodded.

"It was good of you to come down for the clinic."

"I was bored," he admitted. "I'm divorced, living in a furnished condo while I look for a house, with no family nearby and nothing to do. I hang out with Jake a little, but he and Adrianna are having issues so I try to keep my distance."

"Oh, I didn't realize they were having problems."

"They've always had problems. He just gets to ignore them once hockey season starts. I guess there was an incident at the team BBQ last weekend, but since I wasn't there, I only heard about it secondhand from Sergei."

At the mention of his name Dani's stomach rolled a little but she managed to keep her face neutral. "Did he tell you what happened?"

"The story is Addy had too much to drink and made a comment about... Well, you know they've had a bunch of miscarriages, right?"

"No, I didn't know that."

"Yeah, and she really wants a baby, so supposedly they had an argument and she told him if he was a real man, his little swimmers would be stronger or something to that effect. Sergei said he only heard part of it but apparently Coach Sylvester said they had to go to couples counseling. Jake didn't want to talk about it on the phone."

She grimaced. "I'm kind of glad I wasn't there. You never know how to behave in those situations, or whose side you should be on."

"Jake told me everyone asked about you but all Sergei would say was that you were training for the Olympics and that you're just friends." His blue eyes found hers. "Is that true?"

"Yes. We decided it would be too hard to be together with me here and then at the Olympics in Seattle."

"So you're single?"

His eyes burned with something she couldn't quite read and she looked away, suddenly uncomfortable and embarrassed, unsure what to say. Sergei was the only mature, attractive man who'd ever been genuinely interested in her and she had zero experience telling guys who weren't idiotic college students that she didn't want to go out with them.

"Hey, if you're not interested, it's no problem," he said when she didn't answer right away.

"I'm sorry," she whispered. "It's just... I'm still..."

"You're still hung up on Sergei."

She nodded miserably. "I'm really sorry. You're good-looking and sweet and we're friends but it probably would be a disaster with both of us on the rebound."

"Wait, if you're still hung up on Sergei, why'd you break up with him?" He frowned. "When we talked, he made it sound like you dumped him?"

She smiled sadly. "He did that because I asked him to, because I didn't want anyone to know my first-ever boyfriend dumped me."

"He was your first boyfriend?" Aaron looked shocked.

"Why do you look so surprised?"

"Because you're beautiful. How could guys not be all over you?"

"I guess because I'm too much of a tomboy and they don't like women who can out-skate, out-run and out-lift them."

He laughed, a hearty sound that rang through the restaurant. "Then they're pussies who didn't deserve you," he said in a quiet voice. "But tell me what happened. Sergei wasn't acting like a guy who did the dumping. In fact, he seemed pretty bummed."

"It's complicated. We're complicated. Geographically, it's my fault. I can't be with him and Niko. I want to be here in Colorado Springs—not many people get the chance to compete in the Olympics, you know? And then I have a job offer with the Sidewinders as an assistant trainer, which is really tough to get. So that's a big obstacle. But emotionally, it's all on him. He's gun-shy after two marriages, doesn't think he's good enough for me or some bullshit. We could compromise on things like careers and locations, after the Olympics is over, but his inability to commit again? That's all him. I won't give up everything for a guy who says he'll never love me."

Aaron made a face. "Then he's a dumbass who doesn't deserve you, either. Except there has to be something else going on. He was really bummed, but I thought it was because you'd dumped him."

"It doesn't really matter. He won't commit and I refuse to give up everything for a guy who doesn't know what he wants."

Aaron was thoughtful for a bit. "We could...make him jealous."

"We?"

He smiled. "I'm here and if we go somewhere a little high profile after dinner, we'll probably end up on social media. It happens to me a lot. We don't have to actually do anything, he'll just think we are. Or he'll think I'm moving in on his girl. Nothing gets a guy thinking straight more than jealousy. And, since I live in Alaska too and it can't possibly be serious, he'll think I'm using you and get really riled up!"

She frowned. "I don't know if that's a good idea. Why would you want to upset him like that if he's your friend and teammate?"

Aaron laughed. "Because he's being obtuse and the truth, if it was to get ugly, is that nothing has happened between us. Nor will it, unless you were truly interested, and even then, I would talk to him about it first because that's the kind of man I am. However, in the interest of playing matchmaker, I'm willing to be a short-term sacrificial lamb."

"You're sweet, but even if you made him jealous, I don't see that we have a future. What good will making him jealous do?"

"It might shake him up enough to make him admit to the feelings he doesn't want to accept, make him realize he's a dumbass?"

She lowered her eyes for a moment but couldn't help the wistful feeling that whipped through her. Maybe this would work? It probably wouldn't, for a million different reasons, but going out with Aaron couldn't be a bad thing. There was the off-chance it would change Sergei's mind about her being better off without him, but if it didn't, it would still be fun to be out with an attractive, interesting man. A man who wasn't Sergei. Just to see. She wasn't going to sleep with him or anything, but there was nothing stopping her from having an evening of drinks and conversation with someone other than Sergei. After all, he was her first and only everything, so maybe that played into her feelings for him. A casual date with a friend might be just what she needed.

"Let's do it," she said after a slight hesitation.

THEY WENT to a popular club downtown, where the cover charge alone was fifty dollars per person. She'd never been to a place like this and her eyes widened as she took in the women wearing more jewelry than she'd ever seen in her life, the expensive bottles of champagne, and the number of easily recognizable celebrities.

"Wow," she breathed against Aaron's ear. "This is wild."

He grinned. "Great place to see and be seen."

"Nothing over-the-top, Aaron," she warned, meeting his eyes. "We can be here together, sitting together, opening doors for me or whatever, but I'm not going to do something to embarrass Sergei."

"Absolutely not," he said somberly. "He's my *friend*. I'm doing this for him, not to be a dick. We've already talked about the fact that you're not interested —I would never do anything like that."

"I would like to dance, though," she admitted.

"Fast or slow?" he teased.

"Fast!"

He pulled her onto the dance floor. A popular hip-hop song was playing and they found it easy to get into the rhythm. He twirled her around a few times, smiling down at her, and Dani started to relax. He wasn't Sergei, but she was enjoying his company. He was funny and good-looking, a nice guy who definitely wouldn't stay single long. It was possible to imagine dating a guy like Aaron, but when he moved up behind her, his front pressed to her back, longing slowly burned through her. Not for just anyone, though. Her body ached to be touched, but she wasn't even capable of fantasizing about anyone but Sergei. Having Aaron pressed up against her made her uncomfortable, though she loved to dance. Well, at least now she knew.

Without making it obvious, she danced away from him, eventually finding her way back so that they were face-to-face again. This was better, and Aaron didn't seem to mind. Thank goodness. She wasn't nearly as naïve as she'd been a few months ago, but she wasn't ready to dip her foot in any kind of dating pool either. Just the last twenty minutes with Aaron had proven that.

Eventually they made their way to a table and he ordered a beer while she got a white wine spritzer. It wasn't her favorite, but lower calorie than most other drinks and she was conscious of everything she put in her mouth right now. She burned a ridiculous number of calories everyday, but she needed to be at the top of her game, which meant paying attention to every detail.

"Dani?"

She turned her head, realizing Aaron had been talking to her. "Sorry, what did you say?"

"I asked if you were having fun?"

"Just thinking about the time and not staying out too late."

"No worries. I figured we'd stay an hour and then head out."

"Thank you."

He reached out to brush his knuckles across her cheek. "You're a great girl. I hope Sergei figures that out before someone snatches you out from under him."

She blushed but nodded her head. "Me, too."

29

The next few days were busy and Dani had forgotten about her "date" with Aaron the moment she'd gotten home the other night. Especially since she'd finally gotten her period, eliminating all thought of being pregnant. Though she was relieved professionally, there was a small part of her that was disappointed too. Having Sergei's baby would be wonderful. She wanted to. She'd always assumed she would have children one day, but not right now, so it was definitely for the best. If only it didn't eliminate her last glimmer of hope that things would work out with Sergei. Her gut told her it was over, no matter how open-ended they'd left things.

Distracting her from her woes was her upcoming trip to Las Vegas. She was anxious to see Zakk, Tiff and the others. It would be quick, but she always felt better when she was near her brother and his family, as well as good friends like Toli and Tessa. It wouldn't heal a broken heart, but it definitely wouldn't hurt either.

She was packing for the trip when her phone buzzed. Seeing it was a text from Aaron, she opened the program and stared at a picture of the two of them from the night at the club. Though she distinctly remembered the moment he'd touched her face, the picture didn't resemble anything like what had really happened. It looked intimate. He was staring down at her with a serious look on his face. If you didn't know what they'd been talking about, it could appear loving, romantic. And she was staring up at him adoringly. Except she'd been thinking of Sergei in that moment, not him, but there was no way to prove it.

Damn, did we really look all cozy like that?
Oh yeah.
Where did you find this?

*Instagram. Someone who was at the club took it and posted it. Eventually I got
tagged, even though no one knows who you are. Except Sergei.*

Did you hear from him?

Oh yeah.

AND?!

He's...unhappy? Can I call you?

Sure.

She picked up when her phone rang. "What did he say?" she asked as soon
as she answered.

"He asked me, and I quote, 'What the fuck were you doing with my girl?' I
told him I took you out to dinner and dancing because you were a little down
after your boyfriend dumped you."

She almost choked. "Aaron! What did he say?"

"He got real quiet and muttered something in Russian. Then he told me to
stay away from you and hung up."

"He hung up on you? Have you talked to him since?"

"Nah, this was about five minutes ago. I texted you right away in case he
called."

"And there's the beep." She sighed.

"You got this, babe," he said quickly. "Play a little hard to get, okay? Make
him work for it."

"Thanks." She disconnected from him and answered her other
line. "Hello?"

"Hey." Sergei's voice was strained.

"How are you?"

"Worried."

"About me?"

"Aaron's just divorced, probably not a good choice for you. I don't know
that you should get involved with him."

She laughed. She couldn't help it. "Did you call to tell me who I can date?"

"No?" He huffed out a breath. "Babe, I care about you and—"

"Aaron and I are friends," she said softly, unwilling to play games with him
despite how much being without him hurt. "He took me out because he said I
needed cheering up, but he's your friend, Sergei. You really think he'd do
something inappropriate with me? Don't you remember what he and Jake did
the night we were at dinner? And the stripper? Aaron's a prankster and you
keep falling for it."

There was a long silence. "Did he doctor that picture where he's touching
your face?"

"No. It was an intimate moment between...*friends*. He was telling me
everything was going to be okay, the things you tell a friend who has feelings
for someone who doesn't return them."

"I'm sorry if that's my fault."

"If? God, you're a pain in my ass. Look, I have to finish packing; we leave for Vegas in the morning. If you're done telling me how to live my life, I have to go."

"All right. Take care of yourself, babe."

"You, too." She disconnected and stared at the phone sadly. Nope, their big plan to make him jealous hadn't worked. He'd been jealous, but not in a good way. He didn't want anyone else to have her, but he didn't want her himself, and that was a big problem.

DANI and the team got to Las Vegas before lunch and checked into their hotel. They had a practice planned with the Sidewinders at three o'clock and Dani couldn't wait to hug her brother. She didn't care what anyone thought or how unprofessional it might be, she desperately needed to bask in the comfort of her brother's strong arms and broad shoulders.

As soon as they got into the arena, she broke away from the team and ran for the locker room, hoping beyond hope Zakk would be there. Luckily, he looked up as she peeked through the doorway and a smile creased his face.

"Hey!" He called out, getting to his feet.

Dani ran across the room and vaulted herself into his chest.

"Hey." He hugged her tightly. "Are you okay?"

"I will be." She closed her eyes and breathed in his scent, even though he was already sweaty.

"Dan?" He used an old nickname as he looked down into her face. "What's wrong?"

Several of the Sidewinders were nearby and she shook her head slightly. "I'm fine. I just needed a hug. I'll see you after practice, okay?"

His eyes reflected his doubt but he wouldn't embarrass her in front of the team. "Of course. Tiff and the kids can't wait to see you."

"Will they be at the exhibition game tomorrow?"

He snorted. "Like I could keep them away?"

"I have to go. See you later?"

"Of course."

She hurried out to find her team, already feeling better. Nothing had changed but a hug from her big brother always made things seem better anyway.

IN THE MORNING, Dani was able to sneak away to have breakfast with Tiff. She loved her hopefully-soon-to-be sister-in-law and was glad they were close enough to talk about anything and everything, including her pregnancy scare and the sinking feeling that she'd lost Sergei.

"You look pale," Tiff said as they sat at the table.

"I don't get outside much."

"I'd be willing to bet there's more to it than that."

"If you're talking about Sergei, you're not wrong."

"Is it over?"

"I think so. He barely calls or texts. We, um, we had a pregnancy scare but it turns out I'm not and I think after I sent him the negative test results he took that as his cue to back off."

"How did he handle the pregnancy news? Before it was negative."

"He told me to keep him informed, that I shouldn't deal with it on my own, but I mean, what else was he going to say? Our brothers are best friends."

"I think there's more to it than that."

"He's stubborn, determined to believe he's not worthy of another chance at love. Until he's ready to let go of that, he's not going to change his mind. I'm going to have to pull up my big girl panties and get over him."

"Do you love him, Dani?"

"Yes. The big jerk." She rested her chin in her hands.

"Did he see the picture of you and Aaron?"

Dani's head snapped up. "How did you know about that?"

Tiff laughed. "The NHL wives network is better than the CIA—never forget that. Kate saw it on Instagram and showed me. We all knew within a few hours."

"No one said anything."

"We were all hoping you were over Sergei. Except Toli. He really wants you to be his new sister-in-law."

Dani smiled at that. "I'd like that, too, but I don't think so. Sergei doesn't think he'll ever fall in love again."

"He's foolish. He already is."

"Yeah, try telling him that."

"I just might." Tiff pursed her lips purposefully.

THE EXHIBITION GAME between the Las Vegas Sidewinders and the U.S. Women's Olympic Hockey team was televised and Sergei, Sara, Aaron, and Jake sat in front of the TV in Sergei's family room to watch. Niko had been allowed to stay up to watch the beginning, and he was bouncing on Sergei's knee as the game started.

"What number is Mommy?" he was asking.

Sergei's gut tightened every time Niko referred to Dani as his mommy, but there was no sign of him stopping, no matter how many times they'd gently tried to redirect him.

"She's number 88," Sara said quietly, not looking at Sergei.

"She is?" Sergei frowned, his stomach dropping. "She's always worn 61, just like Zakk."

"For some dumb reason, she opted to change for the Olympics," Sara murmured, still not looking at him.

"That's Daddy's number," Niko chirped up. "Mommy and Daddy have the same number."

"Buddy, didn't we agree that Dani is Mama D, not Mommy?"

Niko scowled, his blue eyes darkening. "*Nyet.*"

It was never good when Niko reverted to Russian.

"And she scores." Aaron let out a whoop as Dani put the puck in the net behind the team's goalie prospect, who was in net instead of their starting goalies.

"Yay!" Niko wiggled off Sergei's lap and did a dance around the room, shaking his butt in time to the music on the TV.

That's my girl, Sergei thought, even though he had no right to. That she was wearing his number had startled him. She'd worn the same number as Zakk all through high school and college; he'd never dreamed she would change for the Olympics. While it made him happy on one hand, it bothered him on another because it meant she wasn't moving on. Toli had seen her last night and said she was pale and far too thin for someone as athletic as she was. Sergei had lost a few pounds himself and while he'd told himself it was because of the rigorous training schedule during training camp, it was actually because he wasn't eating or sleeping as well as he should have been. Which meant she probably wasn't either and he regretted being responsible for it.

He turned back to the game and tried to focus.

"That number 42 is fast," Aaron commented.

"That's Hailey Dobson, Dani's roommate," Sara said. "She's great. Dani likes her."

"She hot?" Aaron asked, taking out his phone and searching for her on the internet.

"You in heat or what?" Jake laughed.

"It's been a while," Aaron protested. "And the puck bunnies around here are scary."

"I'm pretty sure you won't be getting any from a woman who lives in Colorado," Sara pointed out.

He scowled at her. "Thanks a lot."

"Hey, the prospects are pretty slim for me, too," she protested. "It's not like I'm getting any."

"I'm sure any number of the single guys on the team would be interested in hooking up," Jake chuckled.

She made a face. "Nah, I'm not going to get a reputation as the team's Naughty Nanny or some such bullshit. I didn't do it in Vegas and I'm sure as hell not going to do it here. Girl has to have some pride, you know?"

"Same for guys," Aaron sighed. "Hence why it's been a while."

"I'm certainly not gettin' any," Jake muttered.

Everyone turned to Sergei, who scowled. "Of course not. I don't have time for that kind of shit."

"But you saw Veronika," Sara said quietly.

Silence fell over the room, despite the blaring of the TV.

"I saw her," Sergei said tightly, "but I didn't take her out or sleep with her."

"Isn't she going out with Matt?" Jake asked.

"Apparently he kicked her to the curb and so she showed up here the other day. We sat outside and talked for a while, but I set her straight and sent her home. That's not happening."

"That's not what she thinks."

He frowned. "What do you mean?"

Sara handed him her phone, open to the Instagram page of NikaV. There was a photograph of Sergei's back yard with her feet, in high-heeled sandals, at the bottom of the image, captioned as "Chillin' with @SergeiPetrov88." It was followed by "#PerfectSummerDay."

"You have got to be kidding me," he groaned. "We talked. That's it."

"You better hope Dani hasn't seen this."

"You didn't show her?"

"She's had enough to worry about the last week, and she didn't need anything else."

Sergei wanted to ask what Dani had been worried about, and it occurred to him she'd never updated him about her period. Had she gotten it? Had she gone to a doctor? Were there any more pregnancy test results? He was such an asshole for not following up. Damn, he needed to talk to her, despite his desire to let her go. He kept trying to convince himself he'd done the right thing in telling her he wasn't capable of loving her, but he found reasons to doubt himself almost every day, and it was getting old.

Ten days, he told himself patiently. He'd see her in ten days in Colorado.

30

The team had been busy from the moment they arrived in Denver until they got to the arena, and Dani was chomping at the bit to see Sergei. He hadn't texted or called, so she didn't even know if he was aware she would be there. The team was probably warming up and she took off in that direction, anxious to get to ice level to watch, let him know she was here. Hailey was hot on her heels and they got right up to the glass, grinning as the players skated by.

"Where is he?" Hailey whispered.

"Not sure," Dani whispered back. "He's...there." She motioned with her head and Hailey followed her gaze.

"Damn, he's even hotter in person."

"I know." Dani's hands were a little damp as she waited for Sergei to notice her. It was ridiculous to be so nervous after all they'd been through, but she'd be a wreck until he acknowledged her. Finally, not long before the warm-up period ended, she caught his eye. He froze and for a long moment they stood still, eyes locked, as if there was nothing but the two of them. A strange look crossed his face but it quickly morphed into a smile as he skated towards the glass.

"Hi," he mouthed.

"Hi."

"See you later?" His blue eyes met hers almost hesitantly.

She nodded and he winked at Hailey before skating off.

Hailey giggled. "He winked at me."

"He's cute that way." Dani watched him moving across the ice and made sure she didn't let her little internal sigh of appreciation escape.

"Who's that?" Hailey asked, motioning towards a dark-haired man skating without his helmet.

Dani grinned. "That's Kane Hatcher."

"Hattrick Hatcher?" Hailey's eyes rounded. "I had no idea he was so hot. Wow…he's downright smoldering."

"I guess I never noticed." Dani frowned as she watched him, trying to pay more attention now that Hailey had said something.

"You've got it bad, girlfriend."

"I do. Kane's nice, though. We met at a party on July Fourth and we talked hockey for a while. I didn't really notice how good-looking he was, with Sergei sitting there with his hand up my dress."

"I probably wouldn't notice anyone else if Sergei had his hand up my dress."

They watched for a little while longer before walking back up to the concourse to find the rest of the team and join them in being announced before the game started. They'd been told they would be introduced on the ice, so everyone was excited and Dani lost herself in the moment, forgetting about Sergei and everything except the music, the sound of the crowd, the magic of it all. The teams from both Colorado and Alaska were on the ice when each member of the U.S. Women's Olympic team was introduced, tapping their sticks against the ice in acknowledgement of who they were and what they did.

Dani grinned at Aaron when he held out his hand for a fist bump as she skated past, and the rest of the Blizzard followed suit.

"You're such a show-off," Coach Saunders whispered when she came off the ice.

"I didn't know he was going to do that," she laughed.

"If your eyes shone this bright every day, you'd probably win that gold all by yourself."

THE GAME WENT into overtime and Colorado pulled it out with a goal Aaron never had a chance in stopping, but at least Alaska got a point since an overtime loss wasn't quite as bad as a regulation loss. The rest of the team was frustrated at starting the new season with a loss of any kind, but Sergei wasn't thinking about anything except Dani. He'd texted her and she was meeting him at the hotel bar in thirty minutes; he didn't know what else to do. He hadn't known what he was going to say or do when they saw each other tonight, but if he was going to truly end things, he needed to do it in person. He owed her that much even though it was going to be the hardest thing he'd ever done.

He saw her the moment she stepped into the bar and got to his feet to greet her. To his surprise she closed the space between them in four long steps, throwing her arms around him and resting her head on his shoulder.

"Sergei." She said his name as if it were part of her, as if it brought her some sort of pleasure to say it, and he loved the way it sounded.

"Hi." Damn, it felt good to hold her and he temporarily forgot all about breaking up, saying goodbye, all of it.

"I missed you."

"I missed you, too." Was she thinner? He held her tighter and thought she'd lost weight, but she'd been thin before so he wasn't sure.

She slowly pulled away, her eyes on his. "Did you want to stay here or go up to your room? I didn't know if you were allowed to be out this late?"

"I'm okay for now. Let's get a drink."

"Okay."

They ordered drinks and took them to a small table in the back, affording them a modicum of privacy. Sergei wasn't even sure how to approach what he'd wanted to say, but he had to. When she'd been introduced as part of the U.S. Olympic team before the game tonight his heart had nearly burst from his chest with pride. She was following a dream, doing what she was meant to do, and he absolutely refused to get in the way of that. It would also be true of the job waiting for her with the Sidewinders. She was smart, educated and talented, but getting a job as an Assistant Trainer for an NHL team wasn't easy, especially for a woman. If she gave it up, that chance might never come again, and he refused to be the reason she didn't take it. No, even though it was tearing his heart out, he had to do what was best for her, not what he wanted.

"You look like there's a lot on your mind," she said softly, reaching for his hand.

He squeezed her fingers, wanting desperately to hold on to her warmth as long as possible. "There is." He had at least a thousand things he wanted to tell her, but none of them would make the end result any more palatable.

"Just say it, Sergei." She slowly pulled her hand away and rested it in her lap, though her eyes never left his. "I have a feeling I know what's coming, so don't delay the inevitable."

"It's time, honey," he said. "Time for us to let this go. For you to go do all the things you were meant to do without being tied to a guy in Alaska."

"Even if that's what I want?"

"I can't promise you a future, and you deserve so much better."

"You keep saying that, but what could possibly be better than what we had all summer?" she protested. "We were happy. We had fun. We had incredible sex. I love your son... What else is there?"

"Dani, sweetheart, you're beautiful and caring, everything a guy could ever want, and when we're together, everything is stupidly easy. The thing is, if I'm being honest, I don't know if I'll ever be ready to marry you, to give you the love you've given me. Just thinking about getting married again makes me uncomfortable and I want you to have everything you want. I couldn't bear to see you become a trainer at some gym instead of working for a hockey team, doing what you love, and I won't let you give that up for a guy who isn't even willing to try."

"You're not willing to try what?" she asked in a soft whisper.

"Marriage, the happily-ever-after I know you want. It scares me. I've shouldered that responsibility twice before and let down two good, loving women. It's shown me that I don't defend the things I love—I corrupt and eventually lose them. I love you enough to not want that for you."

"And that's your final answer? Your decision is made?"

"I'm sorry." He was the world's biggest asshole; he saw the unspoken sentiment in her eyes.

"Are you?"

"More than you know."

"If that was true, you wouldn't be doing this."

"Someday you'll see I was right. I should have done this in Vegas, because leaving you hanging was wrong of me. It's not fair to have one foot in, one foot out, like a relationship is some kind of hokey-pokey dance with your feelings."

Dani didn't say anything, her big green eyes merely focused on his, something so inscrutable in them he wanted to throw his arms around her and tell her how he really felt. Anything to make that look disappear. He couldn't, but he wanted to.

"Is that it?" she asked after a while. "Is that all you have to say?"

He wanted to laugh, because there was so much more he had to say, but none of it would help. Nothing would make this any easier. "I never meant to hurt you. I hope you know that."

"Is that what you're telling yourself to make yourself feel better?" She dug in her purse and put a five-dollar bill on the table. "That's for my beer. I have to go."

He opened his mouth to protest, but that would only add insult to injury. She was hurt and angry, and he wouldn't minimize her feelings by trying to act like the big man over five bucks.

"How are you getting back to your hotel?"

"Cab."

"Let me—"

"No." She got to her feet. "I'm perfectly capable of getting a cab on my own."

"I know." He stood too, frowning slightly as she turned away. "Dani."

"Yes?" She stopped moving but didn't turn around.

"I hope you know our time together was special to me." He needed to stop talking, to let her go and get this over with, but it was harder than he'd anticipated.

"It was special to me too."

"You're too important to me to be my on-again, off-again hook-up. You mean more to me than that." He needed to stop talking, but he didn't want her to feel used. God, he was an idiot and mucking things up more than he'd ever thought possible.

"Good to know." She finally turned, her green eyes finding his in the dimly lit room. "Take care of yourself, Sergei. I hope you find whatever it is you're looking for."

There was no way to respond to that, so he didn't, subconsciously reaching out to gently push a lock of hair out of her face. Their eyes locked and he saw a shimmer of tears brimming in her eyes. It was time to let her leave, before he did something selfish, something that would ultimately hurt her much more than what he'd done tonight.

"I'm truly sorry, sweetheart," he managed to choke out.

"I know." She turned and walked out of the bar.

He watched her disappear out the front doors of the hotel and then sank back into his chair.

"Was that Dani getting into a cab?" Aaron asked as he, Jake and Kane came into the bar.

"Yeah." Sergei cleared his throat. "You guys wanna have a drink?"

"Absolutely." Aaron clapped a hand on his shoulder. "You okay?"

"Yeah." Sergei managed a smile. "I just told her it was best if we didn't see each other anymore. You know, with the Olympics and all, it's better all around."

Jake raised his eyebrows but didn't say anything.

"Oh, this is going to be a long night," Kane chuckled, raising his hand to get the bartender's attention.

"Tequila or whiskey?" Aaron asked Sergei. "You're the dumb-ass who let the best thing that ever happened to you go, so you get to pick."

Sergei scowled. "Jack Daniel's. Straight up."

"Make that four," Aaron told the bartender.

"Probably should make it eight," Jake added.

"You want to talk or just drink?" Kane asked.

"Jesus fuck," Sergei muttered. "What the hell makes you think I want to talk? Unless it's about hockey or Jake's latest marriage counseling session, drinking is the only thing on my mind right now."

"Drinking it is." Jake raised his glass and the others clinked theirs against it.

31

The rest of the trip was a blur for Dani, but she put Sergei out of her mind and focused entirely on herself and the Olympic team. When they got back to Colorado Springs she threw herself into hockey, working harder than ever before. She turned to meditation and melatonin to help her sleep at night, and though it got better, she still didn't sleep as well as she should. She was doing the best she could and everyone close to her respected her request that they not discuss Sergei at all. Instead, she lived and breathed hockey. Once in a while, late at night, she'd allow herself a few minutes of self-pity, to miss and yearn and ache for him, but then she would fall asleep and by morning she was on track again. At least she thought so.

"How long are you going to keep this up?" Hailey asked her as they got ready for practice one morning a few weeks later.

"Keep what up?" Dani asked without glancing up.

"Pretending your heart isn't broken. Pretending you sleep at night. Pretending you're okay."

Dani shrugged. "Until I literally can't. There's nothing I can do about a broken heart, so what's the point of wallowing in it? I loved him and he didn't love me back. Happens every day. At least I've got hockey, good friends and a supportive family. In time, I won't even think about him anymore."

Hailey's blue eyes darkened. "If you truly love him, it won't be that easy."

"It's not easy. That's why I don't sleep well and stay busy from the minute I get up until I collapse at night. Anything else and I might fall apart."

"Have you talked to him at all?"

"No. Just to Niko."

"What does Sara say?"

"She said he's been pretty quiet but he's not home that much. He's not spending a lot of time with Niko, either, so she's frustrated, but when she said something to him, he just doubled her next paycheck. She tried to give it back and he said it was the equivalent of combat pay, that he knew he was a pain in the ass right now and she'd earned it. She actually used a little of it to pay for a babysitter so she could have some time to herself because his travel schedule is brutal."

"Yeah, their schedule is nuts."

"Well, not my problem. I feel bad for Sara but she said she won't leave Niko until they find someone she likes because he's interviewed a few more nannies and they all suck. Her words, not mine."

"Has your sister-in-law or anyone said—"

Dani held up a hand. "Hailey, please. I truly don't want to talk about Sergei. It just breaks my heart all over again."

Hailey sighed. "I know, hon, but you're a mess. I mean, look in the mirror. Those dark circles under your eyes are noticeable, especially at practice when you're hot and sweaty. Everyone's wondering if you're okay."

"I'm fine." Dani took a deep breath and looked up. "Please nip any gossip in the bud. That's not going to make him love me and it's definitely not going to help us win a gold medal in Seattle. Can you do that for me?"

"I can try, but no one can miss how tired and sad you look."

Dani groaned. She didn't know what to do about that.

SEVENTEEN DAYS. Sergei had never been on a seventeen-day road trip before and it sucked. He was exhausted, jet-lagged and grumpy, with a three-year-old who wouldn't stop talking, a nanny who was annoyed with him, and a heart so filled with anger he didn't know how in holy hell he was going to keep this up. It wasn't so bad on the road because hockey took up a lot of his time, but as soon as he got home, reality came crashing back and it sucked.

"But where's my present?" Niko was demanding, tugging at his leg. "You promised, Daddy!"

"Let's eat some pancakes first," Sara said, trying to redirect him because she was now accustomed to Sergei's dark moods and did her best to keep Niko from being subjected to them. He definitely didn't pay her enough for all she'd done in the last six weeks or so.

"I hate pancakes," Niko fussed, frowning and giving her stink eye. "They're not good like Mommy's!"

Sara sighed. "This is Mommy's recipe and they're exactly the same, Niko. She taught me how to make them just for you."

"*Nyet.*" He stuck out his lower lip. "I hate pancakes and I hate you and I hate Daddy, too!" He stormed out of the room and Sara sighed.

Sergei glanced at her. "How long has he been having tantrums like this?"

"A few weeks. He picks up on your mood and because he's a toddler, it escalates."

"Damn, I'm sorry, Sara."

"It's okay. He doesn't do this often, but right now he wants your attention and you're not giving it to him so he's acting out. I'll talk him down."

"Thank you. I know it should be me..." He ran a tired hand down his face. "I'm exhausted and today is my only day off. We've got games every other night for the next two weeks and then we'll be on the road. Again. Does anyone even come to Alaska?"

"But then you'll be going to Vegas for Thanksgiving."

He nodded. "That's about the only bright spot in this, seeing my family over the holiday weekend. Are you sure you're okay flying alone with him?"

She smiled. "Of course. Thank you for sending us early so I can spend time with everyone." She didn't mention Dani's name; that never went well.

"Tell Niko if he behaves for you today, I'll take him skating later."

"Sure." She put a comforting hand on his shoulder as she left the room.

Damn, he was being an asshole. Taking out his dark mood on his toddler and the nanny wasn't like him but he couldn't seem to snap out of it. The simple truth was he missed Dani. Her bright eyes and gentle laughter had been what made this house a home, and though Sara did everything he asked of her, she would never replace the woman he loved. Not even on a day-to-day level that only included taking care of Niko and making sure there was food in the kitchen. He still reached for Dani in the middle of the night, picked up the phone to text her about something, bought her gifts he was never going to give her. Yet he couldn't stop. Her words, the loving things she'd said to him, played on repeat in his head.

Maybe I don't see you as broken because when you're with me, you're not.

He had a woman who accepted him just the way he was and had given herself to him completely. Physically, emotionally and sexually. He'd been her first everything. Boyfriend, lover, soul mate. Just thinking about the night he'd taken her virginity got him so hard he nearly had to find a quiet place to relieve the pressure between his legs. His sweet, innocent virgin loved sex and his kid and even Alaska. What the hell was wrong with him? Why was he torturing both of them?

Because it's better for her, he thought with a grimace.

Maybe I don't see you as broken because when you're with me, you're not.

With a growl of frustration, he stomped up to his room and slammed the door.

THE ONE GOOD thing that had come out of his breakup with Dani was his newfound friendship with Jake, Aaron and Kane. The four of them were single, now that Jake and Adrianna were in the midst of a trial separation, and spent most of their days off together. It was nice to have camaraderie on a team again; Sergei had missed it. Though he, Jake and Aaron were struggling, Kane loved the single life. He was younger than the others, though, just twenty-six to Jake and Aaron's thirty and Sergei's thirty-three. He'd had a girlfriend but she hadn't wanted to move to Alaska, so they'd gone their separate ways.

None of them had tried much dating yet, though. While Alaska had a reputation for having far more men than women, the ratio wasn't as extreme as they'd initially thought. Sergei had gone online and found a government site stating that there were approximately 111 men for every 100 women in Anchorage, which wasn't that big of a difference. So the dating pool existed, it just wasn't all that interesting. For him it was because of Dani. Jake was technically still married and unsure what he was going to do so dating wasn't an option yet. Aaron just seemed incredibly picky now that he'd finalized his divorce, and Kane said there were plenty of puck bunnies on the road—he didn't want to shit where he slept. Which left them together most of the time.

"That blonde in Chicago was smokin'," Kane teased Aaron one night as they hung out at a sports bar.

Aaron grinned. "It had been too long—I caved to peer pressure and the delightful shade of blue my balls had turned."

The others laughed. "I don't know what color mine are at this point," Sergei grumbled.

"You did that to yourself, my friend," Aaron said.

"Not true. Even if we hadn't broken up, she'd still be in Colorado and I'd be here, with my balls woefully blue."

Jake grimaced. "He has a point."

"You still fucked up. She's special."

Sergei made a face. "I'm aware. That's why I let her go. She deserves better than me."

"That's a pansy-ass excuse if I ever heard one." Kane shook his head. "I mean, she's gorgeous, smart, athletic and loves hockey. I'd fucking kill to meet a woman that looked like her and loves hockey. Other women don't get it. They don't get what we do, how we do it, what it takes... You found the perfect one and let her go."

"You should ask Dani out," Aaron said, deadpan. "I talked to her the other day and she said she's going out on a date Friday night, so she's ready to move on."

Sergei made a sound that was a cross between a growl and a clap of thunder, and Jake had to hang his head to hide his laughter.

"Too bad she's so far away," Kane said.

"You guys think you're funny," Sergei muttered.

"And you fall for it every time," Aaron chuckled before sobering. "But I did talk to her the other day."

Sergei tried to act nonchalant, as if he wasn't interested, so Kane spoke up instead. "Is she really going out on a date Friday?"

Aaron shrugged. "That's what she told me. Guy named Lane. Works as some kind of trainer on the men's team, and that's what she plans to do in the future, so it sounds like they have a lot in common."

"You found it necessary to tell me this?" Sergei asked, his eyes darkening.

"I find it necessary to point out you've made a huge mistake," Aaron corrected. "You love her. I don't give a fuck how much you deny it."

"I never denied it," Sergei said quietly. "That's the whole point. I'm a fucked-up hot mess and she deserves better. I love her enough to know she's better off with someone else."

"But she loves *you*."

"Jesus, is that what we're talking about tonight? I'm tired, horny and have a really cranky kid who cries for his mommy every night. If I wanted aggravation, I could stay home."

"Fine," Aaron waved an impatient hand. "I'll let it go for tonight, but if she has fun Friday night, you're going to be sorry."

Sergei was about to change the subject but then cut his eyes to Aaron. "Wait, do you talk to her often?"

"Well, yeah. We're friends. Is that not allowed?"

"Does she ask about me?"

"Actually, no. Sometimes I mention you and she asks me not to, says it hurts too much."

"Ouch," Kane grimaced.

"However," Aaron cut his eyes to Kane. "She did say her friend Hailey Dobson thinks you're the bee's knees."

"Me?" Kane looked startled.

"Rumor has it she was checking you out during warm-ups in Colorado and told Dani you were the hottest guy on the team."

Kane laughed. "I don't know about all that, but is she cute?"

"Super cute." Aaron got out his phone and pulled up a picture of Hailey and Dani taken a few nights ago.

"Why is Dani sending you pictures?" Sergei asked, trying to mask his annoyance but failing miserably.

"Because she wanted me to show Kane the picture of Hailey."

The two men glared at each other but Sergei turned away first.

"Oh, she's definitely cute," Kane nodded. "How old?"

"Twenty-four." Aaron apparently had been prepped with information. "She was going to go to law school but took a year off for the Olympics."

"Nice." Kane had pulled out his own phone and was looking her up online.

"She meets your hockey criteria," Jake pointed out.

"And looks," Aaron added.

"Brains too," Sergei said. "Although I don't know if that's a selling point for you."

Kane glanced up. "With a girl I'm going to get serious with? Of course."

"Well, now you just have to meet her and convince her you're not a douche canoe," Jake laughed.

"Maybe after the Olympics," Kane said, motioning to the waitress. "In the meantime, enough talk about women. Jesus, I feel the estrogen practically seeping into my skin."

32

Dani got to Las Vegas in the early evening the day before Thanksgiving. They'd had a final practice this morning and then she'd had to rush to finish packing and get to the airport, only to find her flight had been delayed. It had been a long day and she was tired, but looking forward to seeing Sara, Niko, and her family. Sara and Niko had arrived several hours ago and were getting settled at Toli's house, and Dani's parents had arrived yesterday. Sergei was coming in tomorrow, she'd heard. Not that she cared. Well, she cared in the sense she hoped to avoid him, but she felt bad too. Zakk and Tiff were having a separate, private Thanksgiving, just for family and Sara, while Toli and Tessa were hosting the big Sidewinders dinner that included Sergei, Vlad, and all the players whose families were too far away to get home since they only had two days off. She hated being the reason they weren't all together, and Zakk swore that wasn't it, but she knew better. Toli and Zakk were as close as Toli was to his actual brothers; there was no other scenario that would have them spending Thanksgiving apart.

She let out a squeal when she saw Sara waiting for her just outside of baggage claim and ran to hug her.

"It's so good to see you!"

"You, too!" Sara stepped back and looked into her friend's face but Dani held up a finger, stopping her from saying anything.

"Don't. I already know. I look tired. Blah blah fucking blah. I'm fine."

"You keep saying that, maybe you'll actually believe it," Sara chortled, taking her arm as they walked. "The rest of us, however, don't buy it for a second."

"Is Sergei here yet?"

"No, not until morning."

"I don't think I can handle seeing him," Dani whispered as they walked. "I'm good as long as I'm busy and don't think about him, but any reminder sends me over the edge."

"I know, honey. I'll come over as soon as I wake up in the morning and stay with you as much as I can so you don't have to be alone if we run into him. But he'll be there for Thanksgiving."

"I know." Dani got her suitcase and they walked out to the parking garage.

"Niko asks about you constantly, so you might want to stop by and see him before he goes to bed."

"Of course. I miss him."

They talked about hockey and Sara's only class this semester for her master's until they got home. Dani opted to see Niko first, since he should have been in bed already and the rest of her family could wait a few extra minutes.

"Mommy!" His voice echoed through the house as he launched himself at her and she squeezed her eyes shut to stop the tears as she hugged him. She adored this child, despite his stubborn father, and held him against her so he wouldn't see the tears.

"Daddy teached me how to skate backwards," he announced proudly.

"I know, Auntie Sara told me. I can't wait to see."

"Is your hockey finished, Mommy? Can you come home now?"

"Not yet, Pumpkin." She really hated lying to him, but she'd leave it to his father to explain she wasn't coming back.

"Daddy comes home tomorrow. How many hours until tomorrow? Do I have to go to bed? Will you read me the pigeon with the hot dog story? And tomorrow can we have pancakes? I want the ones with the rasping berries in them, okay? 'Cause—"

"It's bedtime, little man," she interrupted with a soft laugh. "Yes, we can have raspberry pancakes tomorrow, but you have to go to bed right now and ask Auntie Sara to bring you across the street to Uncle Zakk's house so I can make them, okay?"

"But you have to read me a story?" His eyes filled with tears. "Please, Mommy? You've been gone for so long."

She blinked rapidly so she wouldn't start crying again. "Okay. One story. Let's go." She didn't look at anyone as she followed Niko up the stairs. There was way too much raw emotion on her face and she didn't want anyone to see it. She hadn't counted on it being this hard to see Niko and hear him call her *Mommy*. She'd asked Sara about that and she'd said that no matter how many times they tried to get him to call her *Mama D* again, he simply ignored them, often responding with his most insolent *Nyet*.

As promised, Dani made breakfast for Niko and the rest of the family. He and Sara walked over when they got up and Dani was just pouring the first round onto the griddle. The twins loved her pancakes, too, though they preferred them without raspberries, so she had two separate batches. Her mother was making bacon and Tiff was cutting up fruit. Niko talked nonstop, insisting he sit next to Dani and even helping her load the dishwasher when they were finished since he refused to be away from her. Sara was trying to get him to go back over to Toli's to wait for his father when the door opened and Toli came in. With Sergei right behind him.

"Daddy!"

Niko raced into his father's arms and Dani was frozen in place, unable to turn away though her heart screamed in agony at Sergei's presence.

Everyone exchanged casual greetings and Dani was about to go upstairs to her room when Sergei approached her.

"Hey."

"Hi." She didn't dare look into his eyes for fear of losing her breakfast.

"How are you?"

"I'm good. How about you?" This was the phoniest conversation ever.

"Doing well."

"Daddy, aren't you going to grown-up kiss Mommy?" Niko demanded, tugging at his father's jeans.

"Buddy, we don't have to kiss—"

"You said it's how grown-ups kiss!"

Sergei sighed but leaned over and pressed a chaste kiss on Dani's cheek. "Okay?"

"Yay!" Niko's eyes twinkled and Dani had to smile at his innocence.

"Sorry," Sergei murmured as Niko ran off to go play.

"It's okay." Dani turned to go upstairs.

"I hope it's okay we're both here," he said before she could get away.

"We share family, so it's not the first nor will it be the last time, but I don't mind at all. It gives me time with Niko."

"He misses you."

"He'll get past it once you start dating someone."

"I don't have any plans for that," he said.

"Eventually you will. Anyway, see you later." She took the stairs two at a time and firmly shut her bedroom door behind her.

DESPITE THE SEPARATE FAMILY DINNERS, there was no way to truly stay apart because everyone was in and out of each other's houses day and night. The matchmaking going on would have been comical had it not been for how uncomfortable it made Dani. Every time Sergei turned around, somehow the only empty seat in the vicinity was the one next to Dani. Even when she was surrounded by children, which seemed to happen a lot, he somehow wound up next to her. Which wasn't a bad thing for him, but it made her noticeably unhappy. He wanted to comfort her, tell her it was okay, but it wasn't. Nothing that had happened was okay. Though no one said or did anything overt, he was acutely aware that Zakk and the entire Cloutier clan was a little colder than when he'd seen them in August. Toli and Vlad were okay, of course, but Tessa and Rachel seemed almost painfully polite. He'd mucked up everything with Dani and now his son was miserable, part of his family was upset with him and even his brothers thought he was an idiot. Did no one understand he'd done this for *her*? So she would have a better future than anything he could offer her?

Just one more day, he thought wearily. It was evening now and the women had all gone shopping for the big Black Friday sales that now apparently started on Thanksgiving, so if he managed to get through tomorrow without any incidents, he would be on a plane to the East Coast on Saturday for another long road trip. Since Alaska was so far away, management let them fly solo to away games if they were either just before or just after a holiday. They also had a couple of extra days off around Christmas, even though it meant a busier schedule starting in the new year. The logistics of having a team in Alaska were daunting, but they made allowances to make it easier for both the players and their families.

If he'd been smart, he would have just stayed in Anchorage for Thanksgiving, but that wouldn't have been any fun for Sara and Niko, and if he was being honest with himself, he'd jump at any chance to see Dani. It was purely self-inflicted torture, probably for both of them, but he couldn't help himself. His need for her had only gotten stronger since they'd been apart, making him wonder how the hell to forget her. It certainly wouldn't be easy with their mutual friends and family so closely intertwined, and he'd come to the conclusion that being selfless wasn't any fun at all. It was time to get back into the puck-bunny game, for his sake as well as hers. If some mindless sex could take his mind off of her, it would keep him from reaching out to her as well. Tomorrow he was going to call a couple of the single guys on the Sidewinders to go looking for some female companionship. If he didn't, he might fall to his knees and beg Dani to forgive him for being a jerk.

WITH SERGEI out for the evening, Dani spent time at Toli and Tessa's, playing with Niko and the other kids. Being with Niko was a poignant reminder of what she'd lost in Sergei, but breaking up with the father didn't mean she stopped loving his son, so she was enjoying the time with him. It wasn't easy to be around Sergei, though, and she was looking forward to getting back to Colorado. She had another date with Lane planned for next week, but she wasn't looking forward to it. He was nice, good-looking, intelligent and they had a lot in common. He just wasn't Sergei. He'd only kissed her so far and it had been so underwhelming she had zero desire to try again, much less do anything else. They were going to the movies next weekend, though, and she'd promised herself she wouldn't cancel.

"Mommy, when are you coming home?" Niko was asking as she tucked him into bed.

"I don't know, Pumpkin." She smoothed his hair back off his forehead and pressed her lips there. "I'm playing hockey for a few more months."

"I want you to read to me every night."

"Doesn't Auntie Sara read to you?"

"Not the same."

"Well, sometimes I'll read to you over the phone, okay? But for now, you have to go to sleep."

"Will you stay until I fall asleep?"

She bit her lip but nodded. "Of course."

SERGEI GOT HOME LATE. He'd had a good time but was a little drunk and a whole lot frustrated. There hadn't been a single woman, anywhere they'd went, that he was even remotely interested in. Not even the blonde willing to blow him in the bathroom. This was a new level of sexual frustration for him and the whole thing was exacerbated by the fact that he'd done this to himself. He'd been the one to let go of Dani, regardless of his reason, so he needed to stop feeling sorry for himself. But the woman who'd stuck her tongue in his ear and her hand down his pants had done nothing for him. It had the opposite effect he'd been hoping for, so he'd had a few more shots and called it a night.

Now he was home and staring at his sweet, sleeping son—and the woman he loved fast asleep beside him, a book face down on her chest. Damn. How had this happened? Sara had told him she wasn't sleeping well, and she had dark circles under her eyes, but he hadn't expected this. She couldn't be comfortable on the edge of the little daybed where Niko slept when he was here, but he didn't want to wake her either. He looked around for a blanket and was going to get one when her eyes opened and she sat up, startled.

"Hey. Sorry." He spoke in a whisper since Alex was asleep in the crib.

Dani slowly got out of bed, covered Niko and slipped from the room.

"You don't have to run off on my account." Sergei was still whispering.

"I have to get home. I didn't mean to fall asleep."

"It's okay. I'm sure Niko loved it."

"I think I read him ten stories," she said, covering a yawn. "Anyway, good night."

"Dani..." He called to her as she got to the top of the stairs.

"Yes?" She half-turned.

"Can't we be friends? I still care for you a great deal and I hate having to tiptoe around each other when we're together like this."

"I'm sorry," she said after a slight hesitation. "It's too soon for me. Maybe someday, but not now. At least not the kind of friends we were before."

"I thought you'd moved on?" he asked, though he shouldn't have.

"Aaron busting your balls again to get you riled up?" She shook her head. "You need to stop falling for his antics, but as far as moving on goes, I've gone out on one date with one guy—I'm *trying* to move on. Unlike you, however, I can't turn my feelings on and off just because someone says it's what's best for me. That's not how emotions work. Good night, Sergei."

She disappeared down the stairs and left him staring after her.

33

The silver lining to long, tedious road trips was that Sergei didn't have to do anything but play hockey. He talked to Niko every night when he could, or in the morning when the time difference was too great, but the only thing he had to think about was hockey. Not the future, not how long it had been since he'd gotten laid, and certainly not about Dani. Time, he thought ruefully, didn't move very fast when you had a broken heart.

The other saving grace to all the travel was that Sergei was finally beginning to feel like he was part of a team. He and Aaron had become extremely close, Jake and Kane joined them whenever possible, and even some of the younger guys were a lot of fun both on and off the ice. They'd won seven in a row as Christmas approached and it felt good to head into the break on a winning streak. It was also nice that he'd been invited to several parties over the holidays. He'd sent Sara home to Minnesota yesterday to spend a few days with her family, and he hadn't been looking forward to spending the holidays alone. Luckily, Jake had invited them to his house for Christmas Eve and he would spend the evening with Jake, Aaron, Kane and a few others he got along with. It had been a good way to get through the holiday and today they were going to Mr. Caldwell's house.

There was no valet parking for this party, and he pulled his SUV into a space behind Aaron's pick-up. He got Niko out of the car, along with the bottle of champagne he'd brought, and they headed inside. Niko had been subdued this morning until he'd gotten to Dani's presents, several board games he'd wanted. Of course, that meant Sergei had to play Candy Land and Hungry Hungry Hippos over and over until it was time to leave for Mr. Caldwell's house. He'd never been so grateful for adult interaction. He adored his son but being a single dad during hockey season was exhausting. Sara was wonderful but she wasn't his mother and Niko wasn't nearly as attached to her as he'd gotten to Dani.

Dani. Just thinking about her made him sad. Sad for Niko, sad for himself, sad all around. He'd hoped after a few months he'd stop thinking about her, but that hadn't happened. Niko talked about her every single day, whether it was to ask where she was or when she was coming home or some other random question that tended to make him grit his teeth in frustration. Nothing had changed for him or their situation, so he'd been trying to get past how much he missed her, but it was like all the forces in his life were working against him. Niko brought her up incessantly. Aaron kept in touch with her and updated Sergei on a regular basis, even when Sergei told him not to. Kane and Hailey had become pen pals, introduced on social media via Dani, so even Kane brought up Dani's name whenever possible. It had gotten to the point where Sergei was beginning to question his decision to let her go. Why were so many people invested in their relationship?

"Merry Christmas, Sergei." Gage shook his hand and got down on his haunches to talk to Niko.

"How's it going, big guy? Did Santa bring you lots of stuff?"

Niko scowled. "He didn't bring me what I wanted."

"He didn't?"

Guilt surged through Sergei as he wracked his brain to remember something Niko had asked for that he may have forgotten to buy.

"I wanted Mommy to come home but she didn't." Niko looked down.

Gage glanced up at Sergei in confusion since he knew Niko's mother was dead.

"Buddy, you know Mama D is playing hockey, right?" Sergei kept his voice soft.

"I'm tired of hockey," Niko announced. "No more hockey for anyone." He kicked at an invisible item on the carpeted floors.

"Marcella." Gage turned to one of the women from the catering company. "Do you think you could take Niko to the kitchen and find something he might want to eat? I think there are snowflake cupcakes that might interest him."

The woman smiled. "Of course, Mr. Caldwell. Come along, Niko. There are quite a few treats in the kitchen no one else has seen yet."

Niko still looked a little sullen, but obediently took her hand and let her lead him away.

"Sorry about that," Sergei murmured. "He's having a rough time since Dani left."

"He calls her...mommy?" Gage looked surprised.

"No matter what I say or do, he refuses to call her anything else."

"I take it she's not coming back?"

"She has a job in Las Vegas after the Olympics, and I can't ask her to give up a chance to work for an NHL team. That's not how you treat someone you care about."

Gage's face momentarily changed, something dark shadowing his eyes, but then it was gone and he nodded slowly. "And what does Dani want?"

"I..." Sergei cleared his throat. "I'm not sure. I think she wants me, both Niko and me, but I can't ask her to give up a career opportunity like that to live here in Anchorage. It's not easy being an NHL wife, and for a woman like her to just sit home and raise a family, well, that seems unfair."

"Did you ask her what she wants?"

"She said she would do it, give up the job in Vegas, but I know she doesn't want to. Being the assistant team trainer over there is huge. She's only twenty-three, so I don't want her to wake up in ten years and hate me."

"A long time ago I let someone special walk away. In retrospect, I would do anything to have her back. It's been nearly ten years since she left and I've never gotten over it, never gotten over *her*."

"Unless you want to trade me to Vegas, I don't know how I can do anything but let her go," Sergei responded, since he wasn't sure what else to say.

"I could speak with Lonnie."

Sergei was startled. "You'd do that?"

"He would have to offer me someone special, but that's how deals are made, my friend. If she's that important to you, let me see what I can do."

"I don't know if she still loves me," Sergei admitted helplessly. "I hurt her."

"Talk to her, Sergei. Find out how she feels and let me know." Gage squeezed his shoulder. "Merry Christmas."

"Merry Christmas, sir." Sergei watched him walk away and stared after him for a minute, trying to wrap his head around what he'd just said. Getting traded to the Sidewinders would be ideal, but he wasn't stupid. Sergei was probably the most well-known player on the Blizzard, so they would look for someone even better to trade for and Vegas had too good of a team to break up their chemistry.

He'd just begun moving towards some of the guys gathered around the fireplace when Matt's voice could be heard above all the others.

"And she fucking walked through the bar naked, got down on her knees and blew me right there in front of everyone. Then the guy next to me at the bar gave me a hundred bucks to get her to blow him and—"

"She blew him and you got the money?" Kane made a face. "That's a dick move. What are you, her pimp?"

"Hey, it's not like she needed convincing. She moved right from me to him and then the guy on his other side too. That girl loves to give head. Right, Sergei?" He turned dark eyes to Sergei in a challenge.

"Not sure who you're talking about," Sergei responded flatly.

"Veronika, man. She's smokin', right?"

Sergei shrugged. "Not my type."

"What, you prefer that muscular blonde who's probably got a dick bigger than yours?"

Everyone froze as Sergei's eyes narrowed and he turned slowly to face Matt.

"What did you say?"

"Come on, she has more muscles than I do, for fuck's sake. Did you actually get to fuck her? I mean, she dated that faggot on the Sidewinders too, so she probably has a dick. Did you check when you—" He wasn't able to finish because Sergei's fist shot out and caught him square in the mouth, sending him sprawling.

"What the fuck?!" Matt roared to his feet, but Kane caught him from behind and Jake stepped between them, putting out his hands to stop Sergei from going around him. "Bring it, Petrov. You think it'll get back to her brother that you defended her dyke ass? I'm not afraid of him either."

Sergei had momentarily seen red, but now he remembered everything he'd heard about Matt and took a step back, motioning to Jake that he was okay. "What's funny about this is that *Dani* doesn't need defending. She's a strong, independent woman who can take care of herself. However, if it gets back to her brother that you've been talking shit about her, you might need someone to defend you." He turned and strode toward the kitchen to find Niko. Matt Forbes wasn't worth his energy, though he would never let anyone talk about her like that, no matter who it was.

He tossed and turned that night. Matt was an idiot, but his words had sparked something in Sergei and it was resonating through his subconscious. He'd defended Dani even though she didn't need him to, and maybe that was the difference in her and the two other women he'd loved in his life. Maria had needed him to defend her because she never stood up for herself, especially not in Russia when the other wives teased and made fun of her because she didn't speak the language or share their traditions. Tatiana needed defending from her father, the mob, and a slew of others who had run roughshod over her, and though Sergei had tried, nothing he'd done had ever been enough. It had exhausted him more than he'd ever wanted to admit.

Maybe what made Dani different was that she didn't need him. She wanted him and loved him—at least he hoped so after how hard he'd tried to push her away—but she was perfectly capable of taking care of herself. Danielle Cloutier didn't need defending... All she needed was love. And love was something he had in spades even though he'd been unwilling to admit it.

When he finally dozed off, he dreamed of Tatiana. Their small, intimate wedding day, the day Niko was born, and the day she'd died, her last words to him as she'd faded away forever. *Love you.* The last thing she'd said as the life drained from her body was "love you." He moaned, painful memories ripping through him, making him thrash against the sheets. Then something cool, comforting, rested against his skin.

"Tatiana?" He opened his eyes in surprise.

"What are you doing?" she asked, sitting on the edge of the bed and cocking her head in that curious way she'd always had.

"Trying to sleep," he responded.

"You're fighting it," she corrected, reaching out to smooth his hair out of his face. "Why are you fighting it?"

"What am I fighting?"

"Everything. Guilt. Moving on. Loving Dani. She loves you so much, Sergei. Why won't you let yourself be happy with her and love her back?"

"I do love her, but you…" He stopped, frustrated.

"I'm dead."

"You're right here."

"I'm dead, Sergei, but you still have a lifetime in front of you. Don't waste it. That's not why I stopped my father from killing you. I did that for you to be happy. Don't you see? You were never truly happy with me. I know you loved me, but there was always fear, drama, stress that someone from our past would come after us. That's over now and you can have everything you ever dreamed of if you just give her a chance."

"What about you?" he whispered, tears puddling in his eyes.

"I'm free now, my love. No more stress, no more fear, just love and light and freedom. Goodbye, Sergei. Think about what I've said." She leaned forward and slowly pressed her lips to his.

Sergei jerked awake and sat straight up in bed, looking around wildly.

Just a dream, just a dream, just a dream. He repeated the words until his pounding heart settled and relaxed again. Fuck, that had been too realistic for his own good. Her touch, her voice, it had been real. It wasn't, of course, but it felt that way. It had been eerie, seeing her so vividly, hearing her talking to him in the present tense, as if she were still here. Hearing her talk about Dani was even stranger. But there it was: Even his dead wife wanted him to be with Dani. *Fuck.*

HE MANAGED to get up and pad into the bathroom, relieving himself and then standing under the warm spray of the shower until his skin was pruny and he was a little chilly. He dried off, pulled on sweats and a T-shirt and grabbed his phone. It was after seven in Las Vegas, so Toli would be awake.

"Good morning!" Toli sounded as cheerful as ever when he answered.

"Hey."

"What's up?"

"I need your help."

"Of course. What's wrong?"

"I love her, Toli."

"Duh. Seems like you're the only one who didn't know."

"I need you to help me win her back. I fucked up everything."

"You did."

"I need help coming up with something really big, a way I can surprise her in Seattle."

"Buy her a ring."

"Yeah, yeah, that's a given, but she has to forgive me before I can propose and I think there will be groveling involved. Will you help me or not?"

Toli laughed. "Do you really need to ask?"

34

S ix Weeks Later

AFTER A BIG WIN against the Swedish team, Dani wasn't thinking about anything but hockey and winning a gold medal. They'd been here in Seattle for a week now, and this last win meant they would play for the gold against whoever won in the Canada versus Russia game. She and Hailey were heading in that direction to watch when Coach Saunders caught up to them.

"Can I tag along with you guys?" she muttered, keeping her head down.

"Sure, Coach. What's up?"

"My ex-husband is here and... I just don't want to see him."

"How long have you been divorced?" Hailey asked.

"Legally divorced just two years but separated for nearly ten."

"You were separated eight years before you actually got divorced?"

She nodded. "It's a long story, but despite our differences, there was a lot of love between us. We just couldn't make it work."

"I'm just going to stay single," Hailey said. "All these people with broken hearts make me kind of jittery."

"What about Kane?" Dani teased her. "You two still texting and stuff?"

"Yeah, but he's in Alaska and I'm going home to Massachusetts soon. We haven't even been able to find a time to meet, much less anything else. He's sweet, though, so it's been fun."

"Sweet and fun can be a deadly mixture," Dani murmured.

"Mommy!" The loud cry came from somewhere and though Dani didn't typically react when someone called out *mommy*, Niko's shrill voice was distinct. She turned, catching sight of him with an older woman, someone who looked vaguely familiar. Had Sergei hired a new nanny?

Niko broke away from the woman and ran to Dani, all but vaulting himself the last few feet into her arms.

"Hey, kiddo." She hugged him tightly, assuming Sergei was nearby and cursing her traitorous heart for betraying her by starting to beat faster.

"Hello." The older woman approached her, her blue eyes curious.

"Hi. I'm sorry he ran like that. I didn't know he was coming…"

"You are Danielle?"

"Yes." Dani was curious about how familiar the woman looked.

"I am Anastasia. Petrov." Her English was slow and halting but distinct. "The mother of Sergei."

"The mother…" Dani almost gaped at her. Sergei had said his mother would probably never be allowed to visit the United States, yet here she was.

"This is my grandmama," Niko said proudly. "We comed to watch you win the gold medallions."

"Gold medals," Dani chuckled, blowing a raspberry on his neck and making him squeal with laughter.

"You will walk with me?" Anastasia asked quietly.

Dani briefly glanced at Hailey, but nodded. "Um, yes, of course. I'll meet you guys over at the arena, okay?"

"We'll save you a seat," Hailey called back.

Niko walked between Dani and his grandmother, holding each of their hands.

"Sergei said you weren't able to come to the U.S.," Dani said as they walked.

"My husband and I cannot travel together, but alone, I come. Is not easy for me, but I want to see my grandchildren. I will also go to the Las Vegas."

"But you came to Seattle first?" Dani was confused.

"I come to Seattle because Sergei tells me there is woman he loves. I must meet you, yes?"

"What did Sergei tell you?" Dani asked. "We're not together anymore."

"Yes, but you love him? You love Sergei?"

When Dani hesitated, Niko tugged on her hand. "Don't you love us anymore, Mommy?"

"Of course I love you, sweetie, but your daddy and I play hockey in different cities."

"Niko needs both mama and papa," Anastasia said. "If you love Sergei, you must find the way."

"I tried," Dani said softly, so Niko wouldn't hear everything. "But he sent me away."

"He is…" She murmured something in Russian that Dani couldn't quite decipher. "He had much guilt with loss of wife. He is afraid you will be hurt also."

"I didn't need him to protect me," Dani sighed. "I only need him to love me."

"You will talk, everything will be okay." Anastasia nodded as if it were a done deal.

"Mrs. Petrov, I—"

"Mama," she corrected smoothly, her blue eyes guileless. "Mrs. Petrov is dead long time."

SERGEI, Aaron and Kane arrived in Seattle just as the puck dropped for the start of the gold medal game and they listened to it via a satellite feed on Sergei's phone as the taxi driver navigated traffic. Sergei threw some money at him and they ran through crowds to get to the arena where the game was taking place. Zakk, Toli and a handful of their friends had all arrived earlier and Toli had been texting him updates.

Dani scored the first goal.

Dani threw herself in front of a puck, keeping the Russian team from scoring when the U.S. goalie had been out of position.

Dani assisted on the second goal.

She was everywhere and he hated that he'd missed half the game, but he'd played in Dallas last night and had been on planes all day today trying to get here. She was worth it, he just hoped he wasn't too late. His mother had said they spent a little time together last night and she liked her a lot, but that Dani didn't seem convinced Sergei was coming for her.

He'd flown in everyone he could think of. Sara, his mother, Niko, Tessa, Rachel and some of Dani's other girlfriends. He'd even found tickets to the sold-out gold medal game for Kane and Aaron, so they could attend with him since he needed all the moral support he could get.

"Slow down," Kane teased as they hurried into the arena.

"It's three to one," Aaron said, looking up at the scoreboard just as the Russian team scored again.

"Three to two," Sergei murmured, searching for Dani on the ice.

"There you are." Gage approached them with a grin. "Didn't think you were going to make it. Your girl sure looks good out there."

Sergei took a breath. "She does."

"Come on, let's sit. The second period's almost over, so they've got to get through one more."

"My brother's here," Sergei said. "I need to find him."

"Your brother is sitting with Dani's brother," Kane nudged him. "You might want to sit with us."

Sergei shook his head. "Zakk is going to be my brother-in-law if I have anything to say about it, so we might as well bury the hatchet."

"Don't you think you should bury the hatchet with her before he buries his hatchet in your head?"

"I've got this. You guys will stay after the game, right? You won't abandon me?"

Kane and Aaron nodded. "We got your back, man. No worries."

"What's going on after the game?" Gage asked in confusion.

"He bought a ring," Kane stage-whispered.

"And he's going to propose in front of everyone."

Gage raised his eyebrows, glancing down towards the bench. "Well, this trip just got a lot more interesting. Let's go."

As THE FINAL seconds ticked by, Dani didn't think about anything except keeping their lead. When the final buzzer sounded she found herself on the bottom of a pile of her teammates. They'd done it, won the gold medal, and the cheering from the crowd roared in her ears.

Hailey was tugging her to her feet and then they were all hugging again, crowded close together, laughing and crying. Coach Saunders had just come onto the ice and joined them as the crowd continued to yell, now chanting, "U-S-A-U-S-A..."

Dani spotted her parents and Zakk waving from the area behind the bench and she waved back, a huge smile on her face.

Everything happened in a blur as they waited for the medal ceremony, listening to the national anthem and then the feeling of the medal around her neck. Tears clouded her vision and for a moment everything was stupidly perfect. It wasn't until she had a chance to scan the crowds that she remembered Sergei, and his absence nearly sucked the joy right out of her. She managed a big smile for the cameras but inside her heart constricted painfully, disappointment overwhelming her. His mother had said he was coming, but he hadn't and now—

"Holy shit, Dani, look..." Hailey breathed in her ear.

Dani turned and her eyes widened in shock. Was Sergei skating onto the ice in her direction? He had a huge bouquet of roses and Aaron and Kane were behind him, holding armfuls of even more roses.

"Girl, he's coming for you." Hailey was squeezing her arm. "Oh my god, is that Kane?"

Dani still hadn't moved, unable to do anything but stare at Sergei in utter shock.

He skated to a stop in front of her and her teammates backed away. Even the crowd seemed to grow quiet and Dani felt a rush of emotion.

"Congratulations, sweetheart." Sergei handed her the bouquet.

She took it without thinking, her eyes falling closed as she held them against her face. The fragrant odor wafted into her nostrils like rose-scented Epsom salts and jerked her back to reality.

Kane and Aaron were handing smaller bouquets to each of the other girls and out of the corner of her eye she saw Hailey throw her arms around Kane, but she didn't have time to see what happened next because Sergei had just dropped to one knee in front of her and was holding something out.

"I'm sorry," he whispered, looking into her eyes. "I was scared, guilty, a million other things that were serious but not really relevant. The truth is, just like you once told me, I'm not broken when I'm with you. I'm a better man, better father, better everything with you in my life. Do you think you can forgive me, Dani?"

"I...um..." Tears had gathered in her eyes and she took an inadvertent step back. It was too much. So much emotion, too much to process at once, had her struggling to say anything at all.

"Honey..." He was patiently looking up at her. "Do you still love me?"

"I..." She looked at him, tears falling unchecked down her face. "You have to say it first."

Everything was quiet, as if the entire arena was waiting and watching. Dani was vaguely aware of the silence, the faces of her friends and teammates, of Sergei. So solemn and contrite, his handsome face full of longing and need. He needed her. He'd come for her. It was all she'd been dreaming about for months, but now she was afraid to let herself believe it.

"I love you, Danielle Cloutier. I want you to be my wife." Sergei's voice held no hesitation.

She burst into tears.

"Please don't cry. I'm here. I love you and want to spend the rest of my life showing you how much. Will you marry me? It would be the greatest honor of my life." His gaze never wavered even as the crowd began to chant.

"SAY-YES-SAY-YES-SAY-YES..." The crowd got louder when she hesitated.

"You want to marry me?" she asked at last.

"More than anything. If you want the job with the Sidewinders, we can commute for a couple of years and then I'll retire and move anywhere you want."

She swiped at her tears. "Fat chance, mister. You think I'm letting you live in another city with the Veronika's of the world?"

"Veronika who?" he chuckled. "There's been no one but you since the first time I saw you."

A thousand responses went through Dani's mind, but in the end only one word came out of her mouth. "Yes."

He slid the ring on her finger and the crowd went wild.

Sergei slowly got to his feet and Dani threw herself into his arms. His lips found hers and they kissed as if starving, until the crowd started to hoot and holler all over again. Her teammates were cheering too and she pulled away reluctantly, looking up into his gorgeous face.

"Sergei, are you sure?"

"Absolutely. Can you give me a couple of years to finish my hockey career? Once I retire, I'll follow you anywhere you want to go."

Her eyes glistened. "Do you believe there's anything more important than you and Niko?"

"Not *more* important," he said firmly. "But equally important. I won't have you give up your dreams for me."

"*Loving you* is my dream. You and Niko are the only things that matter. Now that the Olympics is over, I don't care about the job."

"I do."

"I know, but we'll figure it out."

"We have to talk about it. I'm serious. I want you to do what makes you happy. We can compromise on where we live, what we—"

"Stop." She covered his mouth with her hand. "I'll find a job in Anchorage."

"Only if you want to. I've already told Mr. Caldwell I'm going to see if I can get myself traded to the Sidewinders."

"I actually have a better solution." Gage approached them with a grin, his hands in his pockets.

"Mr. Caldwell." Sergei seemed surprised to see him.

"Call me Gage, will you?" Gage said as he turned to Dani. "Dani, would you like to work for the Blizzard?"

Her eyes widened. "Wh-what?"

"We don't currently have an assistant trainer and could use one. If you want it, the job is yours. You don't have to decide right now—"

"Yes!" Dani laughed, reaching out to hug him. "I've already decided—hell yes! Thank you."

"Well, happy engagement present." He winked and turned to go, his eyes resting on Coach Saunders. He didn't speak until she met his gaze and blinked. "Hello, Laurel."

"Hello, Gage." Coach Saunders nodded curtly and then turned to the team. "All right, ladies, we need to get off the ice. We'll have to continue the party elsewhere!"

35

A few hours later everyone gathered in the Presidential suite Mr. Caldwell had rented. He'd ordered a feast and invited Dani's entire team, as well as Sergei's and her friends and families. The team was in high spirits, everyone laughing and indulging in champagne, caviar and other delicacies Dani hadn't even noticed yet. She was still reeling from Sergei's epic surprise.

They'd snuck away to his room where they'd showered and made love twice before digging out clean clothes and heading to the party. There were so many people to talk to, Dani didn't know whom to respond to first, but Sergei kept his hand wrapped around hers as they chatted with everyone.

"Check out Kane and Hailey," Sergei whispered in her ear.

Dani turned and smiled. Hailey was on Kane's lap as they shared a bottle of champagne. "They'd make a cute couple."

"Not as cute as us." He kissed her lightly and she smiled.

"I wish I knew what changed your mind," she said slowly.

"Tatiana."

"Huh?" She looked at him in surprise.

"I had a dream where she spoke to me, told me I was an idiot and how she wanted me to be happy. When I woke up I realized the only way I would be happy is with you because you're my happy."

"You're my happy too."

"I'm sorry I had to hurt you before I could figure this out."

"It's okay." She looped her arms around his neck. "Kiss me, Wayne."

He wiggled his eyebrows. "You know, Maryanne...we still have at least twenty positions left from that book you bought me. We're going to need to work on that."

"We're going to need Niko to stay with your mom then."

"That can be arranged."

"Yeah, well, I'm going to be on *Good Morning America* the day after tomorrow and you're going to be on a road trip."

"We have tonight."

"Hey, you two, we're doing a toast." Toli stuck a champagne flute in each of their hands.

They toasted gold medals, engagements and new jobs and Dani nearly started to cry again. She'd never been as happy as she was right now. She had a gold medal, the man she loved and a job she'd only ever dreamed of. She even had a little boy that called her *mommy*, which was something she hadn't expected to want at this stage of her life, but she did.

"I want babies," she whispered against his ear. "Not yet, but in a few years."

"Okay."

"Say it again," she said.

"Okay?"

"No, silly!" She smacked his arm. "The other thing. You've only said it like ten times so far."

He smiled. "I love you, Danielle Maryanne Cloutier."

"I love you, too, Sergei Wayne Petrov."

SERGEI LEFT the following day since he had to meet up with the Blizzard for their upcoming road trip. Now that the Olympics was over, though, Dani would be able to join him in a week. She and the other members of the team had a handful of promotional appearances to make, but after she and Sergei consulted their calendars they'd decided she would meet up with him in Vancouver and from there they would head home to Anchorage.

Though it was only eight days since they'd had to separate at the Olympics, they couldn't wait to be alone together. They practically raced back to his hotel room, all over each other the moment the door closed behind them. Kissing and touching as if it had been a lot more than a week since they'd been together. He tossed his jacket on the nearest chair and began unbuttoning his shirt, watching intently as she stripped and slowly got to her feet. She walked over to him and pushed the shirt off his shoulders, running her hands over his warm, bare skin. He pulled his belt free of the loops, letting it fall from his hands as she worked on his zipper. His pants dropped to the floor and he stepped out of them, taking his boxers with them.

Now that they were naked, he pulled her in close, tilting his head to kiss her, drinking in her sweet lips. Her mouth opened for him and the second they came together time stood still. There was nothing but the two of them, two hearts, two bodies meeting in a magnetic frenzy of passion. He dug his fingers into her hair, holding her as he kissed her, as if she might slip away at any moment. He was already so hard he could have slid right into her if he had protection.

Shit! He needed to get a condom, but she'd molded her body to his, one hand on his shoulder, the other stroking one of the cheeks of his ass.

"Baby, I need to get protection..." He tried to pull away but she wasn't letting go.

"I'm on the pill now," she whispered against his mouth, tugging him towards the bed.

"Okay." He was surprised but wasn't thinking about anything except being inside her.

"I have a surprise for you," she said, crawling onto the bed on her hands and knees.

"Yeah?" He came up behind her, running his hand down her back.

"Look carefully," she giggled, wiggling her backside.

Something caught his eye and he looked down. Holy hell. She was wearing a plug. It had a small, shiny red cap on the end and seeing it there adorning her beautiful ass got him even harder, which he wouldn't have thought possible.

"Fuck, that's sexy," he moaned.

"I did a little research," she said in a breathy voice. "So I've been wearing it for two weeks, preparing for tonight."

"Fuck." He let out an involuntary growl and yanked her up against him, finding her lips even in this awkward position.

"You were my first everything else and I wanted this to be with you too."

"Jesus, baby." He didn't know what to say so he continued to kiss her, rediscovering every inch of her skin, her breasts, the little strip of curls between her legs. His hands traveled back up and he pulled away long enough to run his finger along her lower lip. "I've missed you, baby."

"Mm, me too."

He teased her with his tongue and lips, occasionally using his teeth to nip at that glorious bottom lip he loved.

"Please," she whispered. "Pretty please."

"Not yet." This time he took possession of her mouth like he meant it, his fingers fisting her long blond hair, demanding she let him control everything. It was rough, carnal, but oh-so fucking sexy and she didn't hesitate. They were still in this awkward position, his front pressed against her back, her head turned almost painfully to let him kiss her. It was time to be inside her, but he wanted her worked up, ready for him. Wearing a plug wasn't enough; he wanted her first anal experience to be far better than the night she'd lost her vaginal virginity.

"Get on your hands and knees, honey." He pushed her down, spreading her legs and using it as an opportunity to touch her creamy skin. "So soft, so sexy..." He traced circles around the points of her spine, sliding down to the crease between her ass. He couldn't decide what he wanted to do first but opted to start with what she knew. There was a bottle of lube and a condom on the bed and he sheathed himself quickly before covering her body with his. He pressed his erection against her tight opening and waited for her to move. She arched back and he pushed inside a little, waiting for her to adjust. Her vagina immediately closed around him, pulling him deeper, and he sank into her in one long, easy thrust. He moved in and out slowly, closing his eyes and listening to the moans and whimpers of pleasure coming from her. He loved this, being inside of her, watching her come alive as he fucked her.

He reached for the lube and slowly pulled out the plug in her ass, earning a long, low moan for his effort. Quickly pulling her cheeks apart, he squirted a liberal amount of lube along her crease and gently eased a finger inside of her. The plug she'd been wearing was bigger, so there was no resistance, and he moved slowly, letting her adjust.

"What do you think?" he whispered, pressing his finger deeper and running his other hand over her back.

"It's hot," she whispered back. "I like it."

He added another finger and her pussy clenched around him like a little vise of pleasure.

"Sergei..." She moaned his name, pushing back against him. "Please, I'm ready."

"You're killing me, my sexy little virgin."

"Not anymore!" she chortled.

He pulled out and slicked up his cock with more lube. Pressing the head against the tight puckered hole, he met with resistance this time. His dick was a lot bigger than the plug she'd been using, so he increased pressure, moving slowly until the head finally moved past the entrance. She was panting, her breath coming in gasps, and he stopped.

"Easy, honey. Just relax. Am I hurting you?"

"N-no...just a little uncomfortable."

He pushed a little deeper and she moaned louder, dropping her head so it rested on a pillow.

"Okay?"

"Oh, fuck, Sergei, it feels like everything back there is going to break open. *Shit.*"

"We can stop." He started to pull away but she was shaking her head.

"No, just, slow down...please. I don't want to stop."

"Whatever you want." He rested against her, letting her adjust to this massive intrusion in a place that had never been touched. He'd fingered her asshole a few times, but nothing like this, and he wished she hadn't been in such a hurry to try, but that's who she was. Anxious to try anything and everything when they were together; one of the many things he loved about her.

"More," she whispered.

He poured more lube between them and rubbed it in, gradually pushing deeper and deeper into her. When his hips were finally rubbing against her backside, she gasped out a breath, fingers digging into the blanket.

"Oh, fuck, oh shit, it's so much…pressure. What do I do?"

"Not everyone likes it," he soothed. "We don't have to keep going."

"I kind of do and kind of don't…just…ahhh…" Her voice changed when his fingers found her clit.

"There you go." He'd used a nice shot of lube and was swirling it around the engorged little nub. "Does that help?"

"Yes…oh, wow…Sergei!" Her hips jerked and she pressed back against him. "Fuck, yes, yes, yes!"

"Easy, honey." He kept his rhythm slow and steady. "Next time we'll use a vibrator on your clit, and you'll be so distracted by that you won't care what I'm doing back here."

"Just keep your finger…ooohhh…oh god."

"That's it, honey." Each time he withdrew she moaned and when he thrust back in she would gasp. Over and over until he nearly lost his mind with need. She was so tight, so hot and wet, he was on the edge of losing control.

"Sergei, please, now… Oh fuck!" Her head reared back and she screamed, her hips thrashing against him as he picked up speed and shot into her with more force than he'd ever managed before.

"Dani! Fuck…" He kept moving, his finger still stroking her clit, loving the way she would clench and spasm with each jerk of his cock. She was an absolute wet dream and he never wanted to stop pulsing inside of her. So he didn't. Until they finally couldn't take any more and collapsed, their breathing labored and a light sheen of sweat covering them both.

He pulled out slowly and got up to dispose of the condom and wash his hands. He hurried back to her, hauling her into his arms and pressing soft, sweet kisses all over her face.

"You're amazing," he whispered. "I never… Shit, no one ever let me go at them like that from behind. Sexiest fucking thing I've ever seen, baby."

"My butt hurts," she giggled, nestling deeper into him. "But I never came so hard. That was intense."

"I can't believe you let me do it."

"You'll always be my first everything."

"And your last too, I hope."

"Oh yeah."

"We still have about fourteen positions left from that book…"

"Then we'd better get started, huh?"

He laughed and drew her closer.

EPILOGUE

Dani arrived at the house in Anchorage three weeks after winning the gold medal at the Olympics. Sara, Anastasia and Niko were waiting for her when the cab dropped her off and they immediately hugged and kissed. Though she'd only lived there about five weeks, it felt like home. She couldn't wait to put her things in Sergei's room and sleep in his bed tonight. Their bed. He was on his way home with the team, so he'd be home late, but she didn't mind waiting up for him. They still had so many things to do and decisions to make but it could all wait until they had a little down time. He wanted to spend time with his mother before she headed to Las Vegas for a week and then went home to Moscow.

"Mommy, can we play Candyland?" Niko demanded after dinner.

"One game but then it's bath- and bedtime."

"Okay." He ran to get the box.

"I am very pleased to spend this time with you," Anastasia said softly. "Maybe I do not come to America again, but these moments are special."

"You'll come when Sergei and I have more children," Dani responded, squeezing her arm. "And maybe for the wedding."

"Sergei has married two times and Toli once, but I am not there for any," she said sadly. "I would like very much to see the wedding of my son."

"We'll talk about it and see what we can do."

"Have you guys set a date?" Sara asked.

"God no, but probably this summer. Why would we wait?"

Sara nodded. "Sounds reasonable. I can't wait to start planning everything."

"Me too," Dani couldn't help letting out a giggle. The thought of marrying

Sergei made her a little delirious every time she looked at the magnificent diamond on her left hand.

"This makes me happy," Anastasia said quietly. "Sergei has been alone too long. Even with Tatiana, sometimes he was alone. Life was difficult and I want only for him to find happiness."

"I'll spend the rest of my life trying to make him happy," Dani said shyly. "He and Niko are everything to me."

"Will you have more babies? Niko needs brothers and sisters."

"Not yet," Dani grinned. "I want more, but I want to work a few years."

"And Sara, what will you do now?" Anastasia asked her. "Where will you go?"

"Nowhere," Dani grinned. "She's going to take care of Niko while I'm at work. She's still in college, so she's not leaving until she finishes her master's."

"This is important, yes?"

"I think so," Sara nodded. "I won't stay forever, but for now, I want to help with Niko."

They chatted amiably until bedtime and then Dani crawled into bed to wait for Sergei, who'd texted he was on his way home.

In the meantime, her phone buzzed with a text from Hailey.

Guess who I hooked up with again last night?

Jack the Ripper?

Very funny.

Kane?

Yup. After the Boston game.

And?

He's pretty amazing, but he lives in Anchorage and I'm going to law school in Boston.

Are you going to see him again?

He said we'll keep in touch, but who knows? He's really great, though. I wish things were different.

You never know—look at me. I never dreamed I'd be living in Anchorage.

Maybe I need a summer nanny job! Ha ha.

That's not a bad idea. We'll work on it.

Okay, have to run. See you later.

Dani closed the text program and smiled to herself. It would be great if she could convince Sara and Hailey to both live in Anchorage. It probably wouldn't happen but it was a nice thought. She closed her eyes and the next thing she knew Sergei was in bed beside her, his naked body warm against hers.

"Hi," she murmured sleepily. "When did you get home?"

"A few minutes ago. Go back to sleep, baby."

"I missed you."

"I missed you too." He pulled her close.

"I think I found a wedding dress."

He chuckled against her ear. "Already? What happened to the tomboy I fell in love with?"

"She's sleepy."

"Me too." He pressed a trail of light kisses along her shoulder. "We can talk about the wedding in the morning."

"Mmm, okay."

"Welcome home, sweetheart."

"Thank you." She nestled deeper into his arms. "I love you."

"I love you too." He kissed her once more as she drifted off to sleep.

If you enjoyed Defending Dani, please consider leaving a review at your retailer of choice. In the meantime, check out an excerpt from "Holding Hailey," Book 2 in the Alaska Blizzard series, on the next page.

EXCERPT FROM "HOLDING HAILEY" (SUBJECT TO CHANGE).

Prologue
February

There shouldn't have been any better feeling in the world than winning a gold medal in the Olympics, but as Hailey Dobson stood on the platform next to her teammates, she had to take a deep breath. She'd dreamed of this day for nearly a decade but now that it was here she was overwhelmed with emotions. There was an unexpected loneliness, causing tears to sting her eyelids. Her father and stepmother hadn't been able to come, and her mother had been dead for a long time, leaving her with the strangest feeling of being alone. It had never felt that way before, no matter how many championships she'd won, so she wasn't sure why it was so poignant tonight.

The music from the national anthem ended and a sudden flurry of activity caught her attention. Turning from her melancholy thoughts she narrowed her eyes slightly as her friend Dani's ex-boyfriend skated onto the ice, flowers in hand, straight towards them. Holy shit, was he going to propose?

She smiled, happy for her friend who'd been so heartbroken after the break-up. Sure enough, Sergei dropped to one knee and was holding out a ring. Hailey's eyes welled with happy tears this time, watching as Dani got teary-eyed as well. By the time she said yes and threw herself into Sergei's arms, half the team was crying and clapping, so she was startled when a some-what familiar voice said, "Hey, babe."

Her head whipped around and she was momentarily dumbfounded. It was *him*. Kane. Kane "Hattrick" Hatcher. Her online crush and pen pal. The hot professional hockey player Dani and Sergei had introduced her to virtually, whom she'd been fantasizing about for months. *Holy shit.*

He was holding out a bouquet of flowers and she took them on autopilot. "Hi," she managed to squeak out just as he engulfed her in a bear hug.

"What a game," he gushed against her ear. "You were fan-fucking-tastic!"

"Thanks." She was grinning from ear-to-ear now, smiling up into his handsome face.

"It's really good to meet you in person," he said, fixing her with a look that made her insides all warm and fuzzy.

"What are you doing here?" she finally managed to ask.

"Well, Sergei had a grand plan for winning Dani back and a few of us came along for moral support. Plus, you know, I have this girl I've been talking to online and figured this would be an awesome excuse to meet her."

"I bet she's really glad you came." Hailey couldn't even express how much it meant to her that he was here, even though he had no idea how sad she'd been until a minute or so ago.

"Well, you said your family couldn't come," he replied, as if reading her mind. "I thought your virtual hook-up had to be better than nothing."

"It's much better," she whispered, impulsively reaching out to hug him again. Damn, he smelled so good, his aftershave permeating the sweat of her equipment. Suddenly cognizant of how bad she must smell, she pulled away.

"Sorry," she chuckled. "I probably smell like ass."

He laughed. "Babe. I play hockey too—nothing I'm not used to."

"That's not the scent I'd like you to associate with me."

"I've got a hotel room you can shower in if you want."

"I can't get away just yet, but yes, definitely. I'll take you up on that."

He closed his big hand around hers and walked with her off the ice.

Several hours later Hailey put a dab of gloss on her lips and fluffed out her hair. Kane was on the other side of the door and this would be his first time seeing her dressed up. They'd exchanged pictures in the months they'd been talking but being together in person was different. She'd pulled on her favorite jeans, a cute sweater that dipped low enough to show a touch of cleavage and had made up her face. It had been years since she'd been this nervous about being with a guy, but Kane was special. From their first phone conversation she'd known he wasn't just looking to get laid. He was probably interested in that too, but they'd had too many intense, intimate conversations for this to boil down to something as simple as sex. He played in the NHL; he probably had women in every city.

Opening the bathroom door, she stepped into his room. He was on his back on the bed, his feet bare and crossed, a magazine in his hands. He glanced over as she walked over to him.

"You look good enough to eat," he said in a husky voice.

"I clean up pretty well," she said, subconsciously licking her lips. He was downright beautiful. All lean muscle with shoulders for days and arms she was already looking forward to having around her.

"You do." His smoldering eyes met hers as he held out his hand.

She took it and let him draw her onto the bed beside him.

"Why'd you have to go make your lips so pretty?" he whispered, leaning towards her. "Now I'm going to have to mess them up."

"That's okay." His breath was warm against her lips and she closed her eyes as he slanted his mouth over hers. It was tender, his lips seeking hers hesitantly, letting her guide the pace. He tasted like cinnamon, his tongue firm and confident against hers, until she forgot everything but him. She'd been waiting months for him to kiss her like this and the real thing was a million times better than her fantasies.

Their phones buzzed at the same time, startling them apart. Kane didn't reach for his right away, though, keeping his eyes on hers and one hand cupping the side of her face.

"I should get that," she whispered. "It might be Coach Saunders."

"Okay." He slowly pulled away and they reached for their phones.

"Party at Gage Caldwell's suite," she murmured, reading a message. "He's hosting the team and our guests."

"Technically he's my boss, so I guess I have to show up," he quipped.

"I don't want to share you," she sighed, resting her head against his chest.

"You don't have to." He closed his arms around her, holding her tighter. "We'll go, have a few drinks to celebrate your win, and then we'll come back here."

"When do you have to leave?" she asked softly.

"Tomorrow afternoon. I have to meet the team in Vancouver."

"We have one day together," she sighed. "I don't want to waste it at a party."

"Time together is never a waste." He lifted her chin and bent his head to hers, taking her mouth again. His touch sent erotic sparks shooting through her and they were both fully dressed; she couldn't begin to imagine what it would be like to be naked with him.

"The sooner we go," he said, reluctantly breaking the kiss. "The sooner we can come back here."

She nodded. "We should do that then."

The party was more fun than they'd anticipated. Gage Caldwell owned the NHL team Kane played for, the Alaska Blizzard, and he'd spared no expense to help the U.S. Women's Olympic hockey team celebrate their win. There was a feast spread out fit for a king and champagne flowed like water from a fountain in the middle of the suite. A light hip-hop beat wafted through the room and guests swayed in time to the music, whether they were sitting, standing, or, in Hailey's case, half-on, half-off Kane's lap.

She was on her fourth or fifth flute of champagne, laughing as Kane told a story about his first NHL game. It was so natural to be with him, she wouldn't have believed it possible that they'd only met in person today. With one of his hands resting on her thigh, the other holding a beer, it was as comfortable as sitting in her own living room with a long-time lover. Just thinking about becoming lovers made her smile because that was happening sooner rather than later and they both knew it. All the months of sexy, flirty texts and phone calls had led up to tonight and he was everything she'd hoped he would be.

"Are you having fun?" he asked, his breath warm against her ear.

"Winning a gold medal is pretty amazing," she admitted. "And being with you is equally wonderful."

"I'm as cool as a gold medal?" he laughed, his eyes warming with pleasure.

"Just about." She pressed her lips to his and they kissed for what had to be the hundredth time today. She couldn't get enough and he seemed to feel the same way. They hadn't stopped touching each other since he'd given her the flowers on the ice, and there was something magical about being together.

"Do I get a gold medal if I make you come a few hundred times?" he murmured against her lips.

"Absolutely."

"Come on, you two," Dani Cloutier, her closest friend on the team, nudged her. "There's plenty of time for that later—come party!"

"I'm five glasses of champagne in," Hailey laughed. "I'm partying just fine."

"We're taking selfies, come play with us. Your boyfriend will be waiting when we're done." She tugged at Hailey's hand and Hailey let her pull her to her feet.

"I'll be right here," Kane called after her.

Three hours and a whole lot of champagne later, Kane and Hailey stumbled into his hotel room, practically ripping their clothes off the second the door closed behind them. Their lips fused together in a heated rush of passion, so anxious to touch, be together, it was hard to think. Kane hadn't been this into a woman in years—maybe not ever—and he struggled to slow down, savor their first time together.

"Hailey... babe... you sure about this?"

Her big brown eyes were hooded, heavy with lust, and her response was to nip his lower lip and slide her hand into his jeans. "What do you think?" she rasped.

"I think you're fucking hot." He scooped her up and tossed her on the bed, pausing to yank off his jeans before joining her. Their lips came together again, a magnetic force guiding them, but he forced himself to go slower. He wanted to watch her strip, enjoy the view of her glorious body as it unwrapped before him like the most decadent present he'd ever received. She whimpered when he pulled away but he just smiled.

"Kane?" she reached for him but he moved away slightly.

"Strip for me, baby. I want to see it all."

Surprise flickered in her eyes but was quickly replaced by a devilish smile. Her jeans were already unbuttoned and her sweater was long gone but she made a show of sliding down the dark blue denim an inch at a time.

"That's it." He leaned back, focusing on the miles of skin coming into view. Sweet Jesus, she had the longest legs he'd ever seen. And damn if they weren't smooth, muscular and shapely. By the time she was in nothing but her bra and panties, his cock was at full staff, ready to salute the first body part it touched.

She licked her lips, her eyes locked on his as she slowly unhooked her bra, but instead of letting it slide off she held it up by pressing her arms against the sides. A naughty smile played on her lips as she whispered, "What do I get for showing you the goods?"

He rumbled out a laugh, glancing down at his raging erection. "You get to see what's hiding in my boxers."

Her eyes widened in faux surprise. "Really? Oh my. It looks... angry."

"Not angry... excited." He slid down his boxers and kicked them free. "See?"

With an impish grin, she let the bra drop but swept her long dark hair over her shoulders, effectively covering her breasts.

"No fair," he teased.

"I'll need a lick before you see anymore."

"I suppose that would be acceptable." He leaned back against the pillows and watched as her wet, pink tongue lapped at his cock, though she didn't touch it with her hands or lips.

"Mmm," she moaned. "So good."

"My turn." He gently brushed her hair back over her shoulders and stared down at the most beautiful pair of breasts he'd seen outside of a porn video. And maybe not even then. They were round and perky, probably a C cup, with raspberry nipples that were currently peaked and ready for his mouth. He didn't hesitate to bend his head and suck one deep, gratified to hear her moan of pleasure. He swirled his tongue around the hard, little nub, alternating sucking and licking until she was squirming against him.

"Kane..." Her voice was hoarse, needy.

"Not yet," he replied, reluctantly pulling away. "I need to see the rest."

She hooked her thumbs into the sides of her panties and tugged them down so painstakingly slowly he almost groaned in frustration, but it was worth the wait. The small patch of brown curls at the apex where her thighs met made his mouth water—he loved a woman who kept it real instead of following the latest fad of shaving everything. He liked pussy any way he could get it, but a well-groomed crotch was his favorite, the happy medium between a bushy forest and completely bare.

"Fuck," he breathed. "You're… perfect."

"I doubt that," she whispered, her eyes fixed on his. "But I like hearing it."

"Perfect as far as I'm concerned," he reiterated, reaching for her. She moved against him eagerly, her lips seeking his. This time he didn't hold back, sliding one arm around her waist and using the other to dig his fingers into the back of her hair.

The kiss intensified, until nothing was between them, not even air. Every inch of skin pressed together, warmth and passion mingling interchangeably. Her skin was like silk, and when one long leg slid between his, his cock stiffened even more. He needed to be inside her now and he reached for the condom he'd thought to grab without breaking their kiss.

"Let me," she whispered, taking it from him. She leaned down, sucking his cock deep until her cheeks hallowed out and he let out a strangled groan.

"Babe, I'm not gonna last if you—"   She released him with a smile, sliding the condom down his shaft with one fluid motion. "I've been waiting for you to fuck me for months—I'm not going to spoil it."

"You like dirty talk?" he asked, pulling her astride him, nipping her ear with his teeth.

"Love it."

"Oh, fuck, I knew there was a reason we clicked." He slid a finger between her legs and sighed when he found her wet and ready. Without any warning, he used two fingers to spread her open and then thrust up deep, sheathing himself in one smooth motion.

"Jesus fucking Christ," she moaned, her head falling back.

"I'm gonna make that pussy rock and roll, baby," he growled, squeezing her ass hard.

"Fuck yeah." Her eyes were closed, mouth partially open as she rocked her hips back and forth.

"That's my girl," he murmured, his lids at half-mast as he watched her grind on his cock. "Take what you want."

"You," she sighed happily. "All of you."

"You've got it all." He thrust up deep again and she moaned. "Now tell me how you want it. Slow and sexy or hardcore fucking?"

"Your choice." Her eyes twinkled. "As long as the next time we do the other."

He growled, sitting up and pushing her onto her back. "Ask and you shall receive." He slid off the bed and pulled her by her feet until her pussy rested right at the edge. Pushing back her spread thighs until her knees were nearly to her shoulders, he snapped his hips forward, bottoming out with a grunt. Before she could move, he pulled out and thrust back in, hard and deep, over and over, until her cries filled the room.

"My name," he panted. "Every time my balls slap against your ass, say my name."

"Kane." Her eyes were closed but her chest was rising and falling in time to his thrusts.

He picked up speed until he was jackhammering into her, harder than he'd ever taken anyone, loving the sound of his name on her lips. When her orgasm crashed over her she screamed like a woman possessed, bucking against him, fingers digging into his forearms. Her pussy convulsed over and over, drawing out his release until he couldn't breathe, couldn't move, couldn't do anything but lose himself in the beautiful woman still calling out his name.

The aftermath left them shattered and raw, poignant emotions taking them on a ride neither had expected. He was incredible. Hailey had never expected sex like this, sex that destroyed the memory of every man before him and created a need she'd never felt before. She had no way of knowing what he was thinking, but the way he'd tenderly pulled her into his arms and was stroking her hair told her he'd been as affected as she was.

The silence wasn't awkward, a strangely comfortable intensity filling the air between them as they basked in each other's warmth. Over the years she'd learned not to trust post-coital intimacy but instead of remaining silent like she usually did, she refused to let a guy like Kane go without telling him what she wanted.

"Was it what you were expecting?" she asked softly, fingers curling into the hair on his chest.

He chuckled. "Hell no. It surpassed every fantasy I'd come up with before we met. It was fucking awesome."

"Kane, if this is going to be a one-off, you need to tell me now. I'm not good at casual sex. I can do once, but if you're looking for a friends-with-benefits thing, I'm not your girl."

His eyes narrowed at he stared down at her in the semi-darkness. "You think that's what this was? Babe, you're not one-off material. I'd never have done this if I wasn't interested in exploring more. We've been building up to something all these months, but we had to meet in person to be sure, and now I'm pretty sure."

"You are?" She was startled.

"Well, yeah. I thought that was pretty obvious."

"I never assume anything. Especially after good sex."

"Good sex?" He laughed. "That was mind-blowing, out-of-this-world, best-I've-ever-had sex. After all that, you can assume anything you want."

She nestled against his shoulder, her body molded to his. "So what happens next?"

"I fuck you as many times as possible until I have to get on that plane tomorrow and then we compare schedules to figure out when and where we can meet up next."

"That sounds—" She couldn't finish her thought because he silenced her with a sweep of his tongue that aroused her to the point of ecstasy.

"The only sound I want to hear is you screaming my name," he whispered.

Read the rest of Kane and Hailey's story on August 30th!
Pre-order today!
www.KatMizera.com/alaska-blizzard

Made in the USA
Columbia, SC
30 January 2023

11249219R00117